Body at Bunco

A Myrtle Clover Mystery

zabeth Spann Craig

A Body at Bunco

Formatting by RikHall.com
Cover Design by Karri Klawiter
Editing by Judy Beatty

Dedication

For my readers. Thank you.

Acknowledgments

Thanks most of all to my family; especially Coleman, Riley, and Elizabeth Ruth. Many thanks to Judy Beatty for editing.

A special thanks to Karri Klawiter for the cover design.

Thanks to Rik Hall for formatting the book for its digital and print releases.

My thanks to Amanda Arrieta for her excellent beta reading.

And thanks as always to the writing community for its support and encouragement.

Chapter One

"Need help, Miz Myrtle?"

As soon as her yardman, Dusty, had asked the question, an irritated look passed across his lean features. Myrtle smiled. Volunteering for more work was usually not in Dusty's game plan.

"As a matter of fact, I do, thank you." Myrtle bumped the door to the metal shed open wider with her hip.

Dusty slouched against the frame of the storage shed, a ragtag figure in frayed, grass-stained khakis, and a floppy hat over lanky gray hair. "We ain't pulling all them gnomes out, are we?"

Myrtle's collection of yard gnomes was extensive, it was true. And the gnomes were an impressive sight when they were arranged throughout her front yard. The sight of their winsome faces infuriated her son, Red, who lived across the street from his octogenarian mother. Which happened to be the whole point.

"Oh, I think that they *all* need to make an appearance, Dusty."

Dusty turned his head and spat a wad of chewing tobacco into a nearby bush. Myrtle wrinkled her nose in distaste. "Red done stepped out of line again?" he asked.

"He certainly has. This time he's really gone too far, Dusty. I need to make a point. Draw a line in the sand."

Dusty scuffed a worn leather boot at the red clay that served as soil in Bradley, North Carolina. "No sand here, Miz Myrtle. Besides, can't you make your point without all them gnomes out? You know I can't mow when they're covering your front yard. I'll have to use the string trimmer and that thing is broke more often than not."

Dusty's grudging willingness to trim around the gnomes was the sole reason for his employment. Aside from that willingness, he was lazy, unpredictable, and coarse.

"You just mowed, so we're in good shape for a week or so." She grunted as she pulled out a particularly winsome gnome that was inexplicably holding a chainsaw.

"Okay. I done finished fixin' the broke spigot, by the way."

Myrtle said, "Wonderful. Now maybe I can actually water the bushes out back. Please make sure you collect all your tools. Last time they were scattered here and yonder. And when you're all done with the gnomes, be sure to lock the gate to the backyard."

Dusty gave an affirming grunt and reached in for a gnome wearing sunglasses and holding a saxophone and glumly carted it off to a prime location in the front of Myrtle's house.

He returned with Myrtle's son Red in tow. "He's onto us, Miz Myrtle," said Dusty with a shrug of a shoulder.

"Keep on going, please, Dusty. Red and I will have a little talk inside over some milk and cookies."

Red's face was thunderous and he ran a hand through his red hair (now with a good deal of gray mixed in) until it stood on end. "Mama, what is this gnome invasion in response to? I've been so busy and *you've* been so busy that I haven't made contact with you for days." Dusty grunted as he carried a scuba diving gnome out of the shed and Red looked at it with distaste. "And I sure don't need any milk and cookies. I've gained several pounds in the last couple of weeks."

Myrtle thought the weight looked fine on him. Red had inherited her own propensity for height and stood several inches over six feet. As a teen, he'd been thin as a rail. He looked much better with the heft of weight on him.

"Oh, these are low-fat cookies," said Myrtle with a dismissive wave of her hand. In fact, they were laden with fat. And sugar. What was the point, otherwise? But sugar helped to sweeten Red's moods, so it was the perfect tool. Except Red seemed as firmly planted in her yard as a tree. She sighed and instead sat down in an old wrought-iron chair on her patio. Red plopped down across from her.

"You should know exactly why the gnomes are gracing my front yard, Red Clover." She paused and waited for light bulbs to go off in Red's head but seeing they weren't forthcoming she snapped, "Sloan Jones. You told Sloan that I was the one correcting all the *Bradley Bugle*'s errors and mailing them into the newsroom. Really, Red. Was that necessary?"

Red looked slightly relieved, as if he thought this was something he could easily handle. "I swear, Mama, I didn't mean anything by it. I just saw the corrected papers lying on Sloan's desk and absently mentioned that I recognized your handiwork. The red pen is a dead giveaway, you know. Ex-schoolteacher and all that. Besides, what was Sloan going to say? It's not like he's going to fire you from the newspaper over something minor like that. He's petrified of you…has been ever since he was your student."

"It's not that he was mad, Red. It's that he was *hurt*. Wounded Sloan is difficult to handle. I was in constant and abject terror that he was going to start crying over the betrayal. And now I have a meeting with him in an hour in the newsroom. That's all I need," said Myrtle.

"If that's the only challenging part of your day it's a blessing, Mama. I had more than that to deal with before breakfast. Such is the life of a small town police chief." On cue, Red's phone rang and he heaved a tremendous sigh. "Chief Clover," he said.

Red listened for a minute and then said, "Miss Mabel, we've talked about this a couple of times. I can't do anything about Miz Tritt's pine tree. Even if it is dropping needles, pine cones, and sticks all over your property, the tree is on *her* property."

Myrtle could hear Mabel's reedy voice say, "But the sticks and pine cones are trespassing on *my* property. And she won't rake or pick them up."

Red was placating. "I tell you what, Miss Mabel. I've got a few minutes before I have to run by for a meeting with the mayor. Just to ease your mind, how about if I run by and take care of those pine cones and sticks for you. Will that help?" He rolled his eyes at Myrtle. "I know it doesn't help the root cause, but it sure might save you some aggravation. How 'bout it? Deal? Great. Be there in half a shake of a lamb's tail."

He hung up and leveled a serious look at Myrtle. "Now that I got Miss Mabel taken care of, how about if we resolve this issue between us? I'm sorry about telling Sloan that you were the phantom editor. I was out of line."

"You certainly were," said Myrtle.

"So can I ask Dusty to start heaving those gnomes back into the shed?" asked Red in a hopeful tone. "I'll tip him."

"Absolutely not. It's completely out of line to give poor Dusty conflicting orders…it will only confuse him. Besides, I've missed seeing the gnomes out there. I love it when children make their parents stop the car to look at them. I'm an attraction."

"You're a *something*," grumbled Red. "All right, I've got to get out of here if I'm going to do yardwork before my meeting. I'll check in with you later." He gave a winking gnome a dirty look as he hurried off. Myrtle might have to keep all the motion detectors running tonight in case Red planned any gnome vandalism.

Dusty was starting to slow down a little, not that he'd gone at any great pace before. "How many gnomes does it take to make a point?" he asked, putting a hand to his back suggestively.

"You already asked me that earlier," said Myrtle. "If you won't do it, then I will. Maybe Puddin can help out, too."

The mention of his wife's name appeared to startle Dusty. Unless it was the juxtaposition of "Puddin" and "help". "She's not here," he said. "Besides, her back is thrown."

"Somebody needs to catch that thrown back of hers," said Myrtle darkly. "It's getting more and more out of whack as my dust and clutter builds up." Myrtle frowned. "You know, I think it's been at least two weeks since Puddin has come over to help me clean. My dust bunnies will be procreating. Give her a call and see if she can run by."

Dusty's brow furrowed, but he obediently fished his phone out of his baggy jeans. "She probably won't be able to make it until late afternoon," he warned.

"Fine. Whenever is fine—I simply want her to come by. The situation is getting dire. Just set it up. I have to head downtown," said Myrtle.

Dusty quickly said, "Want me to drive you there in the truck, Miz Myrtle? It'll just take a second to get there."

"No siree! I want you to lug gnomes around. I can lug *myself* downtown." Myrtle gave him a stern look and he dolefully continued arranging gnomes on Myrtle's front lawn as she walked around the house to the sidewalk and down the tree-lined street to the small downtown.

When she reached the newspaper office, she paused for a second to collect her thoughts before walking into the *Bradley Bugle*. She wished Sloan *would* be mad at her. It was much worse to cause hurt feelings. Then she frowned.

Was it her imagination, or was the office's wooden front door even more battered than usual?

With a sigh, she pushed the door open and entered the shadowy newsroom. As usual, it smelled of old books and paper. There were stacks of printed photographs, old newspapers, and papers on every surface. In the middle of everything was a heavyset balding man. *Bradley Bugle* editor Sloan Jones was ordinarily smiling, even though he was cautious around Myrtle. But now his face was as long as she'd ever seen it. Ordinarily he leapt up from his desk in deference to Myrtle's age and her former position as his English teacher in high school. This time he made a half-hearted effort to rise, before collapsing again in his rolling chair, which squealed in squeaky protest.

"Hi, Miss Myrtle," said Sloan in a pained voice.

Myrtle pressed her lips together. She was almost positive that Sloan's mournfulness was put on to make her feel bad. "Look, sorry about how I handled the proofreading thing." She sat down gingerly in a rolling chair next to Sloan. She didn't much care for chairs that doubled as fair rides.

"You probably can't even help it, Miss Myrtle. Being an English teacher for so many years and all," said Sloan nobly.

His forgiving nature made Myrtle cross. "It's just that, having been *your* teacher, Sloan, I hate to see very basic mistakes in the newspaper. *There, their, and they're* errors. That sort of nonsense. It reflects poorly on me. I'm about to have to start telling people that Doris Penbrook taught you instead of me. And you know it pains me to lie."

Sloan hastily jumped in, likely not wanting to receive any more edits in person. "Here's the thing, Miss Myrtle. The *Bugle* had to let Tilly Morris go a few weeks ago and you know she was the copyeditor. Since then, I've had to take over editing and I'm just not used to doing it. Plus there's the fact that I have no time at all whatsoever. I'm really having to juggle a lot of stuff."

Myrtle grudgingly said, "I suppose I *could* copyedit for you, Sloan. Although that's not really what I was planning on doing with my free time. If you needed me to. And, naturally, for a fee." She got up and moved across from Sloan at his desk, her cane propped up against her, prepared to do business.

Sloan said hurriedly, "And you know that I'd love for you to. That paper would be a hundred percent error-free. But the problem, you see, is that *The Bugle* is going through some hard times. I wouldn't have the funds to pay you. When I told Tilly that I'd have to cut her pay, she walked right out that door." He shifted his bulk again and his chair made that high-pitched squeak.

"I might be bored, but I'm not that bored. I couldn't take on a job like that without compensation and I'm sure that Tilly was unwilling to do so, too. What's happening to the paper, Sloan?" asked Myrtle.

"I'm losing subscribers left and right, which means that I'm losing advertisers left and right. I have a meeting next week with Roger's Automotive. You know that's our biggest advertiser. If we lose them, I don't know what will become of the paper. They usually place a full-page color ad in every issue. Roger's Automotive practically pays for the entire production," said Sloan glumly. "I may have to sell my house and move in with my mother again."

"What's at the bottom of it, do you think? Why would longtime subscribers suddenly unsubscribe?"

Sloan said, "I'm sure it has to do with the fact they can find their news on the internet anytime they want to."

"Yes, but the internet has been around for a while now, Sloan, and you've had plenty of readers before. What's changed? Have you changed the content? Focusing more on stories off the newswire and less local stuff?" asked Myrtle.

It was most definitely the content. People had been muttering about Sloan's changes for months. Half the time now, the paper had the tone of a tabloid instead of a family newspaper in a small town. But she knew if she came right out and told Sloan that, he'd probably not listen.

"I've had some bad luck with staff," admitted Sloan. "My horoscope writer left, I've lost Frannie, who did our recipes, to health troubles. I tried to handle the Good Neighbors column myself, but it was such a pain that I gave it up."

Myrtle shook her head. "You've named the three most popular features in the paper, Sloan. If you don't have those articles, no wonder you're losing readers."

Sloan bit his lip as if he very much wanted to disagree, but didn't want to cross Myrtle. Instead he said in a diplomatic tone, "I don't know, Miss Myrtle. I'm thinking that maybe it's more that people are ready for some *real news*. You know? Maybe they're tired of hearing about Ginny Peters's prize-winning zucchini and Becky Trimble's quilting tips and where the Comptons went on vacation. Maybe they want an in-depth exposé of the new testing over in K-5th grade. Or an in-depth investigative report on whether the oil change place is ripping people off."

"Are they?" mused Myrtle. "I think that's where Red takes the police cruiser."

Sloan's eyes were reproachful for Myrtle's going off topic. "I'm wondering if I need to revamp the whole paper and make it a really newsworthy tool for readers." He threw his hands up in the air and there was a cacophony of chair squeaking. "Who knows? Maybe I need to take it in a *completely* different direction and have it be a tabloid. Stories like: 'It's One A.M. Does Mrs. Smith Know Where Mr. Smith is'?"

Myrtle had never seen Sloan so worked up. Not even

when he'd made a thirty on that English test in tenth grade. "I really believe you're overthinking this, Sloan. Seriously. I haven't heard a single person say that they didn't like the paper's content until recently."

But Sloan had stopped listening. "Miss Myrtle, I need your help. My understanding is that Luella White knows everything going on in Bradley and is the town's biggest gossip. That sounds like the perfect combination. Only problem is that I don't think she wants to work for the paper. Besides, I couldn't afford to pay her, even if she *did* want to work for me. What I really need is for someone to go undercover and use Luella as a source. Then we should be able to get all the news that's fit to print."

Myrtle wrinkled her nose. "And quite a bit of news that's *not* fit to print, too." She paused and then continued suspiciously, "You said you need my help. You're not proposing that *I* go undercover and use Luella White as a source, are you?"

Sloan said meekly, "I sure am, Miss Myrtle. I'd do it myself, except I'd probably stand out if I were trying to hang out with Luella White. I figure you'll be perfect. You can sort of blend into the background when you need to and listen in on Luella's gossip. Then we'll write it in the paper like: *a little bird tells us that Teresa Johnson is leaving her job at the ice cream shop to marry tire salesman Roy Burton. Better get your ice cream while you can! The shop will be closing soon.* Something like that."

"If I did that, Sloan, I'd stand out, too. What are you asking me to do? Flip open a notebook and jot down every salacious thing that comes out of her mouth?"

Sloan smiled hopefully.

"That's not going to work. Besides, where am I going to run into Luella White? She and I hardly run in the same circles," said Myrtle. Myrtle, truth be told, didn't run in *any* circles anymore. "I can't exactly drop by for a visit and hang out on her sofa."

"It should be easy-peasy, Miss Myrtle," said Sloan quickly. "You just cozy up to her at one of her clubs. Since she's new to town, she's joined everything. And if there's one person who has her finger on the pulse of the raging metropolis of Bradley, North Carolina, it's her."

"*She*," corrected Myrtle. Whatever was to become of the *Bradley Bugle* with no copyeditor? "And I don't do clubs." She tapped the floor with her cane to emphasize her point.

Sloan's large face fell comically. "Not garden club?"

"I'm on hiatus."

"Not book club?" asked Sloan rather desperately.

"I haven't read the last few selections. On purpose," said Myrtle firmly.

"Altar guild?"

"I'm Presbyterian."

"Women of the Church, then?" asked Sloan, perspiring a little. "I can't remember if Luella White is Methodist or Presbyterian."

"Women of the Church meet at an inconvenient time," said Myrtle. Right smack in the middle of her favorite soap opera, *Tomorrow's Promise*.

The dismay on Sloan's face made Myrtle relent a little. "Sloan, I'll keep an eye out for her. I'm sure there's a better way. I'll get the *Bradley Bugle*'s subscribers back—and that's a promise."

It was a testament to Myrtle's iron will and complete self-confidence that Sloan slumped in relief at her words.

Chapter Two

Back at home, Myrtle realized it seemed unlikely that she would simply happen to run into Luella White. As she'd told Sloan, they didn't run in the same circles and Myrtle didn't want to start running in Luella's.

She was pulling out pasta sauce, olive oil, and noodles for an early supper when there was a frantic pounding on her front door.

Myrtle cautiously peeked out front, saw her daughter-in-law Elaine holding toddler son Jack, and opened the door. "Mercy, Elaine! Whatever's the matter?"

Something was quite obviously the matter. Elaine's eyes were wild. Upon closer inspection, Myrtle saw that one contributing factor to the wildness was the fact she had half her eye makeup on and half off.

"I'm hosting Bunco tonight, Myrtle. And all our plumbing is backing up! There's water all over the floors. It's coming out of all the sinks, tubs, toilets. We had to shut off the main valve. The toilet was making a percolating noise like a coffeepot. It's a disaster."

Jack reached out to Myrtle, clearly ready to escape from his distraught mother and Myrtle absently pulled the nearly-three year old into her arms before quickly giving his chubby cheek a kiss and setting him down. He'd gotten far too heavy for her. Jack immediately launched into a babbling monologue about trucks and Myrtle nodded, listening to him carefully for a few moments, asking him about the color and type of the trucks. Finally he decided to pretend to *be* a truck and Myrtle had a chance to talk to her daughter-in-law again. "Elaine, what on earth is Bunco? The plumbing I understand."

"It's a game—a dice game. And there are a group of women who play the game once a month at alternating houses," said Elaine.

"Sort of like a bridge club?" Myrtle was trying to follow along, but Elaine was speaking so quickly and seemed so panicky that it was hard.

So it's my turn to host and we're having a plumbing crisis." Elaine blinked hard and Myrtle was suddenly very concerned Elaine might cry. Myrtle didn't handle tears well unless the crying person in question were a compatriot of toddler Jack.

Myrtle saw Red leave his house and head in their direction. "Okay, well, here's Red. Maybe it's not as bad as it seems, Elaine."

But apparently it was. Red's freckled face was grim as he said, "I've called the plumber. It's got to be a main sewer line clog for all the sinks and toilets and tubs to be backed up the way they are. This is going to be a major repair job."

"What could have caused it?" asked Elaine.

"Probably something like a tree's roots growing into the line. We've sure got lots of old trees. And it's been pretty dry lately. It could be that a tree was sending roots farther down looking for moisture," said Red as he absently picked up Jack. He then gave Jack a thoughtful look. "Unless Jack here put something in the toilet that backed up the main line."

Jack beamed at him.

"At any rate," said Myrtle. "It sounds as if you're not going to be having company over tonight—is that right?"

Red looked startled. "Oh no. That's right—you were hosting Bunco tonight, weren't you, Elaine? There's no way we can have those ladies over tonight. Not without restrooms."

"It's all right," said Myrtle. "*I'm* going to host the party. The game. Whatever. Bonkers. I guess we'll need food, right?"

Elaine quickly jumped in. "I've actually got all the food prepared, Myrtle. Well, everything but the hot stuff. I've got veggie dips and some other hors d'oeuvres. So you don't have to fix a thing."

"But no hot foods? I can make something hot to serve, you know. It's no trouble."

Red and Elaine darted uneasy looks at each other.

"Really, Myrtle, it's not necessary. There's no need to cook anything," said Elaine.

"I'll run across the street and get the food that Elaine's prepared," said Red. "You'll see that there's plenty of it, Mama."

Myrtle gave a tight smile. "Anybody would think you were trying to keep me from cooking."

"Of course not!" said Elaine, flushing revealingly. "It's only that we don't want you to go to any trouble."

"I've already said it was no trouble." Myrtle was starting to get annoyed.

Red had set Jack down and was turning around and striding down her walkway to retrieve the food from his house when he stopped. "Well, I'll be. Looks like you've got an angel in disguise pulling up in front of your house, Mama."

Myrtle stepped out on her front porch and squinted. Then she made a face. "That's no angel. That's Puddin. And it's about time, too."

Elaine smiled in relief, either from the change of subject, or Puddin's arrival, or both. "That's good. So now you won't feel like you have to clean up."

Myrtle snorted. "That remains to be seen. You know the level of nonsense I have to deal with from Puddin."

Sure enough, Puddin was moseying up to the front walk, as slow as you please, with a sour expression. Elaine seemed to be trying to keep a straight face. "Hi Puddin," she said to the dumpy, pale housekeeper. "How are you? I haven't seen you around for a while."

Puddin narrowed her eyes as if trying to figure out if that were a knock at her lackadaisical cleaning schedule. Apparently deciding otherwise, she said slowly, "I ain't been doin' too great, truth be told. Been poorly."

"I'm sorry to hear that Puddin. Are you better now?" asked Elaine kindly.

Myrtle rolled her eyes heavenward. Puddin didn't need any encouragement to discuss her real or imaginary health issues. It was for this reason that Myrtle didn't see a flash of black sneak around the backs of Puddin and Elaine and into her house.

"Nope," said Puddin succinctly. She slowly moved into the house.

"Where are your cleaning supplies, Puddin?" snapped Myrtle.

"Supplies?" asked Puddin, half turning around. Her round eyes were perfectly guileless, but Myrtle knew better.

"Yes. Glass cleaner. Floor cleaner. Spray polish. Paper towels. The tools of your trade, for heaven's sake!" She was on the verge of losing her religion over Puddin. Next time, she was going to hide her bleach and ammonia, there was simply no other way around it.

"I done run out, Miz Myrtle. That last cleanin' at your house done finished off my supplies." Puddin conveniently disappeared inside before Myrtle could point out that the cleaning supplies Puddin had depleted during her last visit were originally from Myrtle's cabinet…before Puddin had gone home with them.

"Good luck with all that," said Elaine in a low voice. She picked Jack up and swayed back and forth with him as she frowned at Myrtle. “Are you sure this is okay? I could call everybody and just cancel.”

Red was walking toward them with a couple of brown grocery bags of food. Elaine called out to him, “Did you get the alcohol?”

“That’s going to take a separate trip. Or two,” he said pointedly. He swept past them with the bags and muttered to Myrtle, “This is a heavy-drinking group of game-playing ladies.”

“I have sherry,” said Myrtle to his retreating back.

“Oh, this event will require a lot more than a half-empty bottle of sherry, Mama,” said Red. “Fortunately, they all live close enough to walk home. I think.”

Elaine gave Myrtle an apologetic wince. “I’ll be here to help you out tonight. I think Red can handle the plumber and Jack. It should be a really easy night. We just pull the food out, set out the drinks, and we’re ready to go.” She bounced Jack absently and moved to the side as Red walked by to get the alcohol.

“Don’t we need tables?” asked Myrtle.

Elaine stared at her blankly.

“You know…tables. If we’re playing games. Don’t we need tables?” asked Myrtle. Elaine must really be frazzled because she was staring at her as if she were speaking in tongues.

“Oh! Goodness. Yes, card tables would be good. I’ve got everything else—the dice, the tally sheets, pencils. And five dollars. I think I have five dollars,” mused Elaine. “I wasn’t planning on it since I was originally going to be the hostess and the hostess doesn’t pay in.”

Myrtle felt as though new revelations about the evening were happening at every turn. “Five dollars? What is this…gambling?”

“Well, the winners get a little prize. It’s all small bills, you know. Just for fun. The money goes to whoever has the most Buncos, wins, and losses." Elaine reached over and gave Myrtle a reassuring hug…or, rather, to let Jack give her a hug, since Elaine was still holding him. "You're frowning, Myrtle. It's all so easy! So easy. I'll ask Red to carry over some card tables." She peered thoughtfully into Myrtle's living room. "And maybe we should ask him to move your furniture around a wee bit. Just to make sure there's enough room."

Myrtle nodded. "We could fit a lot more people in if the furniture were all against the wall." Myrtle frowned. "Elaine, I've never played Bonkers. You don't need me to *play*, do you? Just to host."

"No, no. I need you to play. There is some kind of weird virus going around and we've got people calling in sick all over the place," said Elaine, making a face. "And, technically, not that it matters, but it's called *Bunco*."

"I guess I'll need to learn the rules real quick," said Myrtle.

Red overheard this part as he returned with what looked like a staggering amount of alcohol. He let out a peal of laughter. "No, you won't. You know how to play bridge don't you?"

"Of course."

"And you play a mean game of chess," continued Red.

"I've been told so," said Myrtle.

"Then you won't have a problem in the world with Bunco, *believe* me, Mama. It's just throwing dice," said Red, shifting the bags to make them more comfortable.

"Like Yahtzee?"

"Not nearly as academic as Yahtzee. Nowhere *near* as academic as Yahtzee, actually. Really, this game just serves as an excuse for a bunch of nice ladies to get together and drink wine and eat junk food. That's about it."

Elaine made a face at Red and he winked at her as he continued inside to set down the grocery bags of wine. "It's the truth. Although I know y'all have a lot of fun."

Jack squirmed in Elaine's arms and she set him gently down. He walked toward the gnomes, looking back at Myrtle for permission.

"Of *course* you may play with the gnomes, Jack," said Myrtle, beaming at the small boy. "Can you find your favorite out there? The one with the little yellow bird on his shoulder? I don't know where Mr. Dusty put all of them."

Red sauntered back out to the front porch and muttered, "At least *somebody* likes those things."

"Jack isn't the gnomes' only fan," said Myrtle in a complacent tone. "You should spend some time looking out the window. You'd see all sorts of people driving slowly by the house. Like I said before, I'm a tourist attraction."

"Oh boy," said Red glumly.

Elaine smiled as Jack gave a happy cry at finding his favorite gnome and instantly climbing on him. "What did you name the gnome?" asked Elaine.

"Ernie," said Myrtle. "He just looked like an Ernie."

Red snorted. "All right, that's my cue to leave." But when they heard a sudden piercing yell and the sound of glass shattering in Myrtle's house, Red immediately charged inside.

Myrtle was close behind him. A streak of black fur flew past them both.

They ran to the kitchen where Puddin was loudly fussing to the empty room. "Witch cat! Trying to clean and that witch cat jumped out at me."

The kitchen that Puddin was purportedly cleaning was an utter disaster. There was a large, broken bottle of olive oil on the floor alongside a large broken bottle of pasta sauce that had not only spilled all over the floor, but had also splattered up on the cabinets and floorboards.

"Puddin!" gasped Myrtle.

Puddin's small, piggy eyes were blazing with fury.

"That cat jumped out and scared the living daylights out of me!"

Red sighed. "So you had to fling the two messiest things in the kitchen at the floor in reaction to it?"

Myrtle groaned. "I'd been planning to make myself spaghetti for supper. This stuff will take you forever to clean up."

"Isn't my fault!" snapped Puddin defensively. She glared spitefully at the mess on the floor.

"I didn't even know Pasha was inside," said Myrtle. "I know you're not her number one fan. She must have sneaked by me when I was on the porch." Pasha was a black cat that had taken up with Myrtle, and Puddin attributed all manner of wickedness to the feral creature. Pasha had an unerring ability to find the people who didn't like her and mess with their heads a bit. It was a trait Myrtle admired and rather envied. "You probably startled her, Puddin. She wasn't expecting to see you."

"*I* wasn't expectin' to see *her*!"

"I'd better find Pasha," said Myrtle. "She might have gone off to hide, as scared as she was. I don't want to lose her again."

Puddin called after her, "What about the floor? What about the fact that my back is thrown?"

Red followed Myrtle. He said in a low voice, "Puddin is real riled up this time, Mama. And I know you don't want to lose her as a cleaner."

"That's where you're wrong. I'd *love* to lose her as a housekeeper. But the fact is that there isn't another cleaning lady anywhere around who has an opening on her schedule. Or who has a husband who does really cheap yard work." Myrtle stomped to the front door, putting her cane down with more force than usual. "And she riles *me* up. What am I going to do with a disaster in the kitchen and the rest of the house a mess and a Bonko thing to host? I'll have to cook something warm to serve, too."

"It's *Bunco*," said Red. "And I'm sure Elaine will be happy to help Puddin out this one time, seeing as how you're doing her a favor and everything." He paused, significantly. "You know a place where you'd never have to clean again? Or do a lick of yardwork?"

Myrtle raised an eyebrow. "Where *is* this nirvana? Oh wait. Since it's you telling me about it, it must be at Greener Pastures Retirement Home. No thanks. I'll pass."

They'd reached the front door and they paused, staring into the yard. "What do you know?" said Red with a laugh.

"Would you look at that," said Myrtle, smiling.

Pasha, the feral cat who passionately disliked nearly everyone but Myrtle, was sitting curled up in Jack's lap as Jack sat perched against Ernie the bird-loving gnome.

"Why don't I ever have a camera on me at the important moments?" muttered Myrtle.

"You do, Mama. Remember? Your phone has a camera," said Red in the automatic manner of someone who has pointed something out repeatedly in the past. He pulled out his own phone and snapped a photo of the scene. "I'll email it to you."

"Pasha made a friend," she said.

Elaine was sitting on the front porch step. She said, "The cat came tearing out of the house as if chased by monsters or something."

"Or something," said Myrtle. "Puddin can be pretty monstrous sometimes."

"She skidded to a stop when she spotted Jack and curled up right on him as if the two of them had been lifelong friends." They watched as Pasha leaned her head back for Jack to rub her neck. Surprisingly, the little boy very gently petted the black cat. Elaine continued, "What happened in there? Is Puddin okay? That was a lot of yelling."

"Oh, chaos and nonsense as usual. Pasha jumped out and scared Puddin. Puddin threw an olive oil bottle and an unopened jar of pasta sauce on the floor in reaction. So now there is a huge mess in the kitchen where there was already a pretty decent sized mess to start out with. Puddin is acting as if she's going on strike so who knows if she'll even clean up the spill. And that still doesn't help me with the rest of the housework that needs to be done," said Myrtle.

Red, apparently feeling as if he might be recruited, quickly said, "Sorry, but I've got to get back to the house and clean up our *own* mess from the backed-up plumbing. And deal with the plumber and Jack, too."

Elaine said, "Myrtle, I'll help you out. Your house is never as messy as you think it is. I can dust and clean off the counters and run the vacuum. It'll look great. This is going to be a really *fun* evening."

Even though Elaine was fairly speedy at cleaning the house, Myrtle felt the time crunch. Puddin was taking forever to clean up the spills. And Myrtle still needed to cook something. Finally, even Elaine admitted she needed to get back home to change clothes, even though the vacuuming was one main chore that hadn't yet been completed.

Fortunately, as Elaine was walking out, there was a tap on Myrtle's door. Peering out, she saw Miles on her front porch with his level gaze behind his wire-rimmed glasses. He was clutching a plate of brownies.

"Ready to watch the show?" he asked in his serious voice. "Oh, hi Elaine," he said as Elaine darted past with a quick greeting.

"Thank goodness you're here!" Myrtle grabbed the plate of brownies. "I'll put these with the other food that Elaine brought. No time for shows today." She squinted at Miles in appraisal. "Let's see. Should I put you on cooking duty or vacuum duty?"

The words hadn't even fully left her lips when Miles replied with alacrity, "Cooking duty."

Myrtle frowned at him. She had the sneaking suspicion that Miles wasn't completely impressed with her culinary ability. Which sealed Miles's fate for the evening. "No, I think I'd better have you vacuum. Sometimes that cord trips me up. Besides, I need to assess what I have in my fridge and cabinets and see what I can cobble together a meal with."

Miles peeked around the kitchen door and spotted the piqued Puddin muttering dire imprecations under her breath as she swabbed up the spills. He just as quickly ducked his head back out again and obediently fired up the vacuum. Myrtle poked into her cabinets and fridge while trying to skirt the fuming Puddin and the spill, which appeared to be spreading like a viral outbreak instead of being absorbed.

When Miles finished vacuuming, Myrtle consulted him. "Okay, here's what I have. And let's try to work with it since I really don't have time to go to the store. So it's milk, eggs, carrots, broccoli, chocolate chips, crackers, olives, grits, butter, and pimento cheese."

Miles stared at her. "Myrtle, with that odd assortment, the only thing that comes to mind is chocolate chip cookies, assuming you've got staples like sugar and vanilla extract on hand. You should go to the store tomorrow just to get some normal food."

Myrtle snapped her fingers. "Chocolate chip cookies. Quick and easy. Might counteract the effects of some of that heavy drinking. Perfect."

Puddin let out a frustrated wail. "Miz Myrtle, this ain't going to clean up. I done run out of paper towels."

"I didn't even know you were using paper towels! Especially those particular paper towels, which are cheap ones. For heaven's sake, Puddin, go grab those cleaning rags from the closet. I don't have the time or the inclination for your foolishness today."

Puddin sullenly stomped off for the rags.

"Ridiculous," said Myrtle with a snort. "Right when I need to be in here, too." She started pulling out the ingredients for her cookies. But some of the ingredients were in the cabinet where the floor looked especially oily. She'd better wait for Puddin to hand them over to her.

Miles carefully wrapped up the vacuum cleaner cord on the hooks on the back of the vacuum. "Myrtle?" he asked, watching her pull out a cookie sheet.

"Yes, Miles?"

"Why, exactly, are we doing this cleaning and baking?"

"What? Didn't I tell you?" Myrtle scowled again at the olive oil on the floor.

"No, I didn't get the full story. Just that vacuuming needed to happen," said Miles.

"We're playing Bonkers tonight," said Myrtle distractedly, opening the fridge for the butter.

"Excuse me?" asked Miles politely.

"Bonkers. Something like that. Whatever."

"Bunco?" guessed Miles. "I didn't know you were in a group. It doesn't really seem like your scene."

"I'm not in a group. And I don't know what you mean about it *not being my scene*. I do play bridge, you know. Anyway, Elaine, who has had a sudden, dire plumbing fiasco, *is* in a group. I'm hosting and apparently playing, too." Myrtle went back in the fridge for the eggs. "Can you pull out the wine from those bags and put them out on the table with my wineglasses?"

The phone rang right as Myrtle cracked two eggs. "Shoot. Puddin, can you get that?"

Puddin shot her a beleaguered look and struggled up from the floor. She tried to pick up the receiver with the hand that was still clutching the sopping rag. It slipped from her grasp, dangling at the end of the spiral cord. She snatched it back and spat out, "Miz Myrtle's residence, Puddin speakin'."

Myrtle saw Puddin's small eyes gleam as she watched Miles meticulously set out the wine bottles. "What?" asked the housekeeper. "Okay, hold on." She pulled her head away from the receiver. "Miz Myrtle, it's Miz Elaine. She says she had two more calls and two more people can't come. She needs two subs and do you know any?"

Myrtle said some unpleasant words to the eggs, which had cracked in such a way as to allow eggshells in the mixture. "No, I don't know anybody," she muttered.

Puddin coughed in a manner she deemed delicate, but which actually sounded like a prelude to pneumonia. "Mr. Miles and me can play as well as anybody, I reckon."

"What's that?" Myrtle peered at the recipe card and said, "Can you hand me baking powder and sugar, Puddin?"

Puddin's eyes were fixed on the wine table. "I said that I reckon Mr. Miles and I play Bonkers as well as anybody," she repeated in a determined voice, reaching into the cabinet and pulling out some containers and shoving them across the counter to Myrtle.

"Puddin, you might go through all the wine and then who would take you home? As for Miles. ... I think this is supposed to be a hen party."

Miles said with dignity, "I actually have played Bunco several times. Which sounds as if it's several more times than you have, Myrtle."

Myrtle diligently measured out the dry ingredients. "I suppose that desperate times call for desperate measures. Puddin, you may sub tonight as long as you come back tomorrow to help me clean up the mess from the party."

Myrtle carefully made the cookies, despite numerous distractions. She put them in the oven. "I need to go get ready. Puddin, can you keep an eye on these and pull them out when the timer goes off?"

Puddin shot her an exasperated look. "How am I supposed to cook and clean at the same time?"

"I don't know, but I guess you'll figure it out if you're interested in playing tonight."

"Do I look all right?" asked Miles, now looking rather self-consciously down at his khaki pants and button down shirt."

Puddin gave Miles a sideways, appraising look. "Maybe take them ink pens out of yer pocket," directed Puddin. "Kinda nerdy looking."

"Well, he *was* an accountant. That's a fairly nerdy profession," said Myrtle.

Puddin nodded in agreement.

"An engineer," corrected Miles coldly.

"Same thing. The point is that you look fine for tonight. You look fine for really any occasion that might arise, actually. You could even speak to the rotary club in that outfit. But I need to change." Myrtle quickly moved to the back of the house.

Chapter Three

Unfortunately, she also apparently needed to do laundry. In her mind she'd pictured herself pulling out a long, yellow and white shirt dress with a belted waist. It didn't seem to be hanging in her closet, though. Nor did the navy funeral dress, which was her go-to sometimes as a fallback. Racking her brain, she remembered that there had been an unprecedented two days in a row last week when she'd had to wear a dress for longer than the four hour limit when she considered a dress to be clean enough to go right back on the hanger.

Myrtle groaned and opened up the hamper. Maybe she could throw one of the dresses into the dryer real quick with a dryer sheet and it would be fresh again. She discovered that the yellow and white shirt dress appeared to have a large coffee stain on it. The navy one had a hem torn out. Was there some diabolical gremlin determined to sabotage the Bonkers game tonight?

She finally settled on a pair of black slacks and a red, long-sleeved top made out of some sort of blousy material.

"Myrtle?" Miles called from the front of the house.

"Yes? What is it?" It better not be another catastrophe.

"You don't seem to have enough wineglasses for Bunco," observed Miles politely.

"What? I have eight glasses," said Myrtle. She looked at her rumpled appearance in her bedroom mirror and made a face at herself.

"Bunco requires twelve players."

"*What*? Twelve people over here?" This was a vital

piece of information that Elaine had apparently forgotten to transmit.

Miles's voice continued from the front. "If you don't have twelve wineglasses, I can bring some from home."

"Of *course* I don't have twelve wineglasses. Who has twelve wineglasses? We'll be stuffed in here like sardines."

"Okay, I'm off to get my crystal then," said Miles.

Myrtle gave herself a final once-over in the mirror, found she wasn't improved, and decided she was out of time to beautify herself or to bake any more refreshments. There wouldn't be enough cookies to go around, but at least she'd made a stab at it. No wonder there was so much alcohol. Although, under the circumstances, Myrtle might end up making a dent in it herself.

There was a light tap at the door and Elaine came in. She was about as rumpled looking as Myrtle was. "Hope things are going better over here than they are at home. Thanks for this again, Myrtle."

"Oh, it's no problem," said Myrtle automatically. Although, of course, it was. "By the way, who is coming over tonight? Do I know them all?"

"Well, between you and me and Puddin and Miles we make up one of the three tables. I've got Georgia Simpson coming in, you know her from book club," said Elaine.

Myrtle winced. "Glad you told me. Hopefully I can stay far away from Georgia. She wears me out. Big voice, big hair, tattoos."

"That's right. She's a regular. I *thought* that Tippy Chambers was going to have to cancel at the last minute and I'd have to grab Erma from next door to sub. But luckily, Tippy finished whatever it was that was keeping her," said Elaine. She took a large, furry die out of a plastic grocery bag and placed it as a centerpiece on one of the game tables.

"Luckily," said Myrtle darkly. She'd have found a way

to cancel Bonkers if her despised next door neighbor was on the invite list.

"So that leaves the others. There's Mimsy, Poppy, Estelle, Florence, and Alma," ticked off Elaine on her fingers. "I think you might know some of these ladies, although I'm not sure if you know Estelle. She lives in that house with the really modern architecture."

"I know who those women are, but I don't really *know* them. And you've left someone out," said Myrtle. "That's only eleven players."

Elaine knit her brows. "Who am I forgetting? I hope I haven't forgotten that someone wasn't coming or else I really *will* have to grab Erma from next door. We hate playing with ghosts." She frowned. "Oh, I know. Luella. Luella White is the last one."

Myrtle brightened. "Luella White? Wonderful."

"You know her?" asked Elaine.

"I'm supposed to *get* to know her. Sloan Jones at the paper thinks she knows all sorts of juicy gossip that might help get us more readership. I wasn't sure how on earth I was going to spend time with her...until now."

There was another tap on the door and Myrtle grouched, "Grand Central station." It was Miles, carrying a tray with four very prissy-looking crystal wineglasses.

"I ran out of glasses. I didn't realize that I needed twelve," said Myrtle in a meaningful voice to Elaine.

Elaine seemed to miss the subtext. That could, however, be considered understandable under the circumstances and the plumbing nightmare she was experiencing. "Those are lovely glasses, Miles," she said.

He smiled at her. "They don't get a lot of use at my house so it's good to let them actually serve a purpose. They're sort of family heirlooms."

Myrtle eyed the wineglasses warily. They seemed very delicate indeed. "Hope they won't break on my watch. I don't need anything on my conscience. Were they your mother's?"

Miles's dearly departed mother had passed away too young and seemed rather idolized by her son.

"No, I think they belonged to my mother's sister. Or my mother's mother's sister…a maiden aunt who ended up buying her own crystal when she'd given up on getting married. At any rate—they're pretty old," said Miles. He started arranging them on the table with the other glasses and wine bottles.

Myrtle rushed back to the kitchen, pulled out a platter for the cookies and checked on Puddin's progress. Puddin was looking even more disheveled than usual with sprigs of brown hair hanging limply around her face. The red sauce was cleared up (for the most part, although Myrtle still saw a spatter here and there on the counters) but the floor felt a bit oily still. Puddin had indeed pulled the cookies out, although they looked rather crunchy.

There was a knock at the door. Myrtle grumbled, "Why don't they just walk in? It's a party. They were invited. No one's going to shoot them for trespassing."

The knocking continued. "Puddin, can you get that?"

Puddin jumped up quickly. Quickly enough for Myrtle to wonder if she'd really just been lounging around in the kitchen until she heard Myrtle come in. "Okay, Miz Myrtle." She flounced off to get the door. Myrtle could hear her saying, "Playin' the game? Come on in…I'll get her." Then she hollered, "Miz Myrtle, the people are here."

"Puddin is always so wonderfully direct, isn't she?" murmured Miles to Myrtle.

"I wouldn't go so far as to put 'wonderful' and 'Puddin' in the same sentence," said Myrtle.

As everyone entered, Puddin's gaze drifted once more toward the drinks table. "Guess I'd better get myself a wine glass so's I fit in with everybody," she told Myrtle.

Myrtle was too busy trying to herd the cookies onto a platter with her plastic spatula to really listen. Elaine followed her into the kitchen and murmured, "We probably should keep everyone out of the kitchen or else you'll have olive oil tracked all through your house. Here, I'll carry in the cookies for you. Maybe we should put them on a few different plates and scatter them around the room for the guests."

Myrtle knew some of the women who were coming into her house. Actually, since Bradley, North Carolina, was so small, she knew who *all* of them *were*. But she wasn't friends, personally, with most of them. She did recognize Luella White—a small, stern woman with tightly pressed lips, brightly colored clothes, rather too much perfume, and a somewhat disapproving expression on her face. Luella didn't look like the type of woman who was going to gossip easily and freely, despite what Sloan said. Myrtle could only hope she'd join Puddin at the wine table and loosen up a bit.

Miles walked over to join her. Myrtle said, "It looks like the game night starts out as a social hour."

Miles smiled. "The entire night is a social hour, Myrtle. The game is really just an excuse to socialize. The whole point of each round is to roll three dice to get the number of that round. First round, you roll for threes. Second round for twos. If all three dice are the number you're supposed to be rolling for, that's a Bunco."

Myrtle stared at him. "There's got to be more to it than *that*, Miles. Surely, you're missing something. Like the whole point."

"The point is the *socializing*. As I was saying."

Myrtle sighed. "Well, in my head I'm going to be trying to make it harder than it is. I'll be looking for a full house or two of a kind or something. And I guess I need to figure out how to sit near Luella White, if the whole evening is supposed to be about visiting."

Miles raised an inquiring eyebrow. "I didn't realize you and Luella were such good friends."

"I don't even know the woman. But Sloan wants me to extract information from her so that the paper can have a scoop. Or, actually, lots of scoops."

Myrtle turned and startled at the sight of a rather sweaty Dusty very close to her. "Ah! Dusty, you scared me!" she scolded.

"Wasn't trying to. Just telling you I'm done." His gaze was expectant and Myrtle couldn't figure out why.

"Done? With what? Surely not the gnomes—that was ages ago. I thought you'd left for home."

"It took a while. And you have lots of the little guys," said Dusty.

Miles moved away. He must have anticipated a reaction.

"Oh no. Did you put *all* of them out? I'm sure I didn't ask you to put *all* of them out. Just a representative delegation. I never put them all out unless Red's infraction was really unpardonable." Now that she was hosting a party, she found it hard to believe that she'd potentially asked Dusty to put all the gnomes in her yard. It could mean it was rather crowded in both yards and now she had a house full of guests.

Dusty squinted at her, working through the vocabulary. "I was tole to put 'em out. And I did. Feeling I should get a tip for it, too. Lotsa work you know." His narrowed gaze landed on his wife who was gleefully guzzling a large glass of wine out of Miles's prissy crystal and chatting as easily with Bradley socialite Tippy Chalmers as if Puddin were president of the Junior League.

Myrtle said hastily, "We're going to borrow Puddin for a little while to round out a game we're playing. Puddin mentioned she'd subbed for Bunkers before."

Dusty's expression was stony. "So I been slaving out there and she's been partyin'?"

"No, she's been sopping up a catastrophic spill she created. Look, let me just grab my pocketbook and I'll give you a little something extra. I swear, I don't even know how you got all those gnomes to even fit in my yard," she muttered.

"Weren't easy," said Dusty nobly.

"We'll have someone drive Puddin back home," said Myrtle absently as she pawed through her purse looking for cash.

Dusty noted gruffly, "Looks like Mr. Miles is sick."

"What?" Myrtle jerked her head up in time to see Mils carefully spitting into a large paper towel.

"Excuse me," said Miles, grimacing. "Myrtle, these are your cookies?"

"Is there a problem with them?" Myrtle folded her arms in front of her.

"What, exactly, did you put in the batter?" asked Miles delicately.

At that moment there were other coughing sounds and exclamations emanating from the living room.

Myrtle's mind whirled. "Nothing! Nothing special. Just the usual—baking powder, sugar."

Miles closed his eyes. "And apparently other things. It's a shame I couldn't have helped you out. The wine glass crisis distracted me."

His last words were punctuated by a tremendous crash.

A guest named Poppy came in with the remains of one of Miles's heirloom crystal wineglasses. "So sorry," she said solemnly. "It leaped right out of my hand. Someone squealed after they ate something and it scared me."

Miles spotted the ingredients on the counter and said, "Myrtle, this is baking soda, not baking powder." He opened up the white canister next to the baking soda box and said, "And this appears to be salt, not sugar."

Myrtle said darkly, "That Puddin passed them to me. I swear she's trying to sabotage the whole evening. Both she *and* Dusty."

"I'll toss the cookies out," said Miles.

Myrtle said, "And *don't* tell anyone who made them!"

Miles gave her a look that told her that people already had their suspicions.

Myrtle was surprised when everyone rather quickly put their pocketbooks down at various spots at various tables. Elaine said, "The hostess gets to start out at the head, or winning, table and everyone else draws a score sheet out of a pile. If they don't have a star on their sheet they have to sit at the middle table or the losing table."

Myrtle nodded her head although she swore Elaine was speaking gibberish. The hostess rule made sense but the winning and losing tables sounded like something out of *Alice in Wonderland.* She almost felt as if she were at a mad tea party, herself. The volume of laughter and talking in the small room was high and there were already wine bottles in the trashcan. She peered over at the winning table to see if her tablemate might be a March Hare or a dormouse.

To her delight, however, it was Luella White. Since this appeared to be the kind of game one could talk through, or even interrogate a gossiper through, maybe Myrtle could soon return to Sloan with something to report. She sat next to Luella, who was wearing quite a lot of what smelled like expensive perfume and a very brightly-colored blouse with a long, multi-colored skirt.

Luella's eyes narrowed and she gave Myrtle a quick once-over. "So you want to be partners?"

"What?"

"If you sit next to me, we'll be on a team together for the first round." Luella's tone indicated that she wasn't at all sure she wanted to be partnered with someone who seemed baffled by the proceedings.

That had to be better than playing on the *opposite* team in terms of gathering information. "Sure. Why not?" Myrtle scooted her chair under the table. "What's our strategy for winning?"

Luella stared at her, her hard, brown eyes stern. "Strategy? There *is* no strategy for Bunco! There's only luck. And someone who keeps the score well."

"Maybe you should do that part then," said Myrtle. "I'm just a sub."

"I'll handle it," said Luella with a sniff. "It's a big job." She glanced around her. "Where's the fuzzy die?"

Myrtle, who had now finished the bewildered phase and was entering the very cross and irritable stage, asked, "How should I know? I thought fuzzy dice usually dangle from unusual people's rear view mirrors."

"The die starts at the head table and then we pass it to players who get Buncos." Luella rolled her eyes. She appeared to be deeply regretting Myrtle's partnership with her.

Fortunately, Myrtle was able to counteract some of Luella's original impression of her by spotting a large, fuzzy, fuchsia die across the room. "That's got to be it, over there."

Luella jumped up, grabbed the die, and sat back down, tossing it at the center of the table.

Myrtle cleared her throat. A couple of other players looked to be heading their way, so she better fit in her questions while she could. "So, Luella, how are you liking Bradley?"

Luella shrugged a thin shoulder. "It's all right. I moved here because of Mimsy." She gestured to a smiling middle-aged woman at another table. "Mimsy is my only remaining relative." Luella appeared remarkably unmoved as she reported the demise of her entire family.

"I'm sure Mimsy is delighted you're in town," said Myrtle. "I hear you've gotten very involved in a lot of different activities."

Luella said impatiently, "It's the only way to get to know people if you're new in town." She looked thoughtful for a moment. "Say, speaking of getting to know people, you're friends with Miles, aren't you?"

"Friends and neighbors," said Myrtle a bit cautiously. She had a feeling that she knew what was bound to come next.

Luella's voice was somewhat warmer. "So you're *friendly*."

"That's right. We're *friends*," emphasized Myrtle.

"I would love to be introduced to him. He seems like such an intelligent man. And still quite handsome," mulled Luella.

"If you like that sort of highbrow, intellectual look, I suppose," said Myrtle. "He does have a nice collection of antique crystal wineglasses, too."

"Let's get him to play at our table," said Luella quickly.

Myrtle frowned. "I thought that only people with stars on their score cards got to start at the head table."

"Rules are for bending," said Luella. She took out a pen. "You only need to distract him, Myrtle."

But no distracting was necessary, apparently, since Miles was on a mission. "Elaine divided some of the cookies onto another plate so she could have them on two different food tables," he murmured to her. "Trying to track them all down." He laid his score sheet and pencil down on the table and scoured the room. Luella quickly took the opportunity to mark his sheet with a star.

Myrtle sighed. "I think those are they—over on the small table near the hall door. They're hardly poisonous,

Miles. They simply suffered a couple of unfortunate substitutions."

"You didn't eat one," said Miles.

Luella interrupted them. "Looks like you're at our table, sir. And I don't think I've had the pleasure of meeting you."

Miles frowned. "No, actually, I don't have a star on my score sheet." He glanced over at the paper and his frown deepened. "I was *sure* I didn't."

"Maybe you just looked in the wrong spot," said Luella smoothly. She beamed at him. "I'm Luella White. I'm somewhat new to Bradley."

"Nice to meet you," said Miles politely, still looking bemused. "Uh … sorry, I need to do something. One second."

"He seems nice," purred Luella.

But Luella didn't. And Myrtle bristled at the thought of the woman getting her claws into Miles. She wasn't even all that attractive. She wore very loud clothing, rather too much red lipstick and perfume, and looked humorless and tough as nails. Although Luella was probably Miles's age, she looked older.

"What do you think of Bradley so far?" asked Myrtle, trying to get back on track before Miles came back with his high distractibility quotient. "Or, more specifically, what do you think of the people who live here?"

Now she had Luella's attention. She was now giving Myrtle a curious look as she took a large sip of her wine. "Why, don't *you* like the people who live here?" She smiled at Myrtle. The smile told Myrtle that Luella thought she was a very snoopy old woman who was a little too interested in gossip. "What I've found is that people are wrong about small towns. They think that nothing interesting ever happens in a small town. What they have to do is look at the *microcosm* of the small town and they'll find plenty of things going on."

Myrtle affected a confused look although she knew exactly what Luella was talking about. "So…you've found plenty of things going on … aside from the different activities you're in? Is that right?"

Luella now looked a bit scornful. "Not at all. I mean that the *people* have a lot of drama going on. I simply learn about the drama while I'm enjoying the activity." She glanced around the living room and then leaned closer to Myrtle. "Take this crowd—the Bunco players. You probably don't know a lot about the people in your house, do you?"

Miles, having disposed of the rest of the cookies, was now heading their way again. Myrtle said impatiently, "Maybe I'd know more about them if you'd *tell* me about them." She relaxed a bit again as Miles got waylaid by another admirer.

"Take Estelle over there." Luella nodded her head toward an athletic looking woman in her forties with short sandy hair. "She's an interesting case. Do you know what she does for a living?"

Myrtle shook her head.

"Nothing! She calls herself a storm-chaser as if she's some sort of freelance photographer or videographer or something. The truth is that she spends most of her time taking pictures of sunshine and rainbows here in Bradley. Dead broke. And she can't maintain a relationship to save her life. Apparently, she hasn't even *tried* to date for years," said Luella.

Myrtle shrugged. "Sounds like just someone trying to survive a tough economy and facing small town challenges in finding someone to date."

Luella's eyes narrowed. "Or take Florence over there." She gestured to a very fluffy looking old lady wearing a floral dress and a rather bemused smile who was heading in the direction of the kitchen. "I've heard and seen all sorts of scary things about her. Age-related, you know." She smirked at Myrtle.

Myrtle tried subduing her annoyance. "What sorts of scary things? Florence doesn't seem much of a threat to me."

"That's because you're not paying attention," said Luella smoothly. "And then you've got Alma over there. Poor Alma."

Myrtle was starting to get the idea that Luella was actually *not* a gossip. Not strictly a gossip, anyway. She mostly liked feeling important by knowing unpleasant things about people. Maybe she'd share it, maybe not. She simply liked *knowing* it. And Myrtle liked Luella less and less and they went on. Plus she was starting to wonder if she were going to get anything for the newspaper from her. "Do you also have dirt on Mimsy and Poppy? They would be the only other two guests that I'm not as well acquainted with."

Luella scowled at her. "Certainly not. Mimsy is my last living relative, for heaven's sake. Poppy is her best friend. But I can tell you a thing or two about your guest Georgia Simpson." She nodded toward a woman with big hair, tattoos, too much mascara, and a booming laugh.

"No, *I* can tell *you* a thing or two about Georgia Simpson," snapped Myrtle, feeling tired of this game now. "I taught her, for one thing. And she's been in my book club for ages."

"She's literate?" asked Luella doubtfully.

"As I said, I can tell you a thing or two. And anyone who went through my English classes is more than literate, I can assure you." Although Sloan's creative spelling at the newspaper left room for doubt.

Luella shifted a bit in her chair and reached for her purse. "Myrtle, is it all right if I smoke inside?" asked

Luella in her husky voice.

Now Myrtle knew where to attribute the huskiness. And probably the reason behind the generously-applied perfume. "Certainly not," said Myrtle, horrified. "The smoke would get into my curtains and cushions. It'll have to be outside. Although, since we're playing a game, I really don't know where you'll find the time."

Luella said impatiently, "It's not the kind of game where you sit still. We'll all be moving from table to table and getting drinks and eating and using your restroom."

"Then enjoy your smoking break in the backyard," said Myrtle stiffly. She imagined it might be challenging to find a place to stand, if Dusty had truly blanketed the yard in gnomes.

"Break*s*," corrected Luella. "And I may as well take the first one now while everyone's still milling around."

Luella left, looking irked when Miles approached the table. "Serves her right," muttered Myrtle. "What a pill."

Miles murmured, "Making enemies so soon in the evening?"

"You'd do well to make an enemy with that one. She has designs on you, Miles."

"*Designs* on me? I suddenly feel as if I've stepped into a Regency romance."

"Maybe you have," said Myrtle. Elaine came up to fill Myrtle in on a text message update from Red about the plumber. Miles asked a few horrified questions about the issue, which launched Elaine into a gushing monologue on toilets, tubs, sinks, and the perfidy of plumbing in general.

Puddin had trapped Tippy Chambers by the front door and appeared to be forcing the poor woman to listen to a long list of her health problems as she medicated herself heavily with wine.

Mimsy, the middle-aged-last-relative-of Luella's had lost an earring. "Has anyone seen my earring? It's one of my favorites...goes with everything." Several people from the kitchen came to help the group in the living room search for the MIA earring.

An older woman named Florence came up to Myrtle and quietly asked, "Could you tell me where the powder room is?" Myrtle pointed down the short hallway off the living room.

"Honestly, where would anyone *think* the restroom was? This place is no mansion. Isn't it obvious that it's down the hall?" asked Myrtle. She looked at her watch to see that fifteen minutes had gone by since the last time she'd checked. "I think it's time to get this show on the road," she grumbled. "Otherwise, we'll be here all night. People are doing everything *but* playing the game."

Miles pushed his glasses up and looked solemnly at the small bell on their table. "Just ring the bell when you're ready. The head table sets the pace."

"You mean I had the power to start the game all along?" Myrtle felt like Dorothy discovering her ruby slippers could take her home. Elaine stopped talking about plumbing and quickly slipped away to find her table.

Seconds later Myrtle vigorously rang the bell and sure enough, the ladies all obediently headed to their seats like little lambs. Although half of them refilled their drinks before they did.

Miles's partner was the tough, tattooed Georgia. Myrtle smiled at this. Miles was secretly fascinated by the woman. He might pretend it was a horrified fascination, but the truth was that he seemed oddly attracted to her. Maybe his distraction would work in Myrtle's favor, enabling her to win the game. If distraction helped at all with this sort of game.

She *wouldn't* win without a partner, though. Myrtle glanced crossly around her.

"Where is Luella?" she hissed. "How long could it

possibly take to smoke a cigarette?"

Miles took the question seriously and considered it carefully. "Well, I guess it depends on the length of the drags the smoker takes. And perhaps the length of the cigarette itself. It could vary between five and maybe seven minutes."

"Well, this has been much longer than that," said Myrtle. "I think we need to organize a search party."

"Maybe she got lost in the sea of gnomes," suggested Miles with a wicked twinkle in his eyes.

"Dusty wasn't supposed to put all of them out there," grumbled Myrtle. It was always more satisfying to blame someone else than to think about one's own part in a problem. "I declare, no one ever listens to instructions these days."

"I'll track down Luella for you," said Miles.

"No, I will. If you go, she'll view it as a serendipitous opportunity for a liaison." Myrtle grabbed her cane and hurried to the kitchen and out the back door.

Dusty hadn't lied when he'd said he put *all* the gnomes out. They were lined up next to each other and several appeared to be lying on top of other gnomes. It resembled a battlefield, post-battle.

"Where on earth is she?" muttered Myrtle. Luella was small, but she shouldn't disappear amid a herd of gnomes. Myrtle reached back and opened the kitchen door wide, allowing the light from the room to illuminate the outdoors.

And that was when she saw Luella lying on top of the gnomes.

Chapter Four

On closer inspection, Luella appeared to be very dead indeed. Her eyes were wide open and staring lifelessly into the dark. Her mouth was frozen in a snarl. The cigarette she'd been so keen on was lying next to her at the base of a particularly mischievous gnome.

Miles's voice came from behind her. "Any luck, Myrtle? The natives are getting restless in there."

"I found her, all right. But she won't be playing Bonkers tonight. Someone killed her, Miles."

"*What*?"

"Yes." Myrtle squinted into the dark, leaning forward on her cane. She saw a gnome with a large adjustable wrench on its head. "I *told* Dusty to put his tools away! I think that wrench must be the murder weapon."

"I'll get Red," said Miles.

"Just let Elaine know on the way out...she'll need to go over to be with Jack," said Myrtle. A cool breeze came up and Myrtle shivered. "I believe I'll wait for Red inside. Just to be on the safe side."

The nice thing about having a police chief across the street from you is that it takes seconds for him to arrive. Myrtle didn't have to tell everyone that they weren't playing the game because someone had gotten herself killed in the backyard. Red did it. And the announcement didn't have quite the stunning, silencing effect that Myrtle had expected. Perhaps everyone was anaesthetized with wine.

Florence Ainsworth, after returning from her powder room expedition, fell asleep shortly before the awful discovery and was peacefully snoring with her head on her chest. She startled awake, however, at Red's deep voice speaking loudly in the small space. "What number are we on?" she asked drowsily. Tippy Chambers had to whisper an explanation and then the old woman looked abashed at having the bad manners to nap during a murder.

Although Red's face was grim when he made his announcement, it was even grimmer when he told the group that he had a call out to the state police to bring a forensic team. "While I'm waiting on them, I'll need to talk to everyone here, privately. Everyone should make sure that they stay put until I've told them they're clear to leave."

Luella's last living relative, Mimsy, had instantly choked up when hearing the news. But while listening to Red, her tears dried up and her eyes opened wide. "But…surely you don't think one of *us* did it, Red! We're all here to play Bunco and have a fun night."

"That's right," said tattooed Georgia. "Nobody set out to murder anyone tonight. Shouldn't you be searching the neighborhood for the bad guy?"

Red narrowed his eyes. "I'm not making any wild accusations here, I'm only following protocol. It's too early for me to say anything. I'm simply not ruling anything out."

Mimsy said in a pleading tone, "But maybe it wasn't even foul play. Maybe she simply stumbled and fell. It's…well, it's a little crowded out there."

"I'm afraid it *was* foul play, judging from what I saw," said Red in a more gentle voice. "Her wound wasn't accidental."

Myrtle murmured to Miles, "Not to mention the fact that there was a bloody wrench nearby."

Miles nodded. "Do you think it was someone here, then?" he asked her quietly.

"I sure do. My yard is fenced in with a privacy fence. I made sure Dusty locked the side gate. What murderous vagrant is going to scale a tall fence to kill a woman who doesn't even have her purse on her? No, someone in this house did it. And I have to say that Luella wasn't the nicest person in the world. Nobody is probably upset about this except Mimsy over there."

Mimsy had resumed quietly sobbing into a tissue.

Red said, "Mama, if I could speak with you first." He looked around him at the packed kitchen and living room. "I guess I'll have to commandeer the back bedroom for questioning."

Myrtle followed him to the bedroom. Red took out a notebook. "It is unfortunate that you've got a body once again in your backyard, Mama. And most unfortunate that you discovered it."

Myrtle sniffed. "It's a hostess's job to keep track of her guests. And discover bodies, if it comes down to it."

Red let that one go. "Okay. So please tell me that the Bunco game was at least underway so that there was some sort of structure going on and maybe I can figure out the murderer easier."

"I wish I *could* tell you that, Red. But no, all those women were wandering here and yonder. It was like trying to herd cats to get them to play the game."

"Can you at least help me eliminate *anybody* from suspicion?" pleaded Red.

Myrtle pursed her lips. "I can't see Elaine killing her."

Red glared at her. "I could have reached that conclusion myself, Mama. And I'll go ahead and spare you the trouble and eliminate Miles and you."

"Well, now, Luella apparently had the hots for Miles," said Myrtle. "Although I don't suppose that's a motive for murder. Unless Miles had such revulsion for the prospect that he was driven to kill. That could be considered manslaughter, I'm guessing."

"Okay, silliness aside. We know Miles didn't have

anything to do with Luella's sudden death in your backyard. Just give me something. Who was Luella's partner tonight? At least, starting out, since partners change."

Myrtle said, "I was." She really hated giving Red any actual information, since she felt whatever she knew gave her a head start. And she did so love figuring out the killer before Red could.

"Finally! Something we can work with. All right, so did you have an opportunity to talk to Luella at all?" asked Red.

Myrtle sighed. "She gossiped a little about the people in the room. Apparently, she was all about spreading rumors, which seems like a terrific motive for murder in a small town. Other than that, she was only interested in talking about Miles or smoking cigarettes. Technically, smoking is what killed her. If she hadn't taken that smoke break, she'd be inside drinking wine and playing Bonkers right now."

"Who, specifically, did she mention having gossip on?" asked Red, ignoring Myrtle's anti-smoking community service message.

"Oh, let's see. There was Estelle, the storm chaser, who is broke. And Florence, who she hinted has some age-related issues. And then there was Alma. But I don't have any details because Luella didn't want to spill the beans—she just wanted to feel smug."

Red raised his eyebrows. "Still. That's quite a bit of information to have worked out of the woman in a short span of time, Mama. I'm impressed."

"I was goading her into it. Which is all your fault!" hissed Myrtle, shooting her son an annoyed look.

"*My* fault? How on earth is it my fault?" asked Red.

"You're the one who tattled to Sloan about my correcting the newspaper. That sparked him to analyze *The*

Bradley Bugle's stats. Which made him reach the conclusion that the paper needed more local stories … particularly of the salacious variety. Sloan believed that Luella might have the scoop on everyone in Bradley. Which led him to ask me to interrogate Luella." Myrtle shrugged as if this line of progression made perfect sense.

"Let's get back to tonight," urged Red. "We've been able to eliminate you, Miles, and Elaine. Anyone else?"

"I guess Georgia Simpson, too. She's so loud that I could easily keep track of her. I heard that laugh right behind me the entire time after she entered my house. Miles can probably back me up on that, since he's fascinated by her. He likely had one eye on her the whole time," said Myrtle.

Red seemed bemused by this. "I wouldn't put Miles and Georgia together."

"Perhaps he had a memorable childhood experience involving a tattooed lady at the circus," said Myrtle.

"Anyone else, Mama? Think it through for me. I know how observant you are."

It was a sign of Red's desperation that he used the word *observant* instead of his go-to word *nosy* to describe his mother's activities. It was a smart move, too. It actually made her want to help him, instead of begrudging him the information.

"I'd like to imagine that Puddin could be responsible for this mess, judging from the other messes that she spearheaded today. But I can't. Puddin is an utter disgrace, but I don't think she goes around murdering people with Dusty's rusty tools. And I can assure you that she did nothing but drink from a large glass of wine and corner Tippy Chambers at my front door the entire time. Tippy couldn't even sit down or move into the room. Puddin acted as if she and Tippy were the very best of friends," said Myrtle rolling her eyes. "In other words—Puddin and

Tippy are out unless they were able to perform some sort of magical sleight of hand."

Red jotted down notes. "Okay. I'm sure the SBI will be here any minute to help me take statements and they'll have forensics with them. I asked Elaine to make sure everyone kept away from the kitchen and the backyard. Everyone should just stay relaxed and seated in there until we're all done and can tell them to leave. I'm sure you'll want to get back in there and play hostess."

Myrtle intended on playing reporter, instead. This should be exactly the kind of story that Sloan was looking for to boost individual paper sales and maybe even loop in some new subscribers.

But Myrtle hadn't counted on the appeal of alcohol in this stressful circumstance. As soon as poisoning was completely ruled out as a possible method, the Bunco ladies headed over to the wine table and proceeded to deplete the remaining reserves. Fortunately, Miles assured Myrtle in a low voice that he'd already announced that he was the designated driver for anyone who needed a ride home.

Once the state police arrived, things didn't improve. They were rather rude, Myrtle thought. One of the SBI officers made snide statements about having to weave carefully around garden gnomes to look for evidence. It all seemed to take a very long time, too—the statement gathering, the wine drinking, the forensics. Things finally improved only when Myrtle's favorite police officer, Lieutenant Perkins appeared on the scene.

Despite the fact that it was getting fairly late in the evening, Lieutenant Perkins wore a crisp white button down shirt, a pair of dark slacks that appeared to be recently ironed, and a red and gold tie. His super-short military-style haircut was official looking and professional. In comparison, Red was looking rough in his rumpled uniform, his five o'clock shadow, and circles under his eyes.

Lieutenant Perkins, usually a stoic man, smiled fondly at Myrtle and she couldn't resist giving him an impish hug. Red rolled his eyes. He felt that Myrtle was constantly pumping the detective for information whenever he was helping with a case.

Just to prove him wrong, Myrtle asked, "How are things going for you, Lieutenant? How's the family?" The detective had finally married over a year ago. For a long while it had seemed as though he were married to his job, instead. She'd been glad when Red had told her he'd finally settled down with a nice girl.

He surreptitiously glanced around him before pulling out his phone. "I've got a couple of pictures," he said. He handed the phone to Myrtle.

Her eyes opened wide. "Of a baby! What a lovely little girl. How old is she?"

"She was born two weeks ago," he said with a smile.

"And you look less sleep-deprived than Red does! That's amazing."

She glanced at Red, but he appeared to be studiously ignoring her as he spoke to one of the forensic team.

The detective became serious again. "But let's talk about how *you're* doing. Another body on your property. That's got to be upsetting, Mrs. Clover."

"Oh, it is. Believe me. But I absolve myself of any responsibility. I discouraged her from smoking, you know. Maybe not with my words, but *certainly* with my facial expression."

Lieutenant Perkins's eyes narrowed in confusion. "Smoking? But your son was saying this was no natural death."

"The smoking was a direct cause of her demise, Lieutenant. If Luella White hadn't stepped out for a smoking break, she'd be alive this very moment," said

Myrtle.

The detective nodded, thinking this through. What Myrtle liked best about Lieutenant Perkins is that he was never dismissive of her ideas. In fact, in previous cases, he'd even encouraged her to share her ideas with him.

"Very true. And you know I always appreciate your keeping your eyes and ears open for me during a case. But what I most want is for you to stay safe. This murder hit very close to home this time," he said.

"It doesn't get any closer than this," agreed Myrtle. She watched as a technician called him away. She decided it was time to go ahead and keep her eyes and ears open. Much as she liked Lieutenant Perkins, however, she wasn't completely sure she would share any information with him. It was very pleasant to solve cases all by herself.

Myrtle noticed that Mimsy Kessler was very quiet throughout the process and her pale face was pinched with stress. Myrtle sat down across from her. "Mimsy, this must be a terrible shock for you. Luella was just telling me that you were her only living relative. Did she move to Bradley to be closer to you?"

Mimsy nodded, swallowing hard before speaking. "She did. I think she was tired of living away from family. But Luella had a really fabulous life—at some point I will get to the point of being able to celebrate her life and avoid dwelling on her violent death. She traveled everywhere, you know. She had some sort of big bank job before she moved here that meant she was over in Asia or Europe a lot. She used to send me postcards." Mimsy choked up again. "I didn't even really get to see her tonight at all. I wanted to talk to her, but I thought we'd just catch up later."

"Where were you tonight instead of visiting with Luella?" asked Myrtle innocently, trying hard not to sound as if she were giving Mimsy the third degree.

Mimsy seemed not to notice Myrtle's nosiness. "You know—just around, talking to everyone. Getting food. Refilling my wine glass. Around and about."

So she certainly would have opportunity. And if Luella had had such a big bank job and Mimsy were indeed her only living relative…then the financial motive was there, too.

By the time the questioning was over, Luella's body had been removed, and the SBI had left, it was much later than she'd thought it would be. Myrtle remembered that she needed to feed Pasha and opened up a can of tuna to put outside. Her eyes opened wide as Pasha rushed past her and bounded into Myrtle's house and up on Myrtle's bed, blinking at her. Pasha *never* spent the night inside. But here she was, appearing ready and willing to curl up with her while they slept.

Amazingly, for once, Myrtle slept the night through and didn't wake up once.

Chapter Five

A tapping sound woke her up the next morning. For once, it was Miles tapping on her front door that woke *Myrtle* up, instead of the other way around.

And, even more shocking, the normally polite Miles didn't even seem to notice that he'd woken her up despite Myrtle's appearance at her front door with sheet lines all over her face and wearing a fluffy pink bathrobe.

"Hi Myrtle," he said solemnly. "I've been worrying over last night and I thought I'd pop over and we could talk over a cup of coffee."

"Sounds good," she grated in her early-morning voice. "As long as you're the one making the coffee, that is."

As Myrtle sat at her kitchen table, her gaze kept drifting over to her backyard. Although she enjoyed investigating, the fact that someone had murdered one of her guests was truly appalling. Committing a crime, literally in Myrtle's backyard, was entirely too disrespectful. At least the crime scene tape around her gnomes had vanished with the state police. But the memories from last night were vivid enough to stick around in her head for a while.

While the coffee perked, Miles swiftly moved around the kitchen, putting out sugar, half and half, and even a plate of store-bought muffins. As he moved, he talked, almost to himself.

"It doesn't all add up to me," he said. "The crime was such a random thing. It wasn't as if Luella were misbehaving. She wasn't even doing anything—she was simply sitting at the table and talking with *you* until she went off for a smoke break. Luella didn't have the opportunity to stir up any trouble or make someone that mad at her."

Myrtle said, "True, but anger against Luella might have been brewing for a while. Maybe someone had been looking for the opportunity to kill her over a period of time."

"But during a Bunco game in a gnome-filled backyard?" Miles looked skeptical.

"Why not? It was perfect timing. Luella was by herself. People were coming and going so much that no one would notice if one person slipped out really quickly." Miles handed Myrtle a coffee cup and she stirred in a couple of teaspoons of sugar.

"Exactly—people were coming and going so much that it would be *easy* for the killer to be seen returning from the scene of the crime." Miles waved his hand around to emphasize his point, sloshing coffee on his arm in the process.

"But think about it, Miles. Luella was a known smoker. She could be counted on to slip outside and take a break. She clearly knew her killer, so she wasn't going to scream in horror when confronted by them. If the killer couldn't find a handy weapon, she could simply pretend that she'd stepped outside to catch up with Luella and skip the attack," said Myrtle.

"Except there *was* a handy weapon."

Myrtle raised an eyebrow. "I hope you aren't suggesting that Dusty left his wrench there on purpose. What are you thinking…that Puddin wielded a wrench at Luella White? Whatever for? Because Luella wouldn't hire Puddin as a housekeeper? I can assure you that Puddin and Dusty don't have the mental capacity to be murderers. Besides, Dusty leaves his tools lying around all the time—

it's incredibly annoying to me. No, the killer was just lucky. She'd have stepped outside, seen a huge wrench lying around, smacked Luella over the head with it, and then probably rubbed the handle off with her shirt or something to get all the prints off."

"It just seems really brazen to me," muttered Miles before taking a sip of coffee.

"Murder is brazen," said Myrtle. "This was just someone taking advantage of an opportunity. This was someone at my party. Let's figure out who it was. And for the sake of time, let's eliminate each other, okay? And any other women who didn't seem to have much of a connection to Luella."

"I would have thought that was almost everyone at your party," said Miles. "That's another reason why I was awake all last night. I simply can't imagine who might be behind this—Mimsy—she's the only one I could logically come up with. She's Luella's last living relative. Luella appeared to be a woman of some means. There could be a financial motive there."

"Exactly. And, although Mimsy did seem very upset last night by Luella's death, we can't go on appearances."

"Although her grief and surprise did seem very genuine," said Miles.

Myrtle resisted the urge to roll her eyes. Miles's gallantry was a real impediment to him.

"So we're agreed that Mimsy has a motive. But do we know if Mimsy had the opportunity to kill Luella?" asked Myrtle. "She was vague about her movements when I asked her about them. You were up and about a bit more than I was, Miles. When Luella took her smoking break, where was Mimsy?"

Miles said, "Well, I was hardly trying to keep track of her. I was talking with you and Elaine about Elaine's plumbing problem, remember? I know she got some wine at some point. I know she was talking to different groups of people. There was a missing earring at one point, I believe. I think she could have slipped out. But I was busy trying to search and destroy those resilient and determined cookies. You should thank your stars that Luella wasn't poisoned. Everyone would have been suspicious that it had something to do with your cookies."

"Very funny. Okay, so Mimsy had opportunity. Tell me your impression of where everyone else was and I'll see if it matches mine," said Myrtle.

Miles was thoughtful. "Tippy couldn't even sit down or go get food or wine because Puddin cornered her at the front door and was telling her a very long story that Tippy was too courteous to cut short."

"I would feel sorry for Tippy except for the fact that she so clearly needs to learn assertiveness," said Myrtle. "Wine apparently brings out the raconteur in Puddin. I'll have to remember to keep her away from the cooking sherry."

Miles took a big sip of his coffee. "Georgia Simpson couldn't have done it. She was close to Tippy and Puddin near the front door. She even asked me for something to eat and drink." His voice, as usual whenever he spoke of the loud, tattooed woman, was awestruck.

"Did she think you were a waiter as you hovered nearby her?" asked Myrtle. "You must have been hovering near her, Miles. You've simply got to curb your admiration of Georgia."

Miles glared at Myrtle's rooster-covered kitchen tablecloth, a bit flushed. "I don't *admire* her per se. She's just very different from everyone else in Bradley."

"And thank heaven for that. Okay, so that leaves…everyone else. Where were Alma, Poppy, Estelle, and Florence?" asked Myrtle.

Miles looked a bit shocked. "Oh, I don't think

Florence had anything to do with this. She's an old lady."

"Miles, you are *speaking* with an old lady and I am quite capable of murder, I assure you. Florence Ainsworth is a good decade younger than I am. She could kill someone with a wrench in a skinny minute, I'm sure."

"But *why*? Why would Florence want to kill Luella? Why would Estelle, Alma, or Poppy, for that matter? I could see Mimsy having a financial motive. But why on earth would these other women want to commit murder?" Miles waved his muffin around, punctuating his question as crumbs flew.

"All I know is that Luella knew things. She somehow, despite her short time in Bradley, had her finger on the pulse of the town. If you'd done something you weren't very proud of, Luella White knew about it. And Luella apparently sometimes didn't mind gossiping, either, although she was disappointingly reserved with me last night. Her gossiping is why Sloan Jones asked me to spend time with Luella…to get the dirt on what was happening around town and put it in the paper," said Myrtle. "I guess her knowledge killed her."

"Were you able to pump information out of her at the table?" asked Miles.

"There was little pumping required. Luella intimated that she knew all kinds of things. It was almost as if she were showing off. Unfortunately, although she named names, she didn't give me the specifics I was looking for. But she mentioned Alma, Florence, and Estelle."

Miles took another thoughtful sip of his coffee. "And so all these people *could* have done it?"

"Sure they could. And apparently they got away with it, too, since no one came forward last night to say that they spotted one of those ladies coming in the back door with a bloody wrench."

"So what's next?" asked Miles. "Are we making the

rounds?"

"Yes indeed we are. Because I'm taking this one seriously. The gall of someone to commit murder while I'm hosting Bonkers! It's appalling." Myrtle fumed.

"All right, well let me get home and get ready for the day." There was another knock at Myrtle's door. "More company? You *are* popular," said Miles.

Myrtle frowned and then sighed. "Oh, it's got to be Puddin. I made that deal with her that she could play if she'd come back and clean. It had better be her, anyway. This place needs cleaning now, for sure, after that party and the police with their dirty shoes."

Miles opened the door and sure enough, Puddin was there. She still had no cleaning supplies, but at least this time she'd brought her trash bag with her—unless it was one of Myrtle's trash bags from a previous visit.

Miles left and Puddin started the slow process of throwing away trash and collecting glasses and plates for the dishwasher. Myrtle said, "I'm going to go ahead and get dressed, Puddin. All those dishes won't fit in the dishwasher, so if you could hand-wash what doesn't, please."

Puddin's response was to give her a mulish look as she shook the trash bag to open it.

By the time Myrtle got dressed and put a dab or two of makeup on, Puddin was still practically in the same spot as she'd been when Myrtle left her. She wasn't washing dishes, either, which to Myrtle was the clear priority. Instead, she was slapping a dishrag resentfully across the coffee table. Dusting was always something of an act of aggression with Puddin.

Myrtle frowned. She needed to redirect Puddin to the important tasks at hand, but motivating her would be impossible unless she found out what was bothering Puddin. When Puddin had something on her mind, she couldn't be reasoned with.

"Puddin, are you feeling all right?"

Puddin jumped violently, clearly not having realized that Myrtle was in the room. "Course I am!"

"No aftereffects from last night?" asked Myrtle.

Puddin gave her the suspicious stare that indicated she hadn't understood what Myrtle said.

Myrtle revised her question. "Your head doesn't ache from the number of alcoholic beverages you consumed?"

Puddin shook her head vigorously. Vigorously enough to make her wince after doing so. Apparently there *was* some sort of physical repercussion that might be affecting her already slack work ethic.

"So, do you have something on your mind then? Because you seem extremely preoccupied, Puddin. I'm thinking you're either nursing a sore head, or dwelling on the events of last evening, or both," said Myrtle. "We need to work through it, whatever it is, so that I can get those dishes washed. Do you want to talk?"

Stupid question. Puddin *always* wanted to talk, especially when the alternative was working. She happily trotted into the kitchen, sitting down at the kitchen table and shoving aside dirty dishes so that she could rest her elbows on the table.

Myrtle sat across from her. "All right. Let's think this through. Puddin, what are your recollections from last night?"

Puddin gave her a sideways squint. "Do what?"

Myrtle tried a different tack. "I mean, what do you remember about last night?" She paused since Puddin was still looking stumped. "Do you remember *anything* from last night?"

Puddin looked indignant. "Didn't drink *that* much! I just didn't know what you meant. You're talking about Miz Luella's murder. I can tell you all about it."

Myrtle sighed. Puddin did love her time in the spotlight. If she had anything at all helpful to offer them, it would likely take forever to get it.

"Let me show you how it was. I know you couldn't really see anything, sitting where you were. I was talking to my friend Tippy…you know Tippy, don't you?" Puddin gloated at counting wealthy socialite Tippy as a friend. "Anyhow, she and I were talking at the door, but I like to look around, right? So this is what I saw." Puddin grabbed the saltshaker, the peppershaker, and the bottle of ketchup from the middle of the table. "This pepper is Alma, right? Alma was sort of hanging out over by the drinks."

"Lingering because…she was drinking a lot? Or why, Puddin?"

Puddin screwed her face up in thought, loving every second of someone needing her insight on something. "I'd say that she was drinkin' *some.* They all was. But I think she was at the drink table so as she could keep shiftin' her eyes over at Miss Luella."

"So she was watching Miss Luella."

"And sort of snarling."

Myrtle was pretty sure Puddin's imagination was running riot since she couldn't quite picture the rather demure Alma as a rabid beast stalking Luella. But she'd let Puddin continue, at least. "Okay, so Alma is the salt shaker. Who else did you see?"

"No, Alma is the *pepper* shaker. Who else did I see? Well, Mr. Miles." Puddin looked a bit cagey now. "You know. He's got the energy sometimes. He had the energy last night and he was all over the house, wasn't he? He kept poking around, acting like he was looking for something. In the living room, in the kitchen, in the back of the house. Him was everywheres."

Hunting the noxious cookies. And perhaps refilling his wine. "All right, yes, I saw him do that, too. But he was trying to help me out. Besides, Miles has no issues with Luella White—he didn't even know the woman."

Puddin raised a straggly eyebrow. "She sure did act like she *wanted* to get to know him. I saw her watchin' him."

"Wishful thinking. So is Miles the ketchup bottle, then? I'm confused," said Myrtle impatiently.

"Naw, because I don't think Mr. Miles has it in him to murder nobody. Too proper. More likely to hire somebody to do the job instead of getting' his own hands all dirty. Naw, *Poppy* is the ketchup bottle." Puddin, pleased at the diorama she was creating, carefully set up the ketchup bottle near the salt shaker, which she laid on its side.

"Let me guess," said Myrtle, rolling her eyes. "Luella is the saltshaker."

But Puddin was distracted by the sight of salt spilling out of the recumbent shaker. She hissed and threw some salt over her left shoulder. "Have to blind the devil standing there," she muttered to herself.

Myrtle leaned her head into her hands. Now *she* was getting a headache. "Really, Puddin. You need to stumble out of the nineteenth century. Your superstitions will be the end of you."

Puddin was now squinting at the salt, pepper, and ketchup in confusion. "Wait," she said slowly. "I think I mighta got this wrong."

"Just give up, Puddin," said Myrtle crossly. "I'm assuming that you didn't see anyone coming out of my backyard wielding a bloody wrench. I believe we're done here."

"Speaking of that, Dusty wants his wrench back that you took," said Puddin, looking stern.

Myrtle always felt as if she'd stepped through the looking glass when she tried having a conversation with Puddin. "That *I* took? I did no such thing! Dusty is being forgetful as usual and leaving his tools scattered around. And this time one of his tools was used as a murder weapon. The SBI has it now and who knows when they'll release it."

"SBI?" Puddin looked suspicious.

"The state police. State Bureau of Investigations. They're examining it for evidence, although Red said it looked to him as if the metal handle was wiped clean of fingerprints. If I were Dusty, I'd want to clean it really well if I used it again. Or just purchase another one."

Puddin said slowly, "Yeah, but that Dusty don't like spending money much. Guess we might have to if the police take too long with it." She frowned at the salt and peppershakers and the ketchup. "Ya know, I feel like something here is wrong."

"There are things on multiple levels wrong here, Puddin. Why don't you just think about it for a while and then get back to me if anything comes to you?" She'd had enough of all this. "And please wash those dishes."

Puddin snapped her fingers. "There was one thing I thought you oughta know. About Miz Florence. That old lady, you know. I clean for her sometimes and one day I seen her crying. She said that Luella was being mean to her. Luella saw Miz Florence hit the gas pedal instead of the brake and run right over a curb downtown."

Myrtle raised her eyebrows. "Did she run into a shop?"

"Naw, she finally hit her brakes before she run into the building. But it was close, Miz Florence said. Then I sat down with Miz Florence for a while, seeing as how she was upset and everything."

This didn't surprise Myrtle a bit, considering Puddin would sit down instead of work any day of the week.

"I tole her that it didn't matter none in Bradley. Tole her that *you* hadn't had a car in well nigh ten year or so and you walk everywhere, even though you have to lean on a cane and all. And that you are much, *much, much* older than she is and still get around great," said Puddin.

"All right, all right, get on with it! I'm old, okay. Got it." Myrtle was now thinking longingly of the *Tomorrow's Promise* episode that she had taped the day before.

"Anyhow, she said that the place she wanted to go was out of town so far that she couldn't walk there if she tried. Said she had a sweetheart she met at a bridge tournament. And she said that her daughter tole her if there was one more report of Miz Florence's bad driving, her daughter was going to take her keys away," said Puddin meaningfully. "And Luella was bein' real spiteful and said she was going to call up her daughter and tell her that Miz Florence was a menace to society. Then Miz Florence's daughter would be taking her keys away, but good."

"Well then, I'd say that Miss Florence's daughter would be signing herself up to chauffeur her mama wherever she wanted to go," said Myrtle.

"Except that Miz Florence's daughter is a Yankee and lives in Cincinnati," said Puddin smoothly. "Said she'd drive her mama anywhere she wanted to go…if she moved there. But Miz Florence don't want to go. She likes her sweetheart."

"And if she moved up north, she'd have to give up that relationship," mused Myrtle, nodding.

"Now I have to go," said Puddin grandly. "I don't have time to sit around and chat. Once I'm finished here, I've got to go clean at Miz Mimsy's house."

As if Puddin were being forced to chat by *Myrtle*, when it was always the other way around. "I didn't realize you cleaned for Mimsy. When did that start?" Because she would have said that Mimsy had too much sense than to hire Puddin for housecleaning.

"Oh, her usual cleaner's been sick for weeks now. So I'm filling in."

Myrtle said, "Keep your eyes and ears open while you're there. Maybe see what Mimsy says while you're there or what visitors she has or what's going on."

Puddin nodded. "I'll be your eyes and ears, Miz Myrtle. What'll you give me in return?" Her small eyes gleamed with avarice.

"If you have *information* for me—*useful* information, then I might be willing to pay you for it. But I get to decide if it's useful or not."

Because all she needed was for Puddin to give her the inside scoop on what Mimsy Kessler had for lunch.

"And be sure to wash those dishes!" Myrtle added.

Chapter Six

When the house was finally fairly clean, and minutes after Puddin's departure, the phone rang. It was Sloan Jones from the paper. "Miss Myrtle, I'm getting ready to put together the paper for tomorrow and just wanted to see if you had anything for me." His voice had a pleading quality to it, a sort of desperation it didn't ordinarily have. Usually, he was very deferential to Myrtle, having been a student of hers many years ago. The paper must be in bad shape, indeed.

"As a matter of fact, I do," said Myrtle.

"Do you? Oh, that's wonderful, Miss Myrtle! You caught up with Luella White then? I knew y'all would hit it off when you finally managed to spend some time with her. You have a lot in common, after all."

Myrtle paused. "Honestly, Sloan, I can't think of a single thing that Luella White and I have in common. We have even less in common now—considering that she's dead and I am most certainly not."

There was a stunned silence on the other end of the line. Then a mournful, "Miss Myrtle, what happened?" His tone implied that Myrtle had been extremely careless with his valued source.

"It has nothing to do with *me*, Sloan! Well, except that she died in my backyard. And that the murder weapon belongs to my handyman. And that one of my guests is apparently a ruthless killer. But I certainly am not at fault in this!" said Myrtle hotly.

"There goes my gossip feature, then," said Sloan

glumly. "Now I'm going to have to rely on what people send in. It will all be about how many cookies the Brownie troop sold and Miss Margaret Williamson's prize begonias at the fair. Say goodbye to the *Bradley Bugle*. I only hate that it's happening on my watch."

"Sloan, for a newsman, you're remarkably unobservant. Have you heard nothing I've been saying? A murder occurred. During a gathering I was hosting. In my very backyard. The suspects are people that most folks in this town will know and I can write the inside scoop. Who cares about the gossip feature when you're sitting on a goldmine? I'll finish up my article and email it over to you in time and I guarantee you it will be a smashing success."

Sloan said a bit doubtfully, "Are you writing it like you usually do, though? I mean, no disrespect intended, Miss Myrtle."

"You mean am I writing it following the highest standards of journalistic integrity? No, because it's for the *Bradley Bugle* and I've given up. I'm sprinkling my own observations in and making my byline read "an Eyewitness Account by Myrtle Clover."

Now Sloan's voice was a bit peppier. "You know, this might work, Miss Myrtle. It's a pity we don't have a story like this every week."

"If we had a story like this *every* week, it wouldn't be news, would it?" asked Myrtle. She glanced at the wall clock. Between Puddin's nonsense with the salt and peppershakers and Sloan, she was getting absolutely nothing done. "No time to chit-chat, Sloan. I have to go talk to some folks. I'll email you the story soon." And she hung up.

Five minutes later, she was walking down Magnolia Lane in the direction of Estelle Rutledge's house. She knew exactly where she lived since Elaine had told her it was the 'modern' house on the block. What Elaine was too kind to say was that it was the house built forty years ago that had aspired, and failed, to look modern for the time. It was boxy, with too many windows, and evoked a sort of treehouse appearance…with no trees in sight on the property. It also was some kind of split-level but the levels were diagonal from each other. It looked as if the house was a victim of a particularly violent earthquake. Most Bradley residents had considered the residence, standing out strikingly as it was among the ranches, something of an eyesore that had been put up with for ages. Myrtle simply believed that the architect had consumed hallucinogenic drugs.

But of course, Estelle, as a newcomer to Bradley, had nothing to do with the construction or design of the house, so Myrtle couldn't hold that against the woman. However, she had chosen, apparently of her own free will, to live there. And that was a strike against her right there.

Myrtle also wanted to find out a bit more about the storm-chasing business. How exactly did one chase storms? Why did one need special equipment to do so? And what made Estelle Rutledge aspire to do such a thing to begin with? How did this hobby or career tie into the case, if it did?

Lost in her thoughts, she didn't hear a sound until there was a small, nudging, familiar dry cough next to her. She glanced to her side to see that Miles was keeping pace with her and had perhaps done so for some time. He gave her a reproachful look. "You know I've always wanted to see the inside of that post-modern mess of a house. And I'm your sidekick, after all. Next time, invite me."

Being caught at being thoughtless always made Myrtle cross. "Yes, all right. Sorry." The sorry was very begrudging. "I just got caught up in my musing and my feet started taking me here." She paused. "And how did you know that's where I was going? Have you been talking to

Wanda?"

Wanda was a psychic and a cousin of Miles, a fact which Miles would rather forget. "No," he said stiffly. "You were simply walking in this direction and she's the only suspect who lives in this direction on Magnolia. What's our excuse for being there? I'm assuming that we're not just going to start accusing Estelle of murder and see what happens next."

"Of course not," snapped Myrtle. But, as a matter of fact, she'd been so lost in her thoughts that she hadn't really come up with a premise for the unexpected visit at all. She fished in her pocketbook for a second. She pulled out a lipstick. "Someone forgot their lipstick and I'm trying to connect it with its owner."

Miles looked doubtful. "Surely that's not a very good reason for a visit? Maybe if it were a cardigan or something. That's one of your lipsticks, isn't it?"

"It *is* one of mine, yes. What if I brought one of my cardigans and someone actually claimed it was theirs? Then I'd be out a cardigan. Besides, a lipstick can be very valuable to a woman. These wicked makeup companies discontinue shades all the time. Trust me, it's a good excuse," said Myrtle.

They walked up to the front door and Myrtle knocked. "Does Estelle even wear makeup?" murmured Miles. "She doesn't really seem the type."

"It's simply a pretext," hissed Myrtle.

Estelle opened the door at once, her face curious and completely makeup free. And surprisingly welcoming. "Miss Myrtle from last night. And…sorry, I don't remember your name. Wait. Is it Niles?"

"Miles," said Miles a bit stiffly.

"That's right. Can I help you with something? Oh wait. Where are my manners? Come inside." Estelle beamed at them and pushed the door open wide and led the way into the dimly lit house. Miles carefully closed the door shut after he and Myrtle walked in. Estelle seemed amazingly eager to visit with them. It made Myrtle wonder if she might perhaps be a little lonely—new to town, living alone. Did one have a team when one was chasing storms? Or was it more of a solo venture?

There was a strong smell of tuna in the house, which Myrtle noticed at once, nose twitching. Miles appeared more distracted by the architecture. There appeared to be stairs at odd places, walls of different sizes and slants, and oddly shaped scattered windows and skylights. "Your home is very interesting," said Miles to Estelle as they followed the middle-aged woman toward what appeared to be a living area. "Did you pick it for the architecture? That is, have you always been interested in modern architectural design?"

Estelle seemed surprised by the question, or maybe it was the shape of her eyebrows and her large, round eyes that gave her a sort of perpetual look of surprise. "It was available and I needed a house in Bradley. That's really why." She motioned vaguely at a sofa and a couple of worn armchairs. "Here, why don't you sit down?" She paused again, thinking, as if she wasn't often in the position of playing hostess. Myrtle wondered how many visitors she got here. "Can I get you something to drink? I can't offer food because I haven't been to the store lately. I just get busy and you know, the next thing I know all I have in the house is a can of tuna."

"Which makes for a very protein-packed breakfast," said Myrtle smoothly as she settled into one of the old armchairs. And certainly explained the pervasive aroma. "Why were you so interested in Bradley? It seems like an odd choice for a professional…meteorologist?"

"Storm chaser," said Estelle. "Oh, I have some working knowledge of meteorology, but I don't have a degree in it. And some of it bores me to tears. What I really enjoy are the big storms—the tornadoes, in particular. I film them and then sell the footage to news organizations."

Myrtle glanced around the living room. Every available surface seemed to have some sort of odd equipment on it. There was something that resembled a radio that she supposed must be a type of weather radio. There were also maps all over the place—real, physical maps. Somehow she'd thought that maybe there would be something on the computer or phone that Estelle would use. An app, maybe. But instead there were state maps littering the sofa that Miles sat on. And a couple of compasses. Did she not use GPS? There were also flashlights and a binocular next to Miles on the sofa cushion. He gazed at them with a bemused expression, finally managing to pull his focus away from the unusual architecture. "Getting ready to go on a trip?" he asked.

"With any luck," said Estelle fervently. She grinned. "Of course, that means that I'm technically wishing bad weather on some poor soul."

"But again—Bradley isn't really known for bad weather, surely. Wouldn't you be more interested in a place like Alabama or Kansas or even Tennessee? They see a lot more tornadoes than we do," said Myrtle.

"I'd rather *chase* them," said Estelle simply. "Not be surrounded by them. And not to have my property destroyed by them."

However, the overall effect of Estelle's residence was that of a home that had been hit by an F4 tornado. But Myrtle managed to smile understandingly. "You've enjoyed Bradley, then? A nice quiet town, isn't it?"

Estelle said, "Ordinarily, yes. Although the murder at your house was a surprise." She looked down at her hands. "At first I thought that someone must be playing a bad joke. For a murder to happen during a Bunco game?" Estelle shrugged her shoulders to indicate the rarity of such an event.

Myrtle, never one to accept blame gladly, said with a slight edge to her voice, "That had nothing to do with me. I'd only met Luella that day. But *you* knew her, didn't you?" She shifted in her seat as a spring started poking her in an unpleasant way.

"I wouldn't say we were *friends*. Unfortunately, I haven't seemed to be able to make very many friends since I've moved here. But, I did know Luella through Bunko. Elaine was nice enough to ask me if I wanted to be part of the group when another member stopped playing."

That sounded like Elaine. So Myrtle was right—Estelle had been lonely here.

"And Mimsy has been especially nice. She's even been bringing fresh vegetables from her garden over and visiting for a little while when she comes," said Estelle.

Miles gave one of those small coughs that indicated he was about to make a point. "Mimsy and Elaine are both very friendly, aren't they? But going back to Luella. Your tone suggests that you didn't really care for Luella very much."

Estelle measured him up with a quick glance before admitting, "Not much, no. I don't have time for people who gossip, you see. And Luella White was gossipy."

"Did she gossip about you?" asked Myrtle quickly.

"It got back to me, sure. It was more like she was making *fun* of me. She wasn't very impressed, apparently, with my being a storm chaser. And when the bank denied my loan application for a real storm chasing van, she spread that around, too."

"How would she have found out about that?" Miles looked alarmed. Myrtle figured that he would probably be up that night worrying about his personal financial business being spread all around Bradley. Maybe she would come over with coffee and cookies this time.

Estelle said, "Luella was the loan officer. She really only worked part time over there, I guess to help them out. She had a banking background of some kind before she moved here. All I know is that I desperately need an outfitted van for my storm chasing. It's the only way I'm going to be able to really make it, big-time. The bankers here have no imagination whatsoever. If you're not trying to open a diner or a pet store, they don't understand your business."

Myrtle said carefully, "Miles and I were trying to recollect exactly how events happened during Bunco and are having a tough time. Where exactly were you sitting, for instance? And where were you during the party?"

Estelle gave her an indulgent smile. Apparently, she thought Myrtle was nosy but was willing to excuse it because of her age. And maybe because Estelle actually had visitors for once. "I'm afraid I don't have much of an alibi, if that's what you're looking for. I don't know anyone well enough at Bunco to just sit and talk the whole time to one person. I talked to Alma a while, talked to Georgia. I got a glass of wine and then a refill. And I ate. I was in the kitchen, in the living room, and even briefly in the restroom."

"And you didn't pop into the backyard and hit Luella on the head with a wrench?" Myrtle allowed her eyes to twinkle to show that she really didn't think Estelle would do such a thing, but she had to ask the question.

"No."

Myrtle felt as if Estelle had more to say. "Do you know of anyone who might have done it? Did you see anything? Was anyone loitering by my back door? Or do you have a guess who might have been so upset by Luella that she might commit murder?"

Estelle hesitated. "I thought Florence Ainsworth spent

a lot of time near the back door. She seemed as if she were propping herself up, actually. I don't think she's really been on top of things lately. But I can't imagine why she might want to murder Luella. That seems like a strange thing for an elderly woman like Florence to do."

Estelle was vastly underestimating the elderly. "So, Florence was in a good position to have done this. But is there anyone that you think might have *wanted* to do it?"

Miles said simply, "Who had a grudge against Luella and why?"

"Alma Wiggins was no fan of Luella's," said Estelle finally. "She has talked to me about her numerous times. Apparently, Luella was spreading gossip about her son."

Miles looked thoughtful. "You know, I want to say that *I* have heard gossip about her son."

"That he was cooking the books at that accounting firm he works at?" asked Estelle.

Miles nodded.

"You see how a small town works?" asked Estelle, looking sad. "There is no evidence at all, according to Alma, that her son is involved in any such thing. He's not been arrested. He's not being investigated. But the owner of the accounting firm is Luella's friend and is making these unfounded allegations which Luella is spreading around."

"What a shame," said Miles indignantly.

Myrtle said, "So Alma was understandably angry with Luella."

Estelle appeared wary. "Yes. But I can't go so far as to say Alma did anything to hurt Luella. Otherwise, I'm gossiping just as much."

Myrtle nodded and then looked over at Miles. "We should probably head out…we've got things to do." They both stood.

Estelle blinked and said in a rush, "Oh. Do you have to? Can't I get you something to drink? An ice water? I was enjoying our visit. And…well, I'm just curious as to why you dropped by."

Myrtle said, "Didn't I say? How silly of me. I…uh…" She rummaged in her pocketbook as Miles looked uncomfortable. "I wanted to see if you left this lipstick at my house. Someone did. So I'm trying to figure it out. With Miles."

"You're investigating, aren't you? Just like a sleuth! The Lipstick Caper, or something." Estelle smiled at her in her engagingly awkward way. "I'm afraid that I don't wear lipstick. But I'm glad you stopped by. And good luck tracking down the owner of the lipstick. It's cool that you're a sleuth…I mean, considering your maturity."

"Estelle was nice," said Miles as they left.

"Except for the fact that she mentioned my *maturity*," grumbled Myrtle. "It makes it sound as if I've just stopped playing with baby dolls. I don't see why people can't just say *old age*. Why dance around the phrase by substituting something as silly as *maturity*?"

Miles decided not to engage in another of Myrtle's word wars. "I did think she was lonely, though. She was awfully thrilled to see us and didn't even care if we were there on a pretext or not. Don't you think so?"

"Most definitely. She's new to the town and is not in a traditional line of work. She doesn't have a family to help her engage with the community. It's got to make it very hard to meet people," said Myrtle. "But she did give us some leads. We've got Florence near the back door and we've got Alma with a grudge. Excellent." There was a bounce to Myrtle's step as they walked down the sidewalk.

"So glad that narrowing down potential murder suspects has made your day," murmured Miles.

"I think we'll visit Alma now," said Myrtle, ignoring him. "We have a definite lead to investigate and it sounds as if she might enjoy a Luella-bashing opportunity."

"Perhaps that's not the right way of phrasing it, under the circumstances," said Miles rather primly.

"And we can dispense with the lipstick charade for Alma," said Myrtle, turning briskly down a side street. "Alma Wiggins appreciates directness and she knows that I work at the *Bradley Bugle*." She glanced at her watch and groaned. "I have to get that story to Sloan."

"Is it ready to send out?" asked Miles.

"Haven't started it yet," said Myrtle.

They approached a large home with peeling white paint. The yard was kept tidy, the front walk to the house neatly swept. But the house itself indicated that its inhabitant might be low on available funds. And, despite the heat, every window of the house was open to let in any passing breeze. Clearly, Alma wasn't wanting to run her air conditioner.

"Was this house *ever* in good repair?" asked Miles in a low voice as they approached the front door.

"It was beautiful when it was Alma's mother's house. But I think Alma's mother's money was completely drained by her health problems and nursing home stay. Alma doesn't have two cents to rub together." Myrtle rapped at the door.

Alma wasn't quite as welcoming as Estelle or perhaps she simply wasn't as desperate for companionship. She opened the front door a crack and peered suspiciously out at Myrtle and Miles. "Y'all aren't collecting for charity, are you? Or a food drive? It's really not a good time. I haven't been sleeping well lately and I'm absolutely exhausted."

Alma might have been an appropriate recipient for charity herself. Myrtle beamed at her, completely ignoring her unfriendliness. "Hi there! No, Miles and I are just running by real quick to visit everyone who was at my house during Luella's murder."

Miles's alarmed look told her should subdue her peppiness, considering the topic of conversation.

Alma said cautiously, "Why is that?"

"Well, you know I write for the *Bugle*. I'm working on a story for them about the murder."

Alma closed the door a fraction of an inch. "The *Bugle* has gone downhill so much that I dropped my subscription. Besides, I don't know anything that can help you," she said dismissively.

"Oh, I'm sure you do," said Myrtle, leaning forward on her cane a bit and peering earnestly at her. "I hear that you might provide me with some insight into Luella. You see, since she was new to town, I didn't have the chance to really make her acquaintance."

"Nor did I," said Alma. "And I didn't *want* the chance to get to know her better. She was an unpleasant woman."

"Yes. I understand that she could be. And that sometimes she gossiped," said Myrtle in a wheedling tone.

Alma's fingers tightened around the edge of the door. "Lies. Not gossip. Gossip implies an element of truth. And she said very unpleasant and untrue things about…my family."

Miles shifted from one foot to the other and said sympathetically, "That's a shame. Do you know if anyone else experienced issues with Luella?"

Myrtle narrowed her eyes at Miles. She hadn't been quite ready to move on from Alma's potential role in the murder. Miles sometimes went off on a tangent. Sidekicks could be a pain.

Alma's reaction to Miles's rather innocuous question was fairly telling. "I told you, I can't help you!" And she slammed the door shut.

Chapter Seven

"Good job, Miles," muttered Myrtle as they slowly walked back toward Myrtle's house. "You frightened her off."

"I wasn't trying to frighten her off!" protested Miles. "I thought *you* were frightening her off, so I was trying to bring the tension down a little by asking her if *other people* had grudges against Luella. How would I know that it would be a trigger for her?"

"What I'd like to know is, *why* was it a trigger? Does Alma know something about last night? Is she trying to protect someone there?"

They thought about this as they walked past Miles's house and on to Myrtle's. Miles said, "I want to say that I've seen Alma and Mimsy together in town sometimes. Maybe they're friends."

"That makes for an unusual friendship. Mimsy seems very outgoing and cheerful and pleasant to be around. She has a nice house and a nice husband and is just…nice," finished Myrtle with a shrug. "But why shouldn't she be nice? It appears she's had a very easy life so far."

"Well, maybe opposites attract in friendship, too," said Miles, giving Myrtle a meaningful look. "Some would say that you and I aren't very much alike."

"Only because I'm assertive and you're passive, Miles. But we can fix that."

Miles seemed displeased by this pronouncement.

They paused on the sidewalk in front of Myrtle's house. Myrtle said, "Okay. So I have to whip out this story for the *Bugle* and email it to Sloan. You come on in and make yourself a sandwich and then we can catch *Tomorrow's Promise* together. After that, maybe we can pop by and see Florence. I'm curious about her issues with Luella."

Miles squinted at Myrtle's house. "You already have a visitor, Myrtle."

Myrtle turned to see Mimsy on her front porch. Mimsy gave her a cheerful wave. "Well, speak of the devil," muttered Myrtle.

"So to speak," said Miles. "I thought we just decided she was a paragon of virtue. Friend to the friendless."

"Not necessarily," said Myrtle. "I think we just determined that she's been blessed." Myrtle waved back to Mimsy. "What's she holding?"

"It appears to be a casserole," said Miles.

"Am I sick?" asked Myrtle with surprise as they walked toward Mimsy.

Mimsy was calling out to them in her lilting voice, "Miss Myrtle, I just feel so terrible about what happened to you that I simply had to come by with food. Here you were, doing a good turn for the Bunco group by hosting and subbing and you end up with a tragedy right in your backyard! You poor thing."

Myrtle smiled at her and unlocked the front door, motioning them all in. "That's very kind of you, Mimsy. But shouldn't I be the one bringing *you* a casserole? After all, it was quite a blow, losing Luella. You appeared to be very close."

Miles winced at the mention of Myrtle preparing food. Myrtle glared at him. Miles seemed to be under the impression that Myrtle couldn't cook. One botched batch of cookies did *not* mean someone was a poor cook.

Mimsy gave Myrtle a fond smile in return. "Aren't you sweet? No, cooking relaxes and distracts me so it was my pleasure to cook this for you. And believe me, I've got plenty of casseroles from caring friends in Bradley, so you needn't trouble yourself."

Miles gave a small sigh. Myrtle assumed it was a relieved one and this time she stepped very slightly on his foot. He quickly removed it and Myrtle said innocently, "Did I tread on you, Miles? Here, why don't we all sit down? Miles, could you stick the casserole in the fridge for me?"

Once Miles had settled next to Mimsy on the sofa, Myrtle said sadly, "You know, Miles and I were just talking about the terrible tragedy. I think discussing something as disturbing as Luella's demise really helps me to work through all my conflicting feelings. I'm trying to place everyone and everything in my head and relive the entire evening so that I can move past it."

Mimsy nodded solemnly. "I'm trying to do the very same thing, Miss Myrtle. Actually, that's one of the reasons I'm here. The doctor said it could be therapeutic for me to talk it over with someone who was there. But everyone else seems to be tiptoeing around the subject so they won't upset me."

Miles coughed. "No danger of that here."

"Which is exactly why I'm visiting," said Mimsy with a small smile. "I was sitting in a folding chair over close to the kitchen at table three. Much of the time I was speaking with Elaine. She had quite a tale involving their plumbing disaster."

Myrtle realized she hadn't checked in with Red and Elaine on how the repairs were going. She made a mental note. "You weren't in the kitchen at all, then?"

"I'm afraid not. I keep thinking that maybe if I'd been with Luella, this never would have happened. Poppy kept trying to tempt me to join her in the kitchen, though," said Mimsy. "She was ditching her diet and wanted an accomplice. But my stomach was off, so I didn't want to push it."

Miles moved very slightly away from Mimsy on the sofa. He was becoming quite germ-phobic. She'd noticed last winter that he refused to shake hands with people during flu season.

"So Poppy was in the kitchen, then," said Myrtle slowly.

Mimsy's eyes grew wide. "Oh, but that doesn't mean anything, surely. Why on earth would Poppy murder poor Luella?"

"You tell us," said Myrtle.

"She wouldn't have. She didn't even know Luella. I think she only met her briefly once. There would be no reason at all," said Mimsy.

"If Poppy didn't have motive, who did?" asked Miles in the thoughtful, slow way he had which made the question completely innocuous. If Myrtle had asked it, she'd have sounded nosy, or worse.

Mimsy looked miserable. "I guess I do. I mean, I'm the only one, surely, who could have really had a motive to kill Luella. I was her only living relative, so it's only natural…I mean…I'm assuming that I will probably be the sole beneficiary of her will. So that means a house and some property and…well…I think Luella was probably pretty well off. That means money could have been a motive." She paused. "I don't think anyone else had a motive. Why would they?"

"We've heard that maybe Alma was upset with Luella. And that Florence and Estelle might have had issues with Luella, too," said Myrtle bluntly.

Mimsy's eyebrows shot up. "Really? I had no idea. Luella was so new to town that it doesn't seem as if she'd have had time to make everyone form an opinion of her one way or another."

"Apparently, she could be abrasive. And a bit of a gossip, too," said Myrtle. "Do you remember where those ladies were during Bonkers?"

"Bunco," said Miles.

"Whatever," said Myrtle.

Mimsy lowered her head, studying her floral skirt as if she could see the party there. "I did notice Alma going into the kitchen. I remember because she came back quickly and her face was flushed. It made me wonder if maybe Alma were coming down with whatever bug I had."

"And Florence?" asked Miles.

"I don't even remember seeing Florence there. Maybe she was in the kitchen a lot," said Mimsy, brow furrowed.

"What about Estelle?" asked Myrtle.

Mimsy said, "I'm not sure where Estelle was, although I do think I spotted her coming out of the kitchen once or twice. But at one point I'd lost my earring and I was focusing on the floor and the tables to see if I could find it."

"You work at the bank, don't you?" asked Myrtle curiously. "Were you the one who turned Estelle down for a loan?"

Mimsy sat back in surprise. Then she just as suddenly resumed her usual pleasant expression. "Unfortunately, I can't confirm or deny that. It's business, you know." She paused, looking thoughtfully at Myrtle and Miles. "You're trying to figure out who did this, aren't you?" Her voice sounded shocked.

Myrtle realized that Mimsy must think of her as a very old lady who just piddled around her house all day.

"Well, I do write for the *Bugle*," said Myrtle. "And I'm writing the news story on the…tragedy. And yes, Miles and I do like investigating. When circumstances allow."

Miles gave Mimsy a reassuring smile since Mimsy looked as if she was discovering an unknown universe where elderly people led exciting and meaningful lives.

Where they perhaps didn't even require consoling casseroles following upsetting events.

"I see," she said slowly, although it was quite evident that she didn't see at all. "Of course."

Mimsy left shortly after that. Miles fastidiously took out a bottle of hand sanitizer and carefully coated his hands in it.

Myrtle rolled her eyes and Miles said, "You might want to have some yourself, Myrtle. Who has time for a stomach bug?"

Put that way, Myrtle decided to reach out a hand for a squirt, herself. "I'm not sure we learned anything from that exchange, Miles. Except, maybe, that Mimsy pities old people."

Miles said, "Myrtle, you're being harsh. Mimsy was simply trying to be nice and bring you a casserole to make up for the fact that you had a bad experience on a night you were kind enough to host her Bunco group." Miles enunciated *Bunco* carefully, in the manner of someone who was making a point.

"All right. You're being charitable, but all right. She's nice enough, I suppose," said Myrtle grudgingly. "But I still don't feel as if it got us anywhere. Except that she admitted she had motive and that Luella had money."

"She did tell us that Alma behaved sort of oddly. That she spent a short time in the kitchen and came out flushed," said Miles. "So Mimsy is the second person to point us in that direction. Estelle also mentioned Alma as a possibility."

"Well, maybe Alma *did* have a stomach virus coming on. That could explain why she didn't want to let us in—maybe she's running back and forth from the restroom or something," said Myrtle.

Miles's response to this was to squirt more hand sanitizer into his palm.

"A distraction is in order, Miles, to get your mind off infectious disease. Let's turn on *Tomorrow's Promise.*"

"I thought you were supposed to write that news story up," said Miles.

"I can do both things at once. I'm *excellent* at multi-tasking," said Myrtle. "Besides, I frequently find the soap opera most illuminating. It's practically a documentary, Miles. It demonstrates the passion inside people—the passion most people try to cover up. And viewing passion reminds me of the baseness of humanity and what they're capable of…which in turn helps me figure out a case."

So Miles made a sandwich and Myrtle sat at the computer and they both watched the show. Myrtle used a laptop and wrote up her news story as she watched.

After the show was finished, Myrtle frowned at the computer. "Is this okay, Miles? Can you read through it?" She handed over the laptop.

Miles carefully peered at the computer screen. "The soap opera plot might have seeped into your story. As well as some strong verbs. I don't believe I've ever seen the words *gallop* and *whimper* in the newspaper before."

"Sloan wanted something vivid and sensational. He's trying to encourage readership." Myrtle rolled her eyes.

Miles said primly, "It's a very lively account. A bit lurid. But I suppose the facts are generally correct."

"It was easy to write a lurid account while engaged in *Tomorrow's Promise*. Because there was something in it today that was pertinent to our case," said Myrtle.

Miles lifted his eyebrows. "Briana's startling transformation from hair stylist to terrorist?"

"Actually … yes."

"Excuse me?" Miles was looking at Myrtle as if rather concerned now about her mental state.

"Well, not that *specifically*. But I do think we're looking at something similar. We're looking for an innocuous woman who has transitioned from someone very harmless to someone very lethal. And something has provided that trigger," said Myrtle thoughtfully.

"Like Briana was radicalized by her next-door neighbor?"

"Right. Except I think we're looking for an event and not a person," said Myrtle.

"So how do we figure out who this innocuous person is?" asked Miles. "Everyone's going to be faking it and pretending they're not the guilty party. Just like Briana."

"Yes, but the stress got to Briana in the end and she started making mistakes. I'd beware of anyone seeming *too* sweet. Like Poppy? All I keep hearing is that she's a wonderful friend to Mimsy and that she doesn't have anything against Luella."

"You sound skeptical."

Myrtle said, "I am. *Everyone* had something against Luella."

"Not *everyone*."

Typical. Miles had an aversion to absolutes. "Right. But so far, all the people at the party who had the *opportunity* to kill Luella also had *motives* to kill her. So why not Poppy?"

Miles said, "So let's pay Miss Poppy a visit then."

"Okay. Just let me email the article to Sloan first."

The phone rang and Miles stood up. "I'll get it." He strode to the kitchen wall phone. "Myrtle Clover's residence," he said into the receiver.

"People will talk," muttered Myrtle.

"Wanda?" asked Miles. "Is something wrong? All right." He listened for a moment. "Yes, she *is* working on her article, as a matter of fact. But we'll come as soon as she's done." He hung up and returned to the living room.

Myrtle said, "Wanda is requesting a visit, I suppose. How did she make the phone call? I thought her phone service was disconnected."

"Apparently, Crazy Dan was able to jumpstart one of the vehicles in their yard and drive her to a payphone outside a gas station," said Miles.

Myrtle nodded and hit *send* on the story. "All right, let's head over there." She picked up her cane.

Miles rolled his eyes. "Myrtle, you already know what Wanda will tell you. I can't imagine why she couldn't tell you on the phone. She's going to tell you that you're in danger and you're going to get irritated because she doesn't give details. Then I'm probably going to end up paying their phone bill for another month or slipping Wanda some cash."

"All of those things will happen, Miles, and it doesn't take a psychic to know it. You're their cousin, so naturally you're going to feel obligated to help, after all. But what I'm looking for is the extra detail, the extra clue. There's always something to wonder about when we leave Wanda's house."

Miles grumbled, "Like how they survive from month to month?"

Myrtle found some food in her pantry and put it in a plastic bag to bring to Wanda and Crazy Dan. "Still need to get to the store," she muttered. But at least she could bring Wanda some odds and ends to eat. It was an odd combination of saltine crackers, peanut butter, pasta noodles, and pickles. But she was sure Wanda would take the food no matter what.

They got in the car and Myrtle fiddled with the radio. "Let's get some music on. You're always so tense when we set out to see Wanda, Miles."

"Only because I feel responsible for them. And very conflicted about what my role should be," said Miles with a sigh. He glanced over at Myrtle's punching of radio station buttons. "I think button three is a good station."

Myrtle hit button three. It appeared to be a public radio station that offered jazz music. Myrtle made a face. "I don't like jazz unless there's a vocalist. If there's no Billie Holiday or Dinah Washington or Louis Armstrong, I'm not interested."

Miles looked scandalized. "Not even *Take Five* by Dave Brubeck?"

"Okay, I'll make an exception for *Take Five*. But that's my only exception." Myrtle continued hitting buttons and making faces until she came to a station that was playing non-lyrical relaxing music. "This is better. Very relaxing and peaceful. Should make your blood pressure go down a little."

"This is elevator music!" Miles appeared even more stressed out.

"There's nothing objectionable about elevator music, Miles. Besides, I think this *isn't* elevator music. We're nowhere near an elevator and it's playing on the radio. I believe this must be New Age," said Myrtle thoughtfully.

Miles reached over and hit the power button. "Let's just think relaxing thoughts. I don't really need music right now."

"So touchy," murmured Myrtle. She watched as they got farther out of town and into the rundown rural area that the old, unmaintained secondary highway led through.

Minutes later, they were pulling into Wanda and Crazy Dan's driveway. Myrtle said, "Everything looks more dilapidated than usual somehow."

Miles said, "Might have something to do with that uprooted pine tree that fell on one of the cars up on cement blocks." He looked up at the pine trees and carefully selected a parking place that was not close to any precarious-looking pines.

Wanda was at the door before they got out of the car.

She pushed at the battered door until it was fully open and then disappeared into the shack.

"I guess we're supposed to go ahead in," said Myrtle. She glanced over at Miles. "Take deep breaths, Miles."

Chapter Eight

Myrtle and Miles entered the dark house. An ancient fan was slowing rotating and blowing the hot air back and forth around the shack. There was a dirty window on the back of the house allowing a modest amount of sunlight through. Wanda plopped full-length onto a slipcovered sofa. She seemed very lethargic, her movements much slower than usual.

Myrtle said briskly, “Okay, let’s get on with it then. Go ahead and give me my special message.”

Wanda narrowed her eyes at Myrtle. “Don’t see no point innit, since you never do listen.”

“But traditions must be observed, Wanda.”

Wanda first gave a prodigiously rattling cough. Then she fixed Myrtle with a baleful expression. “Yer in danger.”

“Noted. Naturally, however, you won’t give me any details as to the quadrant from which this latent danger arises,” said Myrtle briskly.

Wanda shook her head. “It don’t—”

“I know…work that way. We’ve done this little song and dance before, Wanda. Do you at least have some sort of clue to point me in the right direction?” asked Myrtle.

Miles was surreptitiously spreading out a pocket-handkerchief on a portion of a chair and again gingerly sitting down. He looked longingly at the door.

Wanda nodded. “I can give you a clue. Yer totally wrong.”

Myrtle stared at her. “Totally wrong. What on earth does that mean? My outlook toward life is wrong? My politics or religion is wrong? I'm hanging out with the wrong people?" She glanced over at Miles, who was removing what appeared to be hand sanitizer from his pocket.

"Yer wrong about the case. Dead wrong. Ain't nothin' personal with that Luella," croaked Wanda in her gravelly voice.

"Ain't nothin' personal…" Myrtle gave a frustrated sigh. "I believe Luella would say it was personal. After all, she's *dead*. It doesn't get any more personal than being killed by someone you know." She paused. "Unless…are you saying that the wrong person was murdered?"

"It was pretty dark outside," offered Miles.

"But Luella was fairly distinctive. She wore strong perfume and vibrantly-colored clothes. I find it hard to believe that someone would have mistaken Luella for someone else," said Myrtle. She pursed her lips thoughtfully.

Wanda shrugged a skeletal shoulder. "Up to you. Just sayin' yer wrong." She grimaced, placing a hand on her stomach. "Not feelin' so hot."

Miles leapt up with alacrity. "I believe that's our cue, Myrtle. We should let Wanda rest now to recover." He hurriedly pulled some bills out of his wallet and placed them on a cluttered table. "For the phone bill."

"Phone's broke," said Wanda laconically.

Miles pulled out some extra money. "For the phone bill and for a new phone."

Wanda added, "There's broke cars. Everywhere."

Miles looked a bit nervous about this pronouncement and peered doubtfully into his wallet. "You do have quite a few vehicles up on cement blocks, Wanda. Unfortunately, I don't appear to have enough cash on me to counteract this problem."

Wanda shook her head. "Not here. Well, yes, here. But

there will be broke cars everywhere soon. Everywhere. I got visions of 'em."

Miles coughed. "Yes. I see." It was clear that he didn't.

Wanda nodded and gave him a fond, if fairly toothless smile. "And Miles. Don't worry about bein' sick. It don't last long."

Miles's eyes widened in alarm.

"Did you hear that?" asked Miles as they walked back to his car.

"I know. I can't believe that she thinks we're on the wrong track. I mean—how is it not something personal against Luella?" said Myrtle huffily.

"No, I meant the part about it 'not lasting long.' I think Wanda knows that she's passed a virus on to me." Miles's eyes were panicky as he pulled out the hand sanitizer again. He offered it to Myrtle and she shook her head in irritation.

"For heaven's sake, Miles. It's not as if the poor woman has leprosy or Ebola or something. So what if you pick up a bug?"

"What if *you* pick up a bug?" asked Miles icily. "That would rather effectively shut down your little investigation."

"I'm the very picture of health. I *rarely* fall ill." Actually, Myrtle believed that falling ill was a sign of personal weakness. She opened the passenger side of Miles's Volvo and plopped herself inside. "Going back to Luella. I'm trying to remember if Luella could potentially be mistaken for someone else. Could she have borrowed someone's hat? Or jacket? That always seemed to happen in Agatha Christie murders. It would result in a case of mistaken identity."

Miles reluctantly let go of the virus as a conversation thread. "Myrtle, as you mentioned earlier, Luella was hard to mistake for someone else. She wore a lot of expensive perfume and she wore very brightly colored clothing. It's not as if someone would mistake her for poor Florence or someone."

Myrtle snapped her fingers. "Florence. I knew I was forgetting someone. Let's run by and see her on the way back."

"I thought we were planning a trip to see Poppy."

"We are. But we don't even have a possible motive for Poppy to have killed Luella and we know Florence was mad at Luella for tattling about her driving. Let's get all the interviews with suspects who have motives out of the way first," said Myrtle.

"And what excuse do we have for seeing Florence?" asked Miles. "I don't think she's lonely like Estelle. And after the snub we got at Alma's, I'm in the mood for an excellent justification for our visit."

"Lipstick, Miles! Definitely the lipstick ploy for Florence," said Myrtle.

"I just hope she's not sick," muttered Miles.

Florence, fortunately, did not appear to be sick. She blinked at them absently when she answered the door. Then a flood of recognition apparently occurred. "Well, hi! Come on inside and let's have a visit."

They followed Florence in. The elderly woman's house was nearly as cluttered as Wanda's had been. And Florence was looking disheveled herself. Her white hair was pulled up into a bun at the top of her head, but most of the hair in the bun was cascading out. She still wore a dressing gown, although it was afternoon. She smelled heavily of peppermints…as if she'd consumed an entire bag herself.

Miles seemed abashed at their dropping in, which Myrtle assumed was due to the fact that Florence was in a robe. "Uh, we're here because we wondered if you might have accidentally left something at Myrtle's during the

Bunco game."

Florence gave Miles a startled look. "Did I? I'm so sorry."

"Oh, it's no trouble," said Myrtle quickly. "We're not even sure it was yours. It's just this lipstick here." Myrtle held out the tube of lipstick.

Florence immediately took it. "Yes, I think that might be mine. Thank you."

While she was making room on the sofa for them to sit down, Miles gave Myrtle a meaningful look. Florence didn't seem a hundred percent lucid. She even took the lipstick that wasn't hers to begin with. Myrtle guessed that Miles was going to be pushing for them to go soon, believing that Florence would have nothing much to offer in the form of information. But Myrtle had a feeling that she did.

Florence gave Myrtle a wistful look. "Did you drive over here? I thought I saw you driving around the square a few days ago. It's nice that you're still able to get around."

Miles frowned and said in an aside to Myrtle, "The *square*? I thought you were taking my car to some doctor appointment you had in another town."

"I did. And then I decided to take a spin around the square. For fun," said Myrtle breezily. To Florence she said, "I don't have a car any longer, actually, but I still have my license. And it doesn't expire for years. I borrow a car when I want to go somewhere." She paused before deciding to simply jump right in. "I'm sorry about the way the Bonkers ended. But I understand that many people, although they're sorry Luella was dead, weren't very fond of her when she was alive. Was that true?"

Florence's blue eyes darkened. "She was going to tell my daughter that I'd had some trouble in the car recently. But I didn't want her to do that because my daughter wouldn't let me drive any more. And she'd probably make me move up north to be near her."

"But you're not interested in moving, are you?" asked Myrtle.

"Not at all." Florence hesitated and then said, "I've got a friend, you see. He lives about thirty minutes away. We met at a bridge tournament. He's not driving anymore so I drive every day to see him. If my daughter forced me to move or took away my car keys, he and I would never see each other again." She slumped, just thinking of it.

Miles's eyes clouded with concern. "I'm sure that won't happen," he said gruffly.

Miles was such a softy. Myrtle said, "I'm sure it won't happen, too. Because Luella White is dead and she was the one who was going to tattle."

Florence should have become wary at Myrtle's tone and words. Instead, her gaze clouded. "That's right. She's dead. Are you trying to tell me something?"

"I'm just saying that in a lot of ways, it's fortunate for you that she is no longer in the land of the living." Myrtle bit back a sigh as Florence continued not to register understanding. "Florence, what did you see or hear that could help us figure out who is behind Luella's death? Where were you at Bonkers?"

"Bunco," explained Miles helpfully as Florence knit her brows.

"Oh. Well, let's see. I was in the kitchen. I do love kitchens—they're the heart of a house, aren't they? And this kitchen was very cute with lots of red and white checkers on the towels and tablecloth and the rooster clock." Florence brightened as she spoke of the room.

Myrtle brightened, too. It wasn't often that she was praised for her decorating ability. "That was my house, you know."

"Was it? Well, it was precious. At least, the kitchen was." Florence tried to gather her thoughts again. "So I was in the kitchen, eating some of the food. I didn't have any wine, since I was going to drive home." This was stated in a virtuous voice.

"With whom did you talk while in the kitchen?" asked Myrtle. "Did you notice anyone in particular?"

"You," said Florence, smiling at Miles. "You were in the kitchen and I spoke with you."

Myrtle raised an eyebrow at Miles. He gave a small cough. "I was tracking down the cookies."

"Besides Miles. And, specifically, did you see anyone go out the back door?" asked Myrtle.

"Luella," said Florence. She made a face. "And that's when I decided to go back into the living room. I didn't want to see her or have to talk to her."

"Besides Luella." Myrtle felt as though her patience was being sorely taxed.

"Poppy," said Florence simply. Then she frowned. "Isn't Poppy the chubby one?"

Myrtle's head started pounding. "Can you describe her?"

"Younger than me," said Florence with a shrug.

That would apply to everyone at Myrtle's party besides Myrtle.

Florence had nothing more to offer in the way of information so they soon left. Myrtle said, "I agree with Luella—Florence has no business driving a car. Probably didn't have any business driving a car when she was sixteen."

Miles said, "But she did appear to have seen something."

"What good is that, if she can't even remember what she saw? And you'd think she'd have made special note of it, considering that there was a murder that occurred minutes later," said Myrtle in irritation. She opened Miles's car door and then squinted down the street. "Wait a minute.

Is that Alma walking toward us?"

"It is," murmured Miles. "A sighting of the elusive Alma."

"I wonder where she's heading," said Myrtle thoughtfully. "Surely she isn't walking for her health. She's not wearing casual clothing."

"Considering the condition her house was in, maybe she's trying to conserve money by walking instead of driving," said Miles. "Which would be healthier, too."

"Maybe. She has the appearance of a stranded motorist though, somehow." Myrtle and Miles got in the car and peered through the back window. "Do you think she's going to visit Florence?"

"She could be on her way to visit *any* of the suspects," said Miles. "Everyone lives pretty close together here."

Alma continued heading their way. Miles and Myrtle slid down in their seats. But apparently, Miles's mild-mannered Volvo stood out among the other vehicles on the street. As Alma approached, she stared suspiciously at the car.

"I think our cover is blown," said Miles.

"The problem is that we didn't have a cover," said Myrtle. "We might as well just get out and pepper Alma with questions instead of wasting the opportunity."

Myrtle popped out of the car right as Alma was passing it on the sidewalk. "Alma! What a surprise to see you here. You seemed so … busy … when we tried talking to you earlier."

Alma bared her teeth in a smile. "It's just that I didn't have anything to tell you. Period. And I wasn't feeling well."

Myrtle nodded. "Glad you're feeling so much better now. Nice day for a walk? You just don't seem to have your exercise clothes on."

Alma colored. "I'm running an errand. And getting

exercise at the same time."

"Multitasking. How clever of you," murmured Myrtle. She paused. "So who do you think murdered Luella?"

Miles made a gasping sound. For a sidekick, he certainly supplied a lot of sound effects during suspect questioning time.

Alma gave Myrtle a look of dislike. "As I told you, I don't have the foggiest. It was probably that handyman of yours. The one with the wrench. After all, it *was* his tool that was the murder weapon."

Myrtle narrowed her eyes. "Absolutely not. What nonsense. Are you implying that Dusty scaled the fence into my backyard? At his age? And for what motive?"

Alma's mouth turned down resentfully. "Never mind. Nothing will stop you from nosing around. I should have known."

Miles gave Myrtle a sideways glance. He was waiting for Myrtle to give Alma a piece of her mind.

But Myrtle decided to knock Alma more off-balance as her revenge. "You seem very jumpy, Alma. And most flustered when asked about this errand you're running. Where *are* you going?"

She flushed that bright red again. "I'm out of coffee. And now I'm running late." With that, she strode off down the sidewalk.

Miles said dryly, "I'm assuming you don't buy the coffee story."

"Certainly not. The only place to buy coffee in walking distance is that coffeehouse with the pricy java. Alma doesn't look the type to be buying Sumatra, does she? No, if *Alma* ran out of coffee, she'd be headed to the Piggly Wiggly, like everyone else," said Myrtle. "Still, I suppose there's no point in following her or else she won't end up doing whatever it is that she *is* doing."

They got into the car and Miles started the engine.

"You didn't seem to care for Alma much," he observed.

"She was being hateful about Dusty. As if Dusty has the sense to carry out a complicated murder during a party." Myrtle rolled her eyes. "I'm convinced that Alma knows exactly who the murderer is—and that it's not Dusty."

Miles coasted slowly down the street. "I certainly agree with your evaluation of Dusty's mental capabilities." He paused. "So where are we heading now?"

"Poppy, remember? I wanted to see everyone today and really get the ball rolling."

Miles coughed. "If I might make a suggestion? Let's get something to eat before interrogating Poppy. My stomach is starting to complain." He grimaced. "And I hope it's complaining because of lack of food and not because it's getting a virus."

"It's way too early to have gotten a virus. You've only just been in contact with potential carriers. But you know I always enjoy it when you're being fanciful."

Miles pulled into a spot in front of Bo's Diner downtown. On cue, a gaggle of elderly men waved at him from the bench in front of the diner. They were wearing golfing attire in particularly bright colors with violently conflicting patterns on the pants and tops. "Makes me dizzy just looking at them," muttered Myrtle.

"What do you think of Farland?" asked Miles in an idle voice as he braked the car.

"Which one is he again?" asked Myrtle. "They all look the same to me with their bald heads and loud clothing."

Miles's lips tugged at the ends, a sign that he was trying hard not to smile. "The one in the middle. He's rather fond of you. Keeps asking me if I'm sure you and I aren't an 'item' because he'd hate to 'trespass.'"

"As if I were property of some kind!"

Miles continued to bite back the grin. "He hoped I'd investigate your opinion of him."

Myrtle made a face.

"I suppose I'll have to keep that assessment to myself," said Miles.

They got out of the Volvo and headed for the door. Farland leapt from the bench and swung the door open wide, making its bell swing violently and clang loudly. "After you," he said, giving a funny little bow to Myrtle.

She bared her teeth at him in return.

Miles said kindly to him, "Having a good day, Farland?"

Farland seemed taken aback by the question. "Well, same as every other day. Thought I'd take in a little golf. Meet up with the boys and chat for a while."

Myrtle gave Miles a long-suffering glare.

Miles said in a studiously careless way, "Want to join Myrtle and me for chili dogs inside?"

Myrtle reached out and bore down hard on Miles's instep with one of her sensible orthopedic shoes. Miles grunted.

Farland looked wistfully into the restaurant and gave them a regretful smile. "I'd sure love to, but the doctor put the ixnay on the greasy foods. The boys and I are going to drive out to the Costco and eat all the free samples for our lunch. Sometimes that's pretty fun."

"Maybe another time," said Miles in a gasping voice as Myrtle continued applying pressure. Finally, they walked inside.

Chapter Nine

"The very idea, Miles! As if I want a paramour! You shouldn't encourage him. Next thing, he'll be showing up at my door with a box of stale chocolates from the drugstore and flowers he picked from someone's yard on the way over. Is this revenge for some past, forgotten transgression I've made?"

Miles grinned at her and she scowled back.

Her mood was not improved when her least favorite waitress at the diner cooed at her, "Well hi there, sugar plum! How you doin', baby?"

Myrtle winced at the soppy condescension. "Tanya, I'm doing very well. But Miles here may have contracted some vile virus from a local psychic. It's only his cabin fever that drives him out of his house. Here's a helpful tip—seat us at a table where someone else can wait on us."

Tanya's eyes grew wide as she backed away slightly from Miles. "Thanks, darlin'. I'll just do that." And she hastily pointed out a booth on the far side of the diner.

"Nicely done," murmured Miles as they plopped down in the vinyl booth framing a Formica-topped table. Miles picked up a laminated menu and studied it with a furrowed brow.

"Surely you must have memorized the menu by now," chided Myrtle. "It really just comes down to what kind of hot dog you want. A pimento cheese dog, a slaw dog, a chili cheese *and* pimento cheese dog…."

Miles was turning slightly green and clutched the menu with determination. "I was actually thinking about a salad."

Myrtle frowned. "That's like ordering a hamburger at Red Lobster. Why order something that's not their specialty? It might go horribly wrong."

"Ordering a grease-packed chili cheese dog might go horribly wrong," muttered Miles.

Now Myrtle did study the menu. "What about this blackened catfish?"

"It has that Cajun mustard," said Miles miserably.

"Just tell them to leave it off! It's not that big of a deal. For heaven's sake." Myrtle was suddenly distracted as someone entered the diner. "What do you know? It's Poppy."

At that moment, though, a waitress named Cindy, who had a freshly-pressed apron and a good deal of blue eye makeup, arrived with a smile. "What can I get you two today?"

"Three pimento cheese dogs and a side of chili fries," said Myrtle promptly.

"And maybe an antacid," said Miles, still muttering and looking even greener.

"What's that, love?" asked Cindy, looking a bit concerned.

"Sorry. Nothing. Could I have the Cobb salad? With no dressing," said Miles.

Cindy's eyebrows shot up. "No *dressing*?"

Myrtle was sure that the few salads they sold at the diner came slathered in Ranch.

"Let's just put it on the side," said Miles. "I don't want to create a stir in the kitchen."

Cindy left and Myrtle said, "Let's try to catch Poppy's eye and motion her over to our booth."

"So we can grill her in the diner?"

"Diners *are* for grilling, Miles. Don't worry, I won't scare her off. Besides, it looks as if she's waiting for a takeout order and it's so crowded that there's no place for her to stand." Myrtle half-stood, gesturing wildly at Poppy who blinked in confusion before hesitantly heading in their direction.

Poppy's expression looked very solemn. She attempted what appeared to be a smile of greeting, but it didn't quite make it her eyes.

"Poppy looks as if she's heading to the firing squad," said Miles under his breath.

"Poppy *always* looks as if she's heading to the firing squad," said Myrtle. "I think it's just the way her face is engineered. She's nobody's pretty child, poor thing."

Poppy had an unfortunate combination of features. Any one of them, on their own, would have been perfectly fine. Together, however, they conspired to create a generally unattractive effect. She had a pointy nose that wasn't perfectly straight, a weak chin, and mousy hair. Her choice of clothing was nondescript and concealed any figure she might have had. To cap it all off, she'd apparently decided to get her teeth fixed rather late in life and she had braces, as well. She constantly fought weight gain and frequently gave up dieting, with poor results.

Poppy stood by their booth. "It's crowded in the diner today, isn't it?"

"Sit down with us, Poppy, while you're waiting. They must have fallen behind in the kitchen," said Myrtle.

"Oh, I didn't phone my takeaway order in before coming. I should have, but I forgot. So it's my own fault I have to wait. I thought I would bring lunch over to Mimsy and John…John is her husband, you know. I feel so bad about what happened to Luella. I know Mimsy must be crushed." But the way Poppy said *Mimsy must be crushed* sounded a bit doubtful.

"Mimsy was actually so sweet and came by earlier today to bring me a casserole," said Myrtle.

Poppy's eyes widened and her mouth dropped open a little, giving her a somewhat fishlike appearance. "*She* gave *you* a casserole?"

Myrtle could tell that Poppy wondered if her offering from the diner was good enough, considering the object of her kindness was making casseroles for people who weren't even bereaved. "Yes, but she said she was trying to keep busy, or something like that. I guess to keep her mind off of everything. She said she felt bad that I'd hosted the party and that something dreadful had happened."

Poppy frowned. "That *is* bad, now that I think about it. You were doing a good deed, weren't you? And it backfired."

"I'm fine," said Myrtle a little impatiently. She hadn't meant to get off on this tangent. The food would be ready very soon, she was sure, and Poppy would be gone. "Miles and I were trying to piece together what happened to see if we can figure out who's behind this terrible tragedy. Where were you last night, for instance? During the Bonkers party?"

Miles's eyebrows shot up in alarm to let her know she needed to soften her question.

Myrtle revised, "I mean, could you get an idea where everyone else was? If someone might have had the opportunity to kill poor Luella."

Poppy looked even more solemn. "Poor Luella is right. She was very kind to me whenever she saw me…since I'm Mimsy's best friend, you know. She knew I was interested in easy recipes and whenever the bank finished with their magazines, she'd give them to me. She was very nice."

This was something they hadn't heard before. Usually everyone was quick to point out Luella's faults. Myrtle said, "At the game last night, Luella said nice things about you, too." This was a stretch. What Luella had actually said was that she didn't have any gossip about Poppy.

Inaccurate or not, Myrtle's words had the unfortunate effect of bringing Poppy to tears. "She was always nice to me. Poor Luella."

Myrtle anxiously glanced toward the cash register. Poppy's order would surely be up soon. The only reason their own order was taking so long is because Miles ordered odd things from the menu.

"The only problem is that, nice or not, Luella is dead. Someone didn't think that Luella was nice—have you got any ideas who that might have been? What could you see from where you were at the party?"

Poppy knit her brows, which didn't improve her countenance. "I walked around a lot, visiting with everyone. I didn't spend too much time in the kitchen, although I was in there briefly. I *did* notice Alma going into the kitchen from the direction of your back door. But I really hate to point the finger at anyone. She didn't look as if she'd just murdered someone, if that's what you're asking." She brightened. "Has Red checked into whether it might have been some kind of random intruder of some kind?"

Miles cleared his throat. "The problem, you see, is that there is a privacy fence around Myrtle's yard. It seems very unlikely that someone from the outside would be responsible."

Poppy's eyes darkened as she thought some more. "But surely … there must be a gate of some kind?"

"Bolted," said Myrtle firmly. "Mostly to keep my neighbor, Erma Sherman, out."

"Don't you have someone to cut your grass for you? Maybe he left it unbolted after he'd finished with your yard," said Poppy.

Poppy seemed stuck on the intruder theory. And it was getting tedious. "Certainly not," said Myrtle. "Dusty is only careless with his tools, never with gates."

Poppy sighed. "Then if it absolutely can't be a stranger, I suppose I'd have to wonder about Alma. Since I saw her coming from that direction, and all. But I can't for the life of me figure out why she'd do such a thing." She squinted toward the cash register. "It looks like my order is up. I should take it over to Mimsy and John. I feel so terrible for them." She glanced back at Myrtle and Miles and then more closely at Miles. "Are you feeling all right? You're not looking very well."

Miles was indeed looking a bit peaked. He took out a crisply folded handkerchief and gently patted at dots of perspiration that had appeared on his forehead. "I'm all right, thanks. Tell Mimsy hi for us."

As Poppy left, Cindy appeared with their order. Myrtle tucked into her pimento cheese dogs with gusto as Miles picked at his salad. He did not, Myrtle noticed, use a drop of the Ranch dressing. He said, "Well, at least now we don't have to run by and see Poppy."

"You sound relieved," said Myrtle, turning her attention to her chili fries.

"We've done a lot today. I'm ready to go home and put my feet up."

Myrtle said, "You're looking pale, Miles. And you've only pushed your salad around on your plate instead of eating it. Do you think it's possible that this isn't merely your hypochondria at work but an actual virus?"

But now Miles appeared to be in denial. "I'm absolutely fine. I simply need to catch up on some sleep, that's all. I slept horribly last night. And you probably turned in later than you wanted to."

"Right. But I'm feeling fine," she said as she polished off the rest of her food.

Miles looked past Myrtle's shoulder. "Oh no. Looks as if we're about to have more company," he murmured.

"Who?"

"Tippy Chambers and Blanche Clark," said Miles with a groan. "I hate to be impolite, but I really need to get back home."

"Well, don't be a baby about it. I'll tell them that you've got a pressing engagement. Here's some money for my food. While you're paying up front, I'll get rid of them and meet you at your car."

Miles, determinedly pretending not to see or hear the women's approach, bolted for the cash register with the two bills and Myrtle's money. Myrtle shook her head. Men certainly didn't handle being sick well. The few times that Myrtle was under the weather, she was a complete stoic about it.

An arm slid around her neck as she was briefly hugged by Tippy Chambers. Tippy was dressed as if she were about to address the stockholders at an annual meeting…but since she always dressed that way, she didn't look a bit out of place in the diner. Her friend, Blanche Clark, was similarly outfitted except that her look was that of carefully preserved designer clothes.

"Myrtle, I'm so glad to see you," said Tippy. "I was just filling Blanche in on the events at your Bunco night. So tragic. And so worrisome to think that there was a murder taking place just yards away! I feel as if I didn't thank you properly for hosting. Honestly, I was so bewildered by Luella's passing that I completely forgot my manners. I'm so sorry."

Myrtle liked Tippy. She approved of the briskly businesslike way she'd run everything from book club to garden club. Myrtle had respect for efficiency. The only problem was that whenever she was around Tippy, she felt as if she had a food stain on her blouse or something caught in her teeth. There was that generally disheveled feeling that occurred merely by being in proximity to Tippy's perfection. The only thing she could think of that Tippy should improve was her ability to say no to Puddin who trapped her in long-winded conversations.

Blanche said, "I was appalled. … truly appalled to hear the news. I'm so sorry, Miss Myrtle."

"That's kind of both of you," said Myrtle. "But as you can see, I've fully recovered." To the extent that she was able to polish off a plate of pimento cheese dogs and chili fries. At her age, death had lost its ability to shock.

Blanche gave a small cough and Tippy made a smooth segue. "Speaking of appalling…well, this isn't nearly in the same category, of course. But it's something that's startled and worried both Blanche and me and so I wanted to take the opportunity to mention it to you since we've run into you here."

Now Myrtle was concerned. *Did* she have something caught in her teeth?

"It's about the newspaper," said Tippy. "The *Bradley Bugle*."

Myrtle relaxed and let out the pent-up breath she'd been holding. "Oh, that."

Tippy and Blanche seemed to relax too, at Myrtle's casual tone. Blanche said quickly, "It's only that we know you spend a good deal of time there and are connected with the editor. We thought Sloan Jones might listen to you more than he'd listen to a couple of subscribers."

"You're concerned about the paper's content, I'm guessing?" asked Myrtle. She noticed that Miles had finished paying up and was heading out the door.

"That's right," said Tippy. "You see, we really *liked* the Good Neighbors column."

Blanche said, "And I enjoyed hearing about Cheryl and Randy Peterson's trip to the Grand Canyon in the People section."

"And the Rogers boy getting his Eagle Scout award," added Tippy.

"Even the horoscope," said Blanche with a shrug of her thin shoulders. "I miss that, too."

Tippy said, "The tone of the paper seems to have changed, too. Where it was light-hearted and chatty, it's now sort of…sensationalistic." She said the word as if it tasted bad.

Blanche leaned forward and said in a low tone as if speaking of a sacrilege, "And the typos and misspellings are terrible, Miss Myrtle. Really horrible."

This last part was the worst and Myrtle put a hand to her heart as if receiving a mortal blow. "You both know that I have nothing whatsoever to do with the editing of the newspaper, don't you?"

"Naturally," said Tippy briskly. "If you did, the editing would be flawless."

Blanche gave an emphatic nod.

"We don't want to hold you up—I saw Miles leave. But we didn't want to let the opportunity pass without saying that we were worried about the direction the newspaper is moving in," said Tippy.

Myrtle, who'd been sitting in a booth for long enough, pushed up on the table to try to slide over and stand. Tippy solicitously moved over to support her arm. "Thank you ladies," said Myrtle. "I'll be sure to share your thoughts with Sloan.

"Perhaps, though, as your own thoughts," advised Tippy. "Only if you agree with us."

"Of course," said Myrtle a little absently. "The only problem is that he's convinced himself that this is the best way to win readers."

"I'm sure he'll find it's the opposite," said Blanche with a regretful shake of her head.

Myrtle suddenly had a marvelous idea. "This will sound like I've abruptly switched subjects, but do either of you see car shopping in your immediate future?"

Blanche shook her head. Tippy said, "Not for me. But Benton has mentioned replacing his sedan. In fact, I think he was going to start shopping around tomorrow."

Myrtle said, "Tell him that if he goes to Roger's Automotive to be sure and mention that he'll only give them his business if they continue advertising with the *Bradley Bugle*."

Tippy nodded slowly. "I see. So it's a question of losing advertising dollars—this change of approach for the newspaper."

"That's right. And be sure to mention that whenever you hear of someone who might be shopping locally," said Myrtle.

"I'll see what I can do," said Tippy. And she had that steely look in her eye that indicated she meant every word.

"And now I have to catch up with my ride," said Myrtle.

"Tell Miles we said hi," said Blanche with a smile as a waitress approached to show them to a table.

Chapter Ten

As Myrtle walked outside, she saw Miles slumping against his Volvo looking even greener than he had earlier. "Miles! Are you all right?"

"I'm…not so well. And my car won't run."

Myrtle said, "Won't *run*? The engine won't turn over, you mean?"

"No, I mean that it won't drive me anywhere. The transmission has been slipping some lately. I've been good about having the transmission fluid serviced, but there still have been issues."

Myrtle's forte was not automobiles, and as usual, she tuned out the specifics as soon as Miles launched into them. "So, what's the bottom line here, Miles? That the car won't take us home?"

"That's right. Because the gears won't shift at all. The transmission is shot. We'll be walking home." He gave the car a dirty look. "I knew this was going to happen one day, I just wish it had happened in my driveway. And when I wasn't feeling ill."

Myrtle said, "So you need a tow, I suppose. And then you'll get it repaired?"

"No, I think the part is probably worth more than the car at this point. I've had the Volvo for a while now. I'll likely just get something new. But no more Volvos. They seem to stand out here. However, I certainly *don't* want a truck, which seems to be the official vehicle of the town of Bradley." Miles's voice was fretful.

How fortuitous that everyone was going car shopping!

Myrtle planned on steering him toward Roger's Automotive when it was time for him to shop. But now he clearly needed to get some sleep. She reached out and briskly laid her hand on Miles's forehead. "You're burning up, Miles! Let's start walking home. Maybe we can hitch you a ride on the way and get you there faster."

"It's not as if it's far," said Miles.

"Right. But it's going to feel far in your condition. Let's go."

As they were walking slowly toward home, Myrtle leaning on her cane as she supported Miles with her free arm, Sloan Jones from the paper drove up from behind them in his old pickup truck. Myrtle immediately flagged him down and he rolled down his window. "Sloan, we need a favor. Could you drop us back home? Miles isn't feeling well and his car has broken down."

Sloan looked as if he wished that he could wear a protective suit and mask. He hesitated before quickly saying, "Of course, Miss Myrtle. Hop on in."

Although Miles was able to climb rather nimbly into the cab of the truck, Myrtle had the distinct impression that her own ascent would be problematic. This was one unfortunate issue that occurred to a person in his or her eighties. "Never mind about me. I'm going to walk off those pimento cheese dogs. But Sloan…could you run by my house for a minute after you drop off Miles? There's something I wanted to talk to you about."

Now Sloan's face was even more dismayed than it had been at the prospect of riding next to germ-ridden Miles. "Of course, Miss Myrtle. See you then. Will you … well … will you be home by the time I drive there?"

She leveled a haughty look at him. "I'll most certainly beat you there. I'm quite fleet of foot."

He glanced doubtfully at her cane, but then hastily said, "Okay. In a minute then."

And there was nothing left for Myrtle to do but scamper home just as fast as she could.

Myrtle was huffing and puffing as she reached her front door. She rummaged around in her pocketbook until she felt her keys. She was just reaching the key toward the lock when it suddenly swung open, startling her enough to make her step backward.

It was an apologetic Elaine with a squeaky-clean looking Jack. "Myrtle, I'm so sorry. I tried to call you, but you must have your cell phone turned off."

Myrtle guiltily recalled that it was inside her desk in the house. "No worries, Elaine. I guess the battery must have died. Or something."

Elaine nodded absently, frowning in concern. "Myrtle, you sound really out of breath. Are you okay?"

"Fine, just fine! I was simply having a brisk walk, you see. Getting a little exercise. Sloan Jones is about to stop by to talk with me about the paper, too, so I wanted to beat him back home."

Elaine said, "Jack and I were just using your bathroom. Since, well, we don't have any working plumbing right now. I'm sorry. It's not the first time today, either—we've been sort of in and out."

"Oh, please! No problem at all. I was planning to check in with you and see how things were going over there," said Myrtle. She felt a twinge of guilt again. Her investigating, Wanda-visiting and diner-eating had hijacked her day.

Elaine forced a brave smile. "I think the plumbing ordeal is the kind of thing that gets worse before it gets better. At least, I hope that's true. Right now we seem like we're in the worst of it. But at least Jack is clean now." She hesitated. "I think Red is coming by later to get cleaned up. And there's the washing machine, too—I'm afraid I'm going to have to come by and do some laundry."

Myrtle said, still rather breathlessly, "Of course you should. In fact, why don't you bring the laundry and we'll let Jack nap here and you and I can watch *Tomorrow's Promise* together. I taped it."

Elaine raised her eyebrows. "That sounds great, but what about Miles? Isn't he usually your soap opera buddy? I don't want to step on any toes."

"He's indisposed," said Myrtle, making a face. "Not feeling well in the slightest. And he appears to be a truly ghastly patient, from what I can see. Most men are. I think you're a much better soap opera buddy prospect today." She drank from a glass of water she'd filled earlier that day. Maybe she needed to walk briskly more often.

"It's a plan, then," said Elaine, beaming. Then she hesitated. "Not to get into your business, Myrtle, but you might want to stick your list of suspects in a drawer before Red pops by. You know how frazzled he gets when he thinks you're investigating murders."

"Good point," said Myrtle. She was putting the paper away as Elaine and Jack left.

Myrtle was still trying to catch her breath when there was a light tap at her front door. She took another quick gulp of water and headed to the door. Myrtle leaned against it for a second, taking another couple of deep breaths before opening it. "What took you so long?" she asked Sloan breezily.

He gave her an admiring look as he walked into her living room. "I've got to hand it to you, Miss Myrtle. You're speedy. I would have probably had a heart attack if I'd tried to walk home that fast."

Myrtle silently agreed. Sloan, not particularly slim, was huffing and puffing from just walking from his truck to her living room.

Sloan shifted his weight a bit. "So…what can I do for

you, Miss Myrtle?" Before she could answer, he brightened up. "Oh! I meant to tell you that I got the article you emailed me. It was very good. I mean, I did have to spice up the verbs some, but other than that, it was absolutely perfect as-is. I'll run it tomorrow morning."

"Spice them up? My verbs were quite robust, I assure you, Sloan. In fact, I thought they needed toning down."

Sloan seemed excited by the topic and waved his fleshy hands around emphatically as he spoke. "Vibrant writing, Miss Myrtle. I'm really looking for some very vibrant writing for the paper. I want reading the *Bradley Bugle* to be a transformative experience for our readers. I want them to look forward to every edition because it *transports* them somewhere."

"It sounds as if they only want to be transported to the little league game and the Girl Scout cookie booth to me Sloan. I spoke with two avid readers of the paper just minutes ago and they said they miss the old stories—the small town tidbits. The stuff that readers can't get from the *Charlotte Observer*…local happenings. That sort of thing." Myrtle was getting the feeling that things were much worse than she'd thought. Apparently Sloan had taken complete leave of his senses.

Sloan gave her a sorrowful look. "But see, Miss Myrtle, you likely ran into the only two ladies in town who felt that way. They would have searched you out, knowing you'd be a sympathetic ear."

"I didn't say they were ladies!" But naturally, they were.

"Whoever these readers were," said Sloan in a mollifying tone.

"Well, have you gotten any *compliments* on the new direction for the *Bugle*?" asked Myrtle.

Sloan shifted his weight again. "Not yet. But I've been too busy to really be out and about, conducting reader polls."

"If you haven't gotten any compliments, then I think we need to pay special attention to the complaints I've heard. And what do you mean that you've been "too busy to be out and about?" What about rustling up ads for the paper? That requires someone to get out and about."

Sloan studied the ceiling as if seeking divine support or revelation. "Right now I thought I should focus my efforts on the new tone and style for the paper. I'm trying to update the design of it to make it more exciting."

"Okay, so you're changing content and appearance. What about your salesman? Can you make sure he's hitting the road and rustling up ad sales?" asked Myrtle.

"He was a part time worker and needed to find something full-time," said Sloan in the manner of someone glossing something over.

"So he quit." Myrtle sighed. "So you need a proofreader, a salesman, and columnists to write Good Neighbors and the horoscopes. Basically a full staff."

Sloan looked alarmed. "Not all those people! I couldn't pay them. But I do need a salesperson who doesn't expect to make a fortune. Or even someone willing to work part time."

"Well don't look at me! I have no desire to knock on doors and drum up advertisers. The only reason I wanted to get in touch with you was to pass on the valuable information that we got from these subscribers. Before they become *former* subscribers."

But Sloan didn't really appear to be listening. Instead, he kept saying, "It's going to be great—you'll see, Miss Myrtle. We'll be printing extra editions by the time these changes are in place. It's going to be the most popular small town newspaper around."

Myrtle suddenly felt as if she needed an antacid. And she didn't blame those pimento cheese dogs, either.

The next morning, Myrtle woke up very early. It was the time of day where she actually wasn't sure if it were technically very late at night or very early in the morning. She analyzed carefully whether there were even a smidgeon of a chance that she would fall back asleep. Myrtle decided there wasn't. She showered, dressed and even put on makeup.

She was just sitting down to a four A.M. breakfast of buttery cheese grits with sausage links on the side when the front door unlocked and opened. Considering the plumbing issue across the street and the fact that the only people who had keys to her front door were Red and Elaine, Myrtle didn't even bat an eye or feel the slightest hint of concern. She simply went back to the stove and made up a second plate of grits and sausages for whoever was coming in.

It was Red, looking grim. "Saw the lights and figured you were up. Going to use your facilities real quick before heading out. I've had a call."

Myrtle said, "Here, shove some food down before you go in the back. A call … for the same case?" She had a strong feeling it was. And somehow she didn't even feel very surprised when Red nodded.

"It's Alma Wiggins. Her son, Robert, called me. He discovered her body a few minutes ago."

Myrtle realized that she had a very narrow window to find out any more information on Alma's body. "Here," she said quickly, "have a small bowl of grits. You'll focus better with something on your stomach. And you can get to Alma's house in two seconds … she's not going anywhere, anyway."

Red took the bowl she handed him and started shoveling down the grits while standing in her kitchen.

Not wanting to scare him off, she asked delicately, "I suppose Alma's death wasn't from natural causes?"

Red polished off his grits and said quickly, "Unfortunately, no. Not unless she hit herself over the head with a cast iron frying pan." But that's all he'd give her as he ran into the back briefly and then back out her front door.

Myrtle's mind whirled. Ordinarily she'd run over to Miles's house with this new information and they'd dissect it together. But he'd certainly not looked very well when she'd left him yesterday afternoon. She decided to walk to Miles's house and see if any lights were on.

Already fully dressed and ready for her day, she grabbed her cane and a light cardigan and locked the front door behind her. She was glad she'd thought to get the cardigan because it was breezy outside and she shivered a little despite the sweater.

Myrtle saw with delight that there was indeed a light on inside Miles's house. It didn't appear to be a nightlight variety, either. She quietly tapped at the door and paused. She thought she heard snoring sounds. Myrtle tapped again. Then she peeked through the window next to the door. It was covered by sheer curtains, but she could still see Miles's figure, covered by a large blanket and appearing to be sound asleep in a recliner.

Myrtle made a face. It looked as if she would be investigating solo this time. And, even worse, it was too early to start following up with suspects. All she could do was go back home and do her daily crossword puzzle. And wait.

It was eight o'clock when her front doorbell rang. Myrtle had hoped that maybe it was Red coming back by for a shower—and to fill her in. She sighed when she looked out the peephole and saw Puddin there.

Puddin was looking very self-satisfied, too. "Told you I'd be able to find out all about it."

"About what?" asked Myrtle wearily as she headed back to the sofa and plopped down.

"About Miz Mimsy! I told you I'd listen in real good and then you said you'd tip me. Remember?" Puddin put her pudgy hands on her hips.

Myrtle nodded, "I remember. Stop tooting your own horn and tell me what you know. I'll decide what that information is worth."

Puddin sat down next to Myrtle on the sofa and put her feet up on Myrtle's coffee table…until Myrtle's narrowed eyes made Puddin put them back down on the floor again. "So I was cleanin' for Miz Mimsy yesterday, right? And she was talking to Poppy. 'Cause she and Poppy are friends. And she told Poppy that Luella had had a *million dollars*. A million! And Luella's lawyer said Luella was giving it to Mimsy, since she was her only kin, and all." Just in case Myrtle had missed what Puddin considered her most valuable takeaway, she enunciated loudly, "A *mil*—"

"All right! I heard you. Yes, that's a lot of money, it's true. But I already knew that Luella White was a woman of some means. So what else?"

Puddin's pale face fell comically at Myrtle's lack of reaction. "Well, that gives her a lot of motive to kill her kin, don't it? You're just like Poppy. Poppy didn't react much to it either."

"You could see watch Poppy and Mimsy from where you were? What kind of cleaning were you doing?" asked Myrtle, rolling her eyes.

"Baseboards," said Puddin succinctly.

"You never touch the baseboards here!" said Myrtle. "They're covered with dust, grime, and scuff marks."

Puddin had developed ignoring people to an art form. She continued with her story, apparently worried that it wasn't going to be worth a tip. "Miz Mimsy didn't sound all that happy about the money, neither. Sort of weird. Her attitude seemed like it made Poppy mad. It made me sort of mad, too. Why is it the people who don't care about money who end up with it? That's what I want to know."

Myrtle ignored Puddin's philosophic wonderings. "So Poppy was unhappy with Mimsy's attitude? I wonder why."

"Why?" Puddin snorted. "I reckon because she was being such a pill. Poppy was trying to get Miz Mimsy's head screwed back on right, tellin' her that she should travel or get a little place at the beach, or give it all away to poor folk. But Miz Mimsy said that she don't need no more money, that she got plenty. And that made Poppy madder." Puddin's face was gleeful. It was apparently a fascinating workday for her yesterday.

"Did Poppy bring Mimsy food from the diner?" asked Myrtle.

Puddin squinted at Myrtle as if she'd suddenly been blessed with second sight. "That's right. Why? You spying over there, too?"

"No, I was at the diner when Poppy picked up the food," said Myrtle.

Puddin was now looking grouchy that Myrtle knew part of the story without even being told. "So what do you think? Worth something to you?"

Myrtle thought this through. On the face of it, Puddin's information wasn't very insightful. But somehow, Myrtle had a feeling there was something there that she was missing. And it certainly did seem to show that Mimsy didn't care about money or didn't have a financial motive for the crime.

"And you're sure that Mimsy wasn't just faking her lack of interest in the estate?" asked Myrtle.

Puddin squinted suspiciously at the vocabulary, mistrustful as she was at anything that wasn't very plain English. "She weren't fakin' nothin'. She was flat bored with money, and that's the truth."

"All right then." Myrtle got up and walked over to her desk for her pocketbook. She gave Puddin a ten dollar bill. "But you'll get more if you find out more, Puddin. When are you supposed to clean over there next?"

"In a couple days. If her regular housekeeper, Pam, don't get well." Puddin's small, avarice-filled eyes boded ill for Pam if she were to suddenly improve.

Chapter Eleven

Myrtle decided it was certainly late enough in the morning to start her investigation. And clearly, she should start moving toward Alma's house. If Red spotted her in that direction, why she was simply taking her morning walk, that was all. If he spotted her on Alma's property (because sometimes that nice Lieutenant Perkins from the state police would give her a drop or two of information), then she'd simply say that she'd been taking her walk and decided to make a short detour to remind him that he was welcome to shower at her house as soon as he was done with the crime scene.

As she passed Miles's house, though, something made her stop again. Maybe it was that he'd looked so wretchedly pitiful in that recliner earlier. Maybe it was the fact that he'd been so piqued last time when she'd set off investigating on her own, without him as sidekick. Perhaps it was that she was just the slightest bit worried about him. Although she did think that men were ridiculously melodramatic when they were sick.

She tapped lightly on Miles's front door again. Again, there was no response. Myrtle tapped more emphatically and waited again. She glanced around Miles's yard as she waited. He must have been planning to cut his grass either yesterday or today. It was looking too long for Miles. Miles's yard was usually kept in total control—grass a particular, regulation height. Shrubs made to bow to his domination over them. No misbehaving weeds. Everything in order. Miles's yard was now looking decidedly mutinous.

Since there was no response to the second round of tapping, Myrtle attempted to peer through his window and sheer curtains again. It was a lot more difficult now, though, than it was at night. At night, dark outside and light inside, she could see relatively clearly. Here she *thought* she still saw a forlorn figure in the recliner, but she couldn't swear by it. Myrtle recalled that she still had Miles's extra key from the previous summer when he'd left his home and (rather unwisely) his houseplants to her care as he'd traveled. She decided that drastic times called for drastic measures.

Myrtle found the key on her key ring and opened Miles's front door. She walked into Miles's living room, which felt rather stuffy. Sure enough, Miles was in the recliner and he was sound asleep. Or unconscious. At any rate, he wasn't awake.

Myrtle walked over to him. "Miles!" she said, taking him by the shoulder and giving him a little shake. He was perspiring and some of his steel-gray hair was matted to his forehead. He murmured in his sleep, but didn't wake up.

"Fever," muttered Myrtle. And the man didn't have any water or anything to drink near him. Also, from the way the bathroom door was wide open in the back and the light on, it seemed as if Miles had some stomach upset. That, and the fever and the perspiration…he should have water. And saltine crackers. Myrtle firmly believed that everyone should have saltine crackers when they were ill. And fresh air. The stale, stuffy air in the house needed to go.

Myrtle pushed aside the curtains and pulled open a stubborn window. Then she rummaged in the cabinets in Miles's kitchen until she located an ice bucket. She filled it with ice and put it on the floor next to Miles's chair. Then she poked around in the kitchen some more until she located a large thermos, which she filled with water. After filling that, she hesitated before finally deciding that more would be better when it came to fluids and Miles. She found a large water bottle in the back of Miles's container cabinet and filled it with water, too. She put all the water and a large plastic tumbler on the small table next to Miles's chair. To make room, she had to move several volumes of William Faulkner's works.

"Nobody should gorge themselves on Faulkner when they're ill," muttered Myrtle. Too much stream of consciousness could add an element of nausea, even if one weren't nauseated already.

She added to the pile with a plate of saltine crackers, a couple of ibuprofen, and an antacid. Then she wet a washcloth and put it over his forehead. Miles never stirred once during the entire process. Having witnessed enough dead bodies lately, this prompted Myrtle to feel for a pulse. She immediately found a very determined pulse and ceased to be overly concerned.

However, it was very clear that Miles would not be participating in a murder investigation at any point in the immediate future. She located his television remote, turned on the TV, and studied his recordings. It appeared that he hadn't watched the episode of *Tomorrow's Promise* from yesterday afternoon. She started the show and then hit pause and put the remote next to Miles. Finally she washed her hands thoroughly before letting herself back out the front door and locking it carefully behind her.

Remembering the importance of appearing as if she were getting exercise, Myrtle picked up her pace as soon as she reached the sidewalk. Her cane thumped emphatically on the sidewalk as she went. As she walked, she considered a particular similarity between the two murders—the killer was fond of finding a murder weapon on site. It was, in a way, a crime of opportunity. Although, in Alma's case, the killer had clearly broken into her house first to murder her. At Myrtle's house, it really had been a crime of opportunity in every sense of the phrase…Luella happened to go outside, the killer happened to see a heavy wrench that Dusty had happened to forget. At Alma's house, the killer had deliberately broken in before finding a heavy frying pan as a murder weapon.

Alma's house was surrounded with crime scene tape. Myrtle saw that the state police were already showing signs of wrapping things up. She spotted a thin, pale man in his thirties standing nearby. His face was lined with exhaustion as he smoked and stared blankly at the house. Myrtle didn't really know Alma's son Robert, but she couldn't imagine who else the man might be.

Myrtle had also had a lot of experience in small-town gossip. Although there may have been rumors about Alma's son being dishonest, she would only keep it in the back of her mind and try not to let it overly influence her. Because she was about to ask him a lot of questions.

"Robert, isn't it?" asked Myrtle as she walked up to him.

The thin man nodded and quickly put out his cigarette. "That's right. I'm sorry … should I know you?"

"Probably not. I'm Myrtle Clover. I was an acquaintance of your mother's; in fact, she came over to my house night-before-last. My son is the police chief and he told me what had happened before he came here. I'm so sorry about your mother."

Robert nodded again and swallowed as if trying to keep any strong emotion at bay. "Thank you. I don't think it's really hit me yet. It's hard to process."

Myrtle hesitated. "Red had mentioned that her death was suspicious. Is that correct?"

"That's right. She…well, someone murdered her in her own bed. There was a cast iron skillet nearby that was clearly what was used." He paused and looked as though he would really like another cigarette. "I don't understand it. Who would have wanted to kill Mother?"

"I'm not sure, but I'd like to find out. I feel as if this particular murderer might even kill again. There's something very brazen about this crime and the one that was committed earlier … one that appears to be linked to your mother's death." Myrtle cleared her throat and attempted to sound modest. "I've had some success in the past in solving mysteries that have baffled the police. Since your mother was an acquaintance of mine, I'd very much like to try to discover who might have done this."

Whatever Robert might have done or not done in the past, and no matter how exhausted or shocked he might be, Myrtle could tell one thing—he certainly seemed intelligent. His clear blue eyes quickly evaluated Myrtle as well and he nodded slowly. "I see. Sort of a hobby for you, but one you're good at, too. Maybe a friendly competition between you and your son." He peered closer at Myrtle. "Maybe a *not* so friendly competition between you and your son. If it had been a different day and age when you were young, would you have become a police detective?"

Myrtle hadn't really thought about that before. It certainly wouldn't have been a possibility for her when she was a young woman in her twenties. "No, you know, I don't think so. Working at it all day every day would make it work, wouldn't it? And discouraging work, since human nature never seems to really improve. It's better as a part-time job."

Robert tilted his head very slightly to one side, regarding her thoughtfully. "So what did you do instead? Or did you stay at home?"

"I was a teacher. And teaching could be discouraging too, but not usually on a daily basis."

Robert nodded again and then said, "I hope you find

out who's behind this. I rather like the idea of your solving the case instead of the police. Your son was kind to me, but the state police were brusque. They have a job to do, of course. But you actually knew Mother." He ended with a small shrug and the exhaustion swept over his features again.

Myrtle glanced toward Alma's house. She needed to talk to Robert before Red came out and shut her down.

Robert said, "Let's see. First of all, you'll need to eliminate me from your investigation, won't you? Motive. I really haven't got one. Mother didn't have any money to hand down to me. Her land is mortgaged to the hilt. She has a lot of bills that are going to need to be sorted out. At the end of the process, I'll be in worse financial shape than I was at the beginning." He cleared his throat. "And Mother and I got along well. No arguments. We were very fond of each other."

He continued briskly. "You'll want to know where I was last night, too. An alibi. Fortunately for me (and I never thought I'd be saying those words), I was working my shift at the Stop-n-Shop convenience store. A camera was on me the entire time, as is usual at these types of businesses. The police will find, as you would if you could view the footage, that I was working the entire time." He gave a smirk that seemed too sad to actually qualify at the sarcasm level a smirk requires.

Myrtle frowned. "I see. That makes it simple, doesn't it? But I thought you were working in an office."

"I was. I was let go for … performance reasons." Robert was matter-of-fact. "That's the usual excuse these days when an employer wants to let you go. There were rumors, you see, that I'd been defrauding my company. These rumors made my employer nervous, and they decided they didn't need my services anymore."

"But you hadn't been defrauding them?" asked Myrtle.

"No. But, in this town, when suspicion rests on you, the rest of the town somehow makes false charges into truth. And then it's spread around as gossip until everyone is clutching their pocketbooks when you pass them in the grocery aisle." Robert rubbed at his temple with a thin hand.

Myrtle said quietly, "I'd heard these rumors, too. And I heard that your mother was defending you around town. In fact, I'd heard that the reason your mother was so upset with the first victim, Luella White, is because Luella was one of the people who was gossip mongering."

Robert's sharp gaze met hers. "And so Mother was one of the suspects in her death? If you're asking me whether I think she was responsible … no, I can't see her killing someone over something like my reputation. It would have annoyed her. She would have defended me. But she wouldn't *kill* someone over it."

Myrtle said, "Could you tell me what happened tonight? You discovered your mother, didn't you?"

Robert took a deep breath. "I did. I was working my shift at the Stop-n-Shop. Mother always called me to tell me goodnight—even before I had this late-night job. She'd call and briefly tell me about her day and ask how I was doing. Then she'd wish me sweet dreams and that would be the end of the call."

"I'm guessing that you didn't get the phone call tonight," said Myrtle.

"Exactly. And that's what your son … Red, isn't it? That's what he was saying. He asked me if I figured that meant that the crime occurred at her usual bedtime of ten o'clock. But the problem is that after I lost my job at the accounting firm, I needed to switch my cell phone plan to a less expensive plan and give up my smartphone. I started using an old phone I had in a drawer—the kind with a slide-out keyboard. You know the kind?"

Myrtle did indeed. She'd only just stopped using one recently, herself. And she debated whether the smartphone she had was all that intelligent.

Robert continued, staring wearily at Alma's house as he spoke. "I also changed my cell phone providers to go to a less-expensive place. I guess it was less expensive because it didn't have enough cell phone towers to provide coverage in this area. Plus, this sliding phone not only didn't have a data plan, but it never seemed as if it were working a hundred percent, either. It would notify me that I had received calls or text messages. Or I'd have a hard time getting a signal, as I mentioned. So I sometimes didn't get her call."

"What did you do the nights when you didn't?" asked Myrtle. "Did she follow up by calling the store phone?"

"The manager didn't want the store phone used for personal calls because he didn't want the line busy if customers called. Not that they ever call," said Robert with a scoffing laugh. "I'd not wanted to wake Mother by calling her back later, but something was bothering me. Something she'd said earlier in the day. Plus, she'd told me that I really never have to worry about waking her up because she'd been sleeping poorly."

Myrtle nodded. "Actually, your mother mentioned to my friend Miles and me that she was exhausted from insomnia."

"So I called her back when the convenience store was in between customers. At that point, it was probably two o'clock in the morning. No answer. So I tried again about thirty minutes later. No answer."

"So you drove out here?" asked Myrtle.

"No. Unfortunately, I didn't. My shift wasn't over yet and there was no one to take over for me. I've really just started working there and didn't feel as if I could lock the door and run off to my mother's house to check in. So I waited." He gave a frustrated sigh. "And now I'll wonder, if I *had* come here, maybe I'd have interrupted the murderer and saved my mother's life."

Myrtle said quickly, "Or maybe you'd have startled the murderer on his way back out the door and been killed, yourself. There's no sense in what-ifs." They watched for a moment as the state police came outside, carrying equipment. Myrtle asked, "What was it that your mother said that bothered you so much?"

Robert sounded bemused. "I'd been telling her about the new job and how my feet were hurting for standing up so long. She told me that she was expecting some sort of windfall or other and insisted that she'd buy me a pair of new shoes. She sounded elated."

Myrtle stared at him for a moment. Could this be blackmail money she was referring to as a windfall? "Did you have any idea what she meant by the windfall?"

"Absolutely none. Mother was poor as a pauper and it wasn't as if she had any rich relations on their deathbeds. It was also just her general air of excitement. That wasn't her general disposition at all. I kept thinking about it during my shift. I decided I'd quickly run by and check on Mother as soon as I was finished at work. When I did, she didn't answer the door. But I have a key to her house, so I unlocked the door and walked in, calling her name. I found her in the bed. That cast iron skillet was next to her." Robert blankly stared at the house, as if replaying the scene in his head.

"And no evidence of anyone in the house? No one was hiding out there?" asked Myrtle.

"I was so shocked by what I'd seen that the killer could still have been in the house and I never would have known it," said Robert.

"Do you have any idea how the murderer would have gotten in?" asked Myrtle.

"It would have been a piece of cake," said Robert. "Mother tried to cut down on her cooling bills by leaving windows open. She had them open morning and night—anyone could have easily gotten into the house. It did worry me sometimes, but Bradley has always seemed so *safe*."

Small towns always did. But in a small town, feelings could run very high. It wasn't so much the danger that you would be attacked by a stranger—it was the danger you'd be attacked by someone you know.

Myrtle said, "And this will seem like an odd question, but it ties into something your mother spoke to me about only yesterday. Did you happen to notice any fresh coffee in her house? Still in a bag, perhaps? On a counter? Something like that?"

Robert frowned. "Mother wasn't much of a coffee drinker. She might have some in the house if she were expecting guests, but she wouldn't stock it for herself."

"Not a nice Colombian or Sumatra coffee?" asked Myrtle.

"Most certainly *not* a nice Colombian or Sumatra. It would be more along the lines of a Sanka or some other instant coffee."

"So she wasn't one … say … to frequent coffeehouses?" asked Myrtle.

"Mother would have considered that a waste of money," said Robert.

Myrtle had been keeping a watchful eye on Alma's house and now saw Red walking out the front door with Lieutenant Perkins. Her time was short now. Actually, she would prefer not to be spotted by Red or Perkins at all. Best to avoid questions when possible. She asked Robert quickly, "One more thing. While you were in there, I know you received such a horrible shock that you might not have noticed anything. But did you? Did you notice anything that struck you as strange or out of place at all?"

Robert hesitated. "There was one thing. It might be nothing. But there was an earring on Mother's bed."

"An earring? But it wasn't your Mother's? Or didn't seem to be something she'd wear?"

"It definitely wasn't something she'd wear. Mother didn't have pierced ears."

Chapter Twelve

Myrtle was able to slip away and walk fairly briskly back toward her house before Red realized she was there. She had lots to think about and it was just as well that she didn't have to have a battle of wits or wills with Red. It was all bouncing around in her head, wanting to come out. The mention of an earring had reminded her that Mimsy had mentioned losing one at Bunco. Could the two be connected somehow? Ordinarily, she'd discuss her findings with her trusty sidekick. But, said trusty sidekick had been felled by a virus.

Myrtle was about to pass Miles's house when she hesitated. Perhaps he was in need of more help. Perhaps he even needed an appointment at his doctor's office and a ride in the car there. Myrtle walked up to Miles's front door and peered in the side window again. This time she didn't see him slumped in the recliner as she had before. She removed her key from her pocketbook once more and unlocked the door.

"Yoo-hoo!" she called out cautiously. Myrtle certainly didn't want to suffer any embarrassing encounters of Miles in some stage of undress. "Miles! It's Myrtle. I'm checking up on you."

"Coming," said a weak voice from the back of the house. There was the brief sound of water running from the bathroom faucet and some splashing around. Then a very somber and rather frail-looking Miles appeared, shambling toward the recliner.

"Goodness, Miles! You look horrid."

Miles climbed into the recliner and pulled the old, brown blanket over and around him. "I do," he agreed piteously.

"Do you feel as wretched as you look?" asked Myrtle with some concern. She knew that old men were not nearly as robust as old women when it came to illness. They could also be extremely dramatic and play up their misery for the crowd, but this time she thought that Miles possibly wasn't playing things up. And she wasn't in the mood for losing her sidekick.

"It's been a miserable last twelve hours," said Miles. He made a small waving gesture to encompass the saltines and the water next to him. "Thanks for this. I don't know when you came in, but I know you must have been the one who put out food and water for me."

He didn't seem to want to dwell on the idea of food, however, and Myrtle saw that the crackers were untouched. "See here, Miles—I think we need to take you to the doctor," blustered Myrtle.

Miles levied a horrified look at her. "I don't want to go to a doctor while I'm feeling like this! I need to be near a restroom."

"Here's the important question. Have you been able to keep fluids down?"

Miles just turned greener in reply.

"I'll take that as a no. You might be dehydrated or headed down that path. The doctor could prescribe you something to help repress the nausea. Miles, I'm going to take it upon myself to make an appointment for you at your doctor's office," said Myrtle briskly. There clearly would be no discussion of the case's developments while Miles was like this.

"You don't know his number," mumbled Miles.

"It's Doctor Phillips," said Myrtle, flipping through the phone book. "You've mentioned him casually before and I have an *excellent* memory."

"I shouldn't drive in this condition."

"You certainly shouldn't. I will drive you to see Doctor Phillips. In a borrowed car," said Myrtle.

Miles gaped foggily at her.

"You have no car right now, remember? Last I heard, you're transmission-free. Excellent memory, as I mentioned," said Myrtle, tapping her forehead. She dialed the physician's number, made an appointment, and then hung up. "All right, so I'm going to let you rest for a couple of hours before your appointment, during which time I will be procuring a car for us to take to the doctor."

Miles's expression reflected an odd combination of dread and relief.

Myrtle left Miles's house and headed absently in the direction of Red and Elaine's house to see if she could borrow Elaine's minivan. Since she couldn't mull the case over with Miles, Robert's conversation with her kept circling through her head.

It seemed very clear that Alma had some sort of information about Luella's murder and tried to leverage that information by blackmailing the killer. She had certainly not been interested in speaking with Miles and Myrtle when they'd come by. And she apparently was no coffee drinker, either. Myrtle decided she might splurge on some nice coffee and quiz the shop owner about Alma, though. And, of course, she'd have to be on the lookout for women with pierced ears.

But first there was the matter of the car.

And somehow, with all the busyness of the case and despite the fact that Red, Elaine, and little Jack were making use of Myrtle's facilities at all hours of the day and night, it still surprised Myrtle to see a backhoe in Red and Elaine's front yard. A backhoe and half a dozen men who were doing things with dirt and pipes. She saw Jack staring raptly at the backhoe through his living room window. The little boy was obsessed with trucks of all makes and descriptions. This main line plumbing repair job must be a real treat for him—almost like having a symphonic orchestra playing in the front yard would be for Myrtle.

Myrtle waved at Jack, when he managed to pull his eyes away from the construction equipment. His small face lit up and he waved back and seemed to be calling to someone inside, probably Elaine, to announce Myrtle's presence. Sure enough, a smiling, but rather harassed-looking Elaine, greeted Myrtle at the door just as soon as she knocked.

"Is this a waking nightmare for you?" asked Myrtle as she walked into their house.

Elaine always preferred to put the best possible face on everything. An eternal optimist. Myrtle wasn't sure how she did it. "Oh, it's not so bad. Only because you're directly across the street, you know. We'd have to stay in a hotel during the repair if it weren't for you … there would be no way we'd be able to stay in the house with no plumbing."

Myrtle very much liked saving the day. She beamed at Elaine. "Anytime, Elaine. And anything you need."

Elaine said, "Thanks. I'm going to come by in an hour or so and fill up a bunch of containers with water so that I can cook and wash some dishes."

"Whatever you need," Myrtle repeated. "And since we're being so generous with each other, there's something you can help *me* with, actually. Miles is … well, honestly, he seems completely wretched. He has some sort of appalling stomach bug that's got him rather dehydrated. I need to take him to see Doctor Phillips in a couple of hours, but his car is dead. Could I borrow the minivan?"

That harassed look from earlier returned to Elaine's face. "Oh, Myrtle. You know that of *course* I would let you take the car. I'd even offer to drive y'all there, myself.

Especially with all that you're doing for us right now."

"There must be a big *but* coming here," murmured Myrtle. "Some heinous thing has happened to the minivan?"

"It's in the shop," said Elaine. Her eyes were very bright suddenly and Myrtle was afraid that Elaine would suddenly break down—something Myrtle would very much like to avoid happening.

Myrtle said quickly, "I'm sure the car will be just fine. No worries, Elaine! I'll just ask someone else if I can borrow their car."

But Elaine didn't seem to be able to shake the topic. "I'd love to think that the car would get better, but it doesn't appear that's the case. I'm starting to think that Red and I are being punished for some reason." She gave a slightly hysterical laugh. "The garage said the cost of repairs would be several thousand dollars, including labor, and that's more than the minivan is worth. So I think we're going to have to go car shopping. And Red is too tied up with these murders to be able to do anything personal. When it rains, it pours!"

Myrtle reached out and held both of Elaine's hands. "Elaine, I don't want you to worry about this. I will go with you to the car lot. I will help you find a car. Or possibly, we can go look for cars along with Miles. There's apparently an epidemic of immobile vehicles in Bradley."

Elaine looked a bit uncertain. "Myrtle, that's lovely of you, but are you sure? I mean, I know you haven't purchased a car for a while and dealing with car dealers is … well, you know. It's stressful."

"Dealing with Tim Rogers won't be stressful," said Myrtle. "He's a former student of mine. In fact, I taught Tim Rogers twice and both of his younger brothers. He's always *very* deferential to me." Myrtle had big plans now. So Tippy's husband, Benton, needed a new car and he was going to mention that his condition for buying at that dealership was that Roger's Automotive continue advertising with the *Bradley Bugle.* Now both Miles and Elaine needed new cars. It was very, very lucky that some sort of vindictive sprite was attacking her friends' cars. Wanda's voice entered Myrtle's head: *broke cars everywhere.*

Elaine still looked a bit doubtful, but said, "If you're sure, Myrtle, then I'd love it, thanks. Usually Red would go, but with him so tied up and taking the police cruiser all over town … Jack and I have been stranded at the house. He and I want to get me a replacement—an affordable one—as soon as we can."

Myrtle nodded. "Let's go tomorrow. But for now, I have to run. I still need to procure transport to this appointment." She hesitated. "Have you seen Red at all, or is he still at Alma's?"

Elaine blew out a deep breath. "Still over there. Or at the station, I'm not sure which. Can you believe it? Poor Alma. I really can't imagine what's going on … and Red isn't exactly filling me in, either. I guess he thinks I'd just feed information over to you."

Myrtle gave a high-pitched laugh. "How silly!" Of course, Elaine was a terrific informant. It was a pity that Red had caught on, although, she could think of one question to ask Elaine. "Out of the ladies who came to…Bunco, do you remember who has pierced ears?"

Elaine laughed. "Pierced ears? That would be the kind of observation someone who has a lot of time on their hands might make. I'm usually just trying to make sure I don't have my shirt on inside-out."

As Myrtle stepped outside of Elaine's house and waved goodbye to Jack who was still glued to the window, she thought about the car situation. Most of the people she knew seemed fiercely protective of their vehicles … at least they had behaved so in the past when Myrtle had expressed interest in borrowing it. And she needed a car in the immediate future. Which left her with …?

"Hi Myrtle!" a nasal voice sang out from across the street.

Erma Sherman. Ordinarily, the sound of Erma's voice would be enough to send Myrtle hurrying away in the opposite direction as fast as she could go. But today her neighbor may prove useful. She had an old Cadillac that was not the most attractive vehicle on the road but always seemed in working condition. But to borrow it, Myrtle would have to play nice. Or, at least nicer than she usually did with Erma.

"Hi, Erma," said Myrtle, repressing a sigh. "How have you been?"

"How have *you* been?" asked Erma excitedly. "I understand that you've been hosting a den of murderers."

Erma had become distressingly interested in Myrtle's detective work. Erma enjoyed all types of morbid things, as evidenced by her enjoyment of discussing all her grotesque medical ailments. "Certainly not a *den* of murderers. Although there was at least one in the group," said Myrtle coolly.

"And you're figuring out who's behind it, aren't you?" gaped Erma. "Let's see if I have any clues for you this time." She closed her eyes tightly, which was apparently what she did to spur intellectual processes. "I'm trying to remember if I noticed anything unusual during your Bunco party."

Myrtle said, "If you can see into my backyard, then clearly I'm doing something wrong. I do have a privacy fence up and shrubs, to boot. And the gate was locked."

"Was it?" asked Erma. "Are you sure? You know that I think Dusty is a fine yardman, but maybe this time he left the gate unbolted. He was there that afternoon, wasn't he?"

"He was, and no, he didn't. Red checked during his investigation, as did the state police. And I'm assuming that you'd have noticed if someone scaled a six-foot fence on your side."

Erma gave her braying laugh. "Well, I sure hope so! Because I was looking out the window that night, for sure."

This fact did not surprise Myrtle in the least. She decided to change the subject to something that didn't make her stomach hurt. "I'm glad to see you, Erma, because I wanted to ask you a tremendous favor."

"You want to borrow my car?"

Apparently, Erma had gathered that this was the only reason Myrtle might seek out conversation with her or want to ask her anything. "Actually, yes. Miles has contracted some sort of dire virus and I need to drive him over to see his doctor. His car isn't working. Do you need your car for anything today?"

"Nope! I'm going to be a couch potato today. Go toodling around as much as you want! I know how much you and Miles like to spend time together." Erma took the car keys off her key ring, handed them to Myrtle, and leered.

Myrtle's stomach lurched again as Erma's breath assaulted her. Except this was no virus, just normal nausea from dealing with her neighbor. "As good friends do, Erma. I can assure you, however, there will be no toodling around with Miles today. He barely looks well enough to get to the doctor. And now I've really got to go. I have an errand to run in town before the appointment." Myrtle started walking toward downtown Bradley.

"Don't you want to take the car?" called Erma behind her.

"Not now. It's an easy walk," said Myrtle, cane thumping as she headed away as quickly as she could go.

The coffee shop was Myrtle's errand. Although she

strongly suspected that Alma had been lying to her about buying coffee in town, she still wanted to check her statement out. Besides, the coffee shop also sold hot tea and she thought some herbal tea might help ease Miles's stomach complaints.

A bell chimed as she entered the door of the little coffee shop. It was certainly a cheerful place. Jazz music played in the background, cheerful checkered curtains hung in spotless windows. The only things Myrtle had against the shop were the unfortunate lack of available seating and the high prices of the offerings. Her taste in coffee ran a bit cheaper, which was one thing she apparently shared in common with Alma.

The proprietor, a smartly dressed middle-aged woman wearing a jaunty scarf smiled at Myrtle. "May I help you with something?"

Myrtle rested her large pocketbook on the tall counter. "Yes, please. I have a sick friend and wanted some hot tea to help settle his stomach. I was thinking peppermint?"

The woman beamed at her as if at a star pupil. "A smart choice. There isn't a better option here for stomach upset."

The woman busied herself preparing the tea and Myrtle said, "I was also wondering if you could provide me with some information. A friend of mine said she was here yesterday buying coffee. I was wondering if you remembered her."

Without looking at her the woman shook her head. "She wasn't here."

Myrtle frowned at her back. "I haven't described her to you."

"Oh, sorry. That must have sounded rude of me. I mean, she wasn't here because *no one* was here. The shop is closed on Mondays."

A couple of minutes later, the woman handed Myrtle a

cup.

"Here's your friend's tea," she said. "And I'll hold the door for you, since you're juggling a cane and a cup."

It was a bit of juggling. Although the cup did have a top on it, Myrtle still didn't want to drop it on the ground and have the contents explode all over. It had certainly cost enough.

It was Myrtle's complete absorption in the balancing act that prevented her from immediately noticing Poppy Dryden approaching the shop. In fact, it was Poppy who called out to her.

"Need help, Miss Myrtle?"

Although, as Myrtle raised her head to look up at Poppy, she could tell that Poppy was just being nice. Poppy actually appeared to be running late for something. Poppy's general appearance was always a bit disheveled, but her mousy hair hadn't even been combed this morning, as far as Myrtle could discern. "No thanks, Poppy. I can manage it. Where are you off to this morning?"

Poppy pouted. "Work. I watch a class at the church preschool until one. And this morning I'm running behind. I'm not the only teacher in the room, though, so it's okay."

Myrtle arranged her face in an appropriately solemn manner. "Have you heard the terrible news about Alma?"

Poppy looked startled. "What terrible news?"

"I'm afraid she's dead."

Poppy's hand flew up to cover her mouth. "What?"

"Yes. Someone broke into her house and killed her in her own bed. A horrible business," said Myrtle. She did feel very indignant about that part, too. One should feel safe in one's own bed, certainly.

Poppy's face was flushed with an unattractive blotchy stain. "I don't understand it. What is going on in this town?" The hand covering her mouth dropped down to clutch her neck. "I don't know if I even feel safe anymore."

"You didn't happen to see anything unusual near Alma's house did you?" asked Myrtle.

Poppy said, "What do you mean? I wasn't at Alma's house yesterday."

Myrtle said soothingly, "I know you had a very busy day yesterday, that's all. I saw you at Bo's Diner remember? What happened after that?"

Poppy gulped. Her eyes darted back and forth as she thought. "Let's see. I took the takeout bag and then walked out the door to the parking lot."

For heaven's sake. Poppy really *would* be late if Myrtle got the blow-by-blow description of Poppy's tiniest movements for the last eighteen hours. Myrtle interrupted her quickly. "I mean, what *in general* did you do after you left the diner?" Poppy paused and Myrtle said impatiently, "I'm assuming you drove over to Mimsy's house, right? To deliver the hot food?"

"Oh, that's right," said Poppy, sounding relieved at having a clue how to answer. "I gave them the food and I visited for a little while. Then I had to get ready for work."

"For work?" asked Myrtle. "But you said you worked at the preschool."

"And I *do*," said Poppy earnestly. "But I also wait tables at Geronimo's."

Geronimo's was some sort of wings and beer joint that was in nearby Creighton. Actually, it wasn't far from Wanda and Crazy Dan's house. "How late did you work?" asked Myrtle curiously. "Maybe you saw something when you were leaving. Even if it doesn't seem important."

But Poppy was already shaking her head. "I'm sure I didn't. I mean, I was so, so tired. I was just focused on my driving and getting home safely." She swallowed, hard. "Do they have any idea who did it?"

Myrtle's eyes automatically lifted to Poppy's earlobes. Not only was Poppy not wearing earrings, she didn't appear to have her ears pierced at all. "There're working on it. Apparently, though, someone lost an earring in the process."

Poppy knit her brows. "In the process?" she asked slowly. Myrtle wondered if she were slow, period. "You mean … during Alma's …?"

"I'm afraid that's right. In the process of her murder," continued Myrtle smoothly. "Alma wasn't an earring wearer. So it would appear that the person who lost an earring may either have some important information or may somehow be involved in this murder."

Poppy opened and shut her mouth a few times, wordlessly. Finally, she said, "Or maybe it just means a visit. That the person was visiting Alma. Completely innocently."

"In Alma's bedroom?" asked Myrtle skeptically.

Poppy dropped her gaze. But what would Poppy have to be concerned about? She clearly wasn't an earring wearer.

"Well," Poppy said in a rush, "it was nice talking to you, Miss Myrtle. I'm late for work, as I said, so I should run."

Myrtle stared after her as she rushed into the coffee shop. Late enough to rush but not too late for a coffee stop? Or was she merely trying to escape from Myrtle?

Chapter Thirteen

As Myrtle carefully carried the hot tea down the street, she heard another voice calling her name. But this time there was only one person in the world it could be. "Mama!" called the voice again, this time a little impatiently.

"Hi Red," said Myrtle in a calm voice.

"Can I give you a ride?" he asked. He was leaning out of the window of his police cruiser. To be honest, although she'd always considered her son a handsome man, he had certainly looked better. The five o'clock shadow that he sometimes sported at the end of a day had entered into full-beard territory. His eyes were as red as his hair. And the smattering of wrinkles developing on his face were deep crevasses today. "And when I drop you off, maybe I can borrow your shower."

"Most definitely," said Myrtle, nose wrinkling a little. "But can you drop me by Miles's house first? This is tea for him." She got into the passenger seat of the cruiser and made sure to lean as far away from her son as possible.

Red seemed miles away and didn't take notice of the slight. "Miles. Well, that's very nice, Mama. Thinking of your friend like that."

"I'm trying to rehabilitate him. He has some sort of vile virus. As a matter of fact, I'm taking him to the doctor in a little while," said Myrtle.

Red drawled, "And he's a good friend to trust you with driving his car."

"Oh, his car is in the shop. Or should be in the shop. No, I'm borrowing Erma's car." She made a face as she said Erma's name. It tasted foul in her mouth.

Red's eyebrows shot up. "Miles really *must* be sick, if you're reaching out to Erma. Hope he's better soon."

Myrtle coughed delicately. "I was wondering how *your* morning went, Red. With the murder of poor Alma, I mean. I suppose it *is* murder." She added the last bit hastily, remembering that she really shouldn't know so many details of Alma's death.

He glanced at her sideways before directing his attention back on the road. "It is, yes. But nothing that concerns you."

Myrtle laughed lightly. "Why, I didn't say it concerned me. But it *concerns* me, in the other sense of the word. I'm worried about poor Alma and the rest of the ladies who were at my house the other night. Naturally…" she paused, "… did any of Alma's neighbors hear anything unusual?"

"Before you start badgering the poor people, I'll assure you they all slept like the dead last night," said Red as he pulled up into Miles's driveway.

Pooh. "Be right back out," said Myrtle quickly as she climbed out of the car. She was so lost in her thoughts that she nearly rang the doorbell. Remembering herself in time, she peered through the window and saw Miles in his usual spot. In his normal, slumped pose.

She fumbled in her pocketbook with her one free hand until she got her keys. Myrtle opened the door and strode quickly over to Miles. "Here is some herbal tea," she said briskly, making space on the end table next to Miles. There was no response from the slumped figure. "The tea should help settle your stomach." No response. "I secured a car." There might have been a brief fluttering of his closed eyelids. "We're borrowing Erma's car."

Now Miles's eyes flew open. They gazed in steady concern at Myrtle. "I must be hallucinating— not . Erma."

Myrtle beamed at him. It was good that she didn't

have to check her friend's pulse. That would have seemed rather intrusive. "Erma's *car*. You're right—if I'd said that Erma was going *with* us to see Doctor Phillips, that's when you should have worried. We're just borrowing that decrepit vehicle of hers. I'll be back in a little while. Now I have to run. Red is waiting for me."

As she got back into Red's cruiser for the split-second ride back to her own house, Myrtle realized that perhaps Red was just as much of a hypochondriac as Miles was. "So what kind of vile virus is this, Mama? Bronchitis?" he asked hopefully.

"Bronchitis is an infection, not a virus," said Myrtle.

"And not catching, either. Which is why I was hoping that's what he has," said Red.

"No, I'm afraid he's got some sort of stomach virus. And now he's reached the point where he may end up dehydrated if we don't control his symptoms," said Myrtle.

Red sighed as he pulled the car up into Myrtle's driveway. "I have the sudden urge to wipe down the entire inside of this car with antibacterial wipes. You're not going to get close enough to catch this thing, are you? I don't think a virus like that would be good for you."

"I have the constitution of a horse," said Myrtle coldly. "And I'm not going to go gallivanting around catching viruses. I simply don't have the time for one."

Red showed remarkable reserve in not asking what was consuming all of Myrtle's free time. "Okay. Well, at least wash your hands real well when you get inside. I packed a small bag in my car for this shower."

Myrtle opened the passenger door. "I was wondering, Red, if you knew when Luella's body might be released by the medical examiner to the funeral home."

"Already has been," said Red, ducking down as he retrieved his bag from the backseat. "Funeral is set for tomorrow morning at eleven. Graveside service."

"At which cemetery? Perpetual Care? Ingleside? Or Grace Hill?" asked Myrtle over her shoulder as she found the key to her front door. With any luck, it wouldn't be Grace Hill. She'd be setting out pretty early to walk to that cemetery or else she'd be hitching a ride again.

"Grace Hill," said Red succinctly. "Do you want a ride out there? We're having some car issues with Elaine's minivan, but I'm going to be at the funeral. And early."

Myrtle had no real desire to attend the funeral early. She'd rather linger later when there might be a chance to speak with some of Luella's friends. "I'll try to catch a ride with someone else. Thanks, though. If I can't find anybody, I'll give you a call. And, by the way, tomorrow afternoon I'm taking Elaine to go car shopping."

She expected consternation from Red at her announcement, or at least some doubt as to his octogenarian mother's ability to haggle with a car salesman. But instead, Red looked immensely relieved. "Mama, that's wonderful. Thanks. With the way this case is going and with everything else going on, and with Elaine not really enjoying the whole car shopping experience…let's just say I owe you one."

Soon it was time to take Miles to his appointment. She fired up Erma's old Cadillac and thoughtfully supplied a couple of plastic grocery bags to preserve the car's upholstery from any virus-related aftermath.

Miles was looking even worse and leaned on Myrtle heavily as she helped him out to the car. "Have you got your insurance card?" she asked briskly. Miles gave her a helpless look and she shoved him into the car, took out her key, and searched Miles's house until she found his wallet. When she'd returned to the car, he'd already fallen asleep.

It had been a few months since Myrtle had last driven and Erma's car wasn't exactly the minivan, which was the last vehicle Myrtle had driven. She decided that slow and steady won the race and set out at a stately twenty-five miles an hour.

Miles was still asleep when she finally arrived at the doctor's office. Myrtle left him in the car and strode inside the small, brick building.

A cheery receptionist at the front desk beamed at her and chirped, "Good afternoon! Have you got your insurance card, sweetie?"

Myrtle never appreciated endearments from strangers. Especially when the strangers were young enough to be her grandchildren. "Have you got a strong man around?"

The receptionist's eyes clouded. "Well…Doctor Phillips, I suppose."

"No, Doctor Phillips doesn't qualify as a strong man. I've seen him," said Myrtle, pursing her lips. "I suppose you'll have to do. You and a young nurse, perhaps. Your patient is out in the car—very ill. I lugged him into the car, but I want someone else to lug him out of it."

The receptionist suddenly didn't look either cheery or chirpy. "But …"

Myrtle tuned her out, turning her attention to a large bottle of hand sanitizer on the counter and availing herself of a large amount. She carefully chose a seat far away from any other patients and quickly engaged herself in what appeared to be a very old magazine.

Five minutes later, a rather green-looking Miles was unceremoniously dumped into the chair next to her. Myrtle swiftly moved to the next chair over. He turned his head to glance apprehensively around the waiting room. "You don't suppose I could catch anything *else* on top of this virus, do you?"

Myrtle snorted. "Miles, you're clearly the sickest person here. No one wants to get within germ-catching distance of *you*."

Miles nodded and started drowsily dropping off. Then

his eyes opened wide in alarm. "Someone *is* coming over, though."

Myrtle glanced up, expecting to see a nurse to cart Miles away. Instead, she saw Florence Ainsworth walking over. Myrtle held up a cautionary hand. "Florence, Miles is too gentlemanly to ask, so I will. Have you got some sort of contagious disease that you're here to have treated?"

Florence looked vaguely offended. "Not at all. I'm here for my checkup."

"All right. Well, Miles here has a contagious disease that *he's* here to have treated. So you might want to stop right where you are and we can have a bit of a long-distance conversation," said Myrtle. Miles appeared to relax a bit. Actually, more than a bit. He was on the brink of falling asleep again, but fighting it.

Florence settled down into a nearby, but not too nearby, chair. She leaned closer to Myrtle. "Did you hear about poor Alma? What is the world coming to? Will we all be murdered in our beds? What does Red say about all this?"

Miles perked up. "Poor Alma?" He blinked at Florence and Myrtle.

Florence gave him a sad smile and leaned in close to Myrtle. "He seems a bit confused. The poor dear."

Considering the source, Myrtle had to force back a chuckle.

"Alma was murdered last night, Miles. You haven't exactly been in the condition for me to talk with you about it," said Myrtle.

Miles gave her a hurt look. "What happened to her?"

"Oh, stop it with the puppy dog eyes," snapped Myrtle. She turned again to Florence. "It's horrible, isn't it? Red feels it's tied into Luella's death somehow."

"How was she murdered?" asked Miles again in a querulous voice.

Florence said sadly, "Someone broke into her house and killed her as she slept. Smothered her with a pillow."

Myrtle frowned. "Not exactly, Florence. Someone *did* break into her house, although that was a piece of cake considering all the open windows. But she wasn't smothered. She was hit over the head with a cast iron skillet while she slept. Blunt force trauma."

Myrtle could tell that Florence was one of those old ladies who got very defensive when shown to be inaccurate. Florence drew herself up. "I have it on very good authority that she was smothered!"

Myrtle took a deep breath. This was obviously an argument that she wasn't going to win. She continued smoothly, "At any rate, the poor woman is dead now. And we need to figure out who did this before they kill again."

Florence's irritation was clearly forgotten. "Do you think they will? Kill again, I mean?"

"Naturally. They must feel as if they've gotten away with it twice. If they think someone is getting too close to the truth, they'll be motivated to murder again," said Myrtle. She looked closely at Florence. She did have pierced ears, but she was wearing both earrings. Still, Florence would be the type to lose an earring, if anyone would. And she certainly had a motive. She was very keen to keep driving her car.

As if on cue, Florence asked, "Myrtle, are you going to Luella's funeral tomorrow morning? I know you don't have a car, so I wondered if you might want a ride."

Myrtle hesitated. She did need a ride. Was she desperate enough to climb into a car with Florence Ainsworth who was reputed to drive over sidewalks?

Florence seemed to think so. "I'll pick you up thirty minutes before the service. So ten-thirty tomorrow morning." She glanced over at Miles, who was slumped with his chin on his chest, sound asleep. "I guess I'd better be on my way. See you tomorrow, Myrtle." She gathered her keys and left.

She was actually a bit spryer than Myrtle had thought. Certainly capable of bopping someone over the head. The breaking-in-through-a-window part might be a bit tricky, but she was motivated.

"Miles Bradford?" called a nurse.

Miles slept on.

"You're going to have to physically retrieve him," said Myrtle as she complacently picked up her outdated magazine again. There were good things about being old. No one expected much from you.

Forty-five minutes later, they left the doctor's office after the nurses had carefully deposited Miles in Erma's car, prescription for nausea in hand. He immediately fell asleep again as soon as he sat in the car. Myrtle sighed. Good deeds were a hassle. Now she'd have to see if Red could help her get Miles inside. She didn't want to prop him upright as she'd done before.

Fortunately, Red was just dashing out of his house, sandwich in hand, when Myrtle pulled onto Magnolia Lane. She rolled a window down. "Red! Can you give me a hand for a minute?"

Red walked briskly over to meet her in Miles's driveway. "It really is startling to see you in Erma's car, Mama. Alarming, actually."

"Well, you know. In cases of emergency, this kind of thing becomes necessary," said Myrtle. "Now, can you move Miles inside?"

Red stooped over, gently awakened Miles, and then pulled him slowly out of the car. "Here we go," he said in a cheerful voice. "Let's head inside."

Myrtle hurried ahead of them, finding the key and unlocking the door. "Put him in the recliner, Red, if you could. That's where he's been camping out."

Miles mumbled a thank you and dropped down with relief into the recliner. "Okay, Miles," said Myrtle. "I'll be back in a few minutes. I've got to fill that prescription of yours."

Miles had already fallen asleep. He was beginning to resemble the dormouse in *Alice in Wonderland*.

Red said, "That'll be more than a few minutes, Mama. The drugstore was jam-packed with sick folk when I ran in there to get a Coke a little while ago. You'll want to either bring a book or drop it off and return later."

Myrtle made a face. "I don't want to do either one. Miles needs this filled immediately. Maybe the crowds will have cleared by the time I get there." She segued quickly: "You seemed as if you were in a hurry yourself when I spotted you outside. Any developments in the case?"

Red looked tired. And when he was tired, sometimes he was more forthcoming than usual.

He said, "You know, Mama, sometimes I don't particularly like my job. Especially when I feel I've got to hassle people I know and respect. It pains me, it really does."

"Who have you got to hassle? And what exactly does this hassling involve?"

Red rubbed the side of his face. "Everybody, really. I know all these women. Elaine plays Bunco with them every month, for heaven's sake. I wouldn't call any of these ladies hardened criminals. Estelle Rutledge? She only cares about tornadoes. Poppy? She's just a harried soul trying to piece a living together. Florence Ainsworth is a bit batty. And Mimsy Kessler. I've always liked Mimsy. *Everyone* likes Mimsy. She's just *nice*."

Myrtle nodded, her mind whirling. "Are you questioning them all about evidence? Something to do with an earring?"

Red froze. "Okay, Miss Marple. How'd you know

about that?"

"A little bird told me."

Red appeared to be gritting his teeth. She hoped he didn't grind them. That tended to lead to all sorts of dental troubles that he probably couldn't afford. Especially now that he had plumbers at his house twenty-four seven. "Does this bird have a name? You should be glad you gave *me* this little nugget of information. The state police would be asking if you left the earring yourself."

"As if I could climb through windows at my age. Pooh."

"Pooh nothing. You could do anything you set your mind to, Mama."

Myrtle sighed. "The little bird was poor Robert Wiggins. Alma's son noticed the earring since his mother didn't wear them."

Red shook his head. "You're a source of constant amazement. All right, since you've gotten this far, let's hear it."

Myrtle raised her eyebrows. "Hear what?"

"Who you think the owner of the earring is," said Red.

"You want my opinion?" asked Myrtle incredulously. What was more—she didn't really want to share it. Because there was this nagging worry in the back of her head. Something was off, she was sure of it. And some of it surrounded this earring.

Red just looked at her, expectantly.

"Okay. I wonder if maybe it might belong to Mimsy. Out of all your suspects, it seems like the kind of thing she'd wear. Just a guess. And she'd mentioned losing an earring at Bonkers, so I suppose she's lost them before. But I wouldn't read that much into it," said Myrtle quickly. "And now I have to go get that prescription."

"With a book," stressed Red again.

"And I don't have anything to read except this horrid

dystopian novel that Miles gave me." Those words always spurred a sense of panic in Myrtle. She *always* liked to have a stack of books ready for reading.

Red waved a hand around Miles's book-lined living room. "Looks like you're in the right place, Mama. There must be over two hundred books here. I think you can spot something you haven't read."

And he hurried out, leaving Myrtle to mull over the fact that Miles seemed to have an extraordinary attachment to the testosterone-driven literature of Hemingway and Steinbeck. She finally grabbed a dog-eared copy of *Little Men* and hurried out the door.

Chapter Fourteen

After Myrtle had finally gotten the prescription and roused Miles long enough for him to take it, she was ready to put her feet up for a while. Lugging Miles around town, even if she *had* been able to outsource some of the lugging, was still an exhausting process. And she felt as if he were on the right road at last. She'd checked in on him forty-five minutes after that anti-nausea pill and he'd seemed a lot more chipper. And awake.

Myrtle sat down on the sofa and fumbled with the remote to bring up that afternoon's installment of *Tomorrow's Promise.* But her head was still miles away. Wanda had said that Miles wouldn't be sick for very long. She always seemed to know what she was talking about, as hard as that was to believe. There was something else she'd said that had bothered her … that Myrtle was on the wrong track. Myrtle wondered again about that earring.

Myrtle finally managed to put the murders out of her head. She spent the rest of the day watching her soap opera, doing the last couple of days' worth of crossword puzzles, and eating a very simple supper of canned salmon and instant grits. When she turned in that night, she fully expected her usual nocturnal nonsense of nagging insomnia. Instead, though, she slept soundly through until five the next morning. And five was almost like the middle of the day for Myrtle.

She got up, ate a healthy breakfast, and started tracking down her funeral clothes. She'd planned in advance this time since her funeral attire had had various issues for the last couple of funerals she'd attended. She kept finding annoying stains or missing buttons or torn hems. It was quite extraordinary…almost as if some malevolent elf had been sabotaging her wardrobe. Considering the damage to her clothing, you'd think she'd been attending some sort of bacchanalian bachelorette party instead of funeral-going. As she looked in her closet, she also noticed she was very, very low on clean clothing. Myrtle wasn't at all sure when she was going to find time to do some laundry, especially with Elaine popping over all the time to do her own.

And she'd had an epiphany this morning. It was right when she was staring at the severe navy-blue coat dress in her closet. She'd been standing there, frowning at the thing, making sure it didn't have any defects, when it occurred to her that she had a new line of questioning for the remaining, living suspects.

Who has something against Mimsy Kessler?

Because, really, what if Wanda *were* right? What if Myrtle were on the wrong track, trying to find out who had something against Luella White? What if someone had something against *Mimsy* and was trying to set her up as Luella's and Alma's murderers? What if Myrtle weren't merely on the wrong track, but at the entirely wrong station?

Which was when Myrtle switched from her epiphany and back to her funeral dress. It was quite wrinkled as if someone had taken it from the closet, stomped on it vigorously, and hung it back up.

Myrtle was, indeed, so efficient that morning that she was carefully pressed, wore immaculate stockings with no runs, chose sensible jewelry, and had her hair combed and makeup on at ten o'clock. She then commenced to wait for her ten-thirty ride.

The phone rang shortly after ten. She certainly hoped it

wasn't Florence with some hair-brained excuse.

But it was Miles. His voice sounded a lot more like Miles and a lot less than the petulant toddler he had sounded like during his less-lucid moments at the doctor's office yesterday. "Did I dream it, or is there a funeral for Alma Wiggins today?"

"There certainly isn't. She's dead, but no one has the power to hustle her into the ground quite that fast. It's a service for Luella White, our first-murdered. At eleven. I'm leaving for it presently," said Myrtle. "And no, you can't go."

"I was only asking," said Miles a bit coldly.

"You're in no fit condition to be mourning around a graveside. You'll steal all the thunder from the dead by passing out as if you were grief-stricken by Luella's demise. And *then* people will talk."

"I'm sure they're *already* talking," said Miles with a sigh. "Considering she was murdered at your party and all." He paused. "At any rate, I wasn't really calling about going to the funeral. I know better than to try to push myself. I'm certainly too weak from the minor dehydration and it *would* be rather alarming if I were to faint at the funeral. I was only calling to make sure that Alma *was* dead and that I hadn't imagined it in some fit of feverish hallucination. Plus, I wanted to thank you for everything you've done the last couple of days. I know it took time away from your investigation. And—you had to interact with Erma."

"Well, I make sacrifices for friends, Miles. Even unspeakable sacrifices such as dealing with Erma Sherman. And you are my best friend." She moved on briskly, since any hint of raw emotion made her very uncomfortable. "I'll come by after the service to fill you in. Tape *Tomorrow's Promise* and we'll watch it together. I'll let you know when because I've also got to fit in car shopping with Elaine … and I'd take you with me except that I don't think you're completely recovered yet. Now I've got to run since my ride should be here any minute."

But her ride wasn't there. And wasn't. And when it was past the allotted time for Florence to arrive by a good bit, Myrtle called Florence.

"Hello?" asked the old woman cautiously.

"Florence? It's Myrtle. Are you on your way?"

"On my way where?" asked Florence.

"To Luella's funeral!"

"Is that today?" Florence's voice was startled.

"It's in twenty minutes!"

"Oh, mercy! Well, I'm glad you reminded me. I'll see you there, Myrtle." And Florence hung up.

Myrtle stared at the receiver in her hand. Then she quickly redialed Florence. The phone rang and rang and rang until finally a breathless Florence picked up. "Florence! You offered yesterday to drive me to the funeral. I need a ride."

"You do? I did?" Florence was sounding a cross between skeptical and concerned.

"Yes! And we really need to leave now."

Myrtle hung up, grabbed her pocketbook and cane and stood outside her front door. Five minutes later, Florence drove up into the driveway. Actually, Florence drove into the driveway and the grass next to it, hitting a baseball player gnome and sending him flying into a gnome woman bearing a bouquet.

Myrtle sighed and climbed into Florence's front seat.

"Did I hit something?" asked Florence in concern. She was wearing a floral shirt and khaki slacks, which Myrtle did not find particularly funeral-appropriate. These younger folks were always messing with tradition.

"Yes, you knocked a gnome." Florence seemed to want to investigate the gnome's vitals (or perhaps the vitals of her Buick), and Myrtle added impatiently, "There isn't time now, Florence. We have to get to the cemetery. And it's a bit of a drive, which is why I'm not walking."

"Oh, it's not Ingleside then?"

"No, it's Grace Hill. It'll take us about ten minutes to get there," said Myrtle.

Or not. Florence took off like a shot, speeding down the residential streets and downtown Bradley as if she were part of NASCAR. Myrtle clung to the door. "Florence, you could go a bit slower. We're going to end up at Grace Hill permanently if you keep driving like this."

Florence made a very slight correction in speed. The trees alongside the road were still whizzing by at an alarming rate. Myrtle said a brief prayer as Florence bumped the curb. Finally, they arrived at the venerable cemetery. Florence sped through the vine-covered iron gates and down the narrow, winding road that twisted through the graves.

"I think they've already started," said Myrtle, peering ahead at a group assembled around a tent. "Let's just coast in."

No hope of that, though, as Florence hit the accelerator instead of the brake and their tires squealed as they pulled in.

Myrtle's face felt red as she climbed gratefully out of Florence's car. Perhaps she could find an alternate ride home. She would like to attend more church and do a few more Good Deeds before meeting her Maker and it didn't suit her to meet Him today.

There was actually a fairly good crowd at Luella's graveside. This cemetery did have a lot of atmosphere and perhaps that drew people. One felt as if one were almost part of a movie set. There were ancient, tilting, moss-covered tombstones scattered about, Kudzu-covered trees loomed overhead, looking like leafy ghosts. The fact that a good crowd was in attendance was interesting, since Luella had been new to town and wasn't exactly popular with many. She saw Mimsy under the tent in the seated area with her husband. Myrtle craned her head and saw that Mimsy clutched a white tissue that definitely appeared used. She had a Bible in her lap. Her other hand firmly held her husband's.

Since Mimsy was the only represented family, other funeral-goers were sitting under the covering of the tent. Poppy was *not* there, which surprised Myrtle at first. After all, she and Mimsy were such good friends. Wouldn't Poppy want to be there for support? But then she realized that Poppy had made it very clear that she spent a good deal of time at work…and this was most definitely when preschool would be in session.

Estelle was standing toward the edge of the gathering, looking fairly awkward and uncomfortable in black slacks and a white blouse. She kept pulling at the blouse's collar as if it were constricting her neck. Estelle likely didn't spend much time in dressy clothes while chasing storms. And still not a spot of makeup graced her features. She had an ambivalent look on her face as she kept sending flittering glances in the direction of Luella's casket.

Florence said in a too-loud stage whisper, "Want a peppermint?"

Myrtle shot her a disapproving look and pointedly shook her head, keeping her eyes on the minister, who was now into the ashes-to-ashes stage of the proceedings. She needed Miles there. Miles might sometimes be annoyingly loud with cellophane wrappers, but he wouldn't whisper.

"Poor Alma," murmured Florence.

Myrtle rolled her eyes. And one should definitely keep track of whose funeral one was attending. How tiresome. "Poor Luella," she said through gritted teeth.

"Poor Luella, too. But that was a while back," whispered Florence loudly.

"Regardless, we are at *Luella's* funeral," hissed Myrtle.

Florence blinked at her. "Is that so? Well, for heaven's sake. I wouldn't have wanted to come to *Luella's* funeral, you know. I'd only wanted to go to Alma's." She was sounding a bit fussy and her voice rose.

"That's for you to keep to yourself," reprimanded Myrtle. "They'll likely wrap up before you know it."

Despite Luella's apparent wealth, the service was very plain. Myrtle wondered if that was Luella's stated wish or if Mimsy just hadn't been able to pull together anything more elaborate. There was a short homily, a hymn, a prayer, and a wrap-up. Snappiest funeral Myrtle had ever attended. And she'd been to a slew of funerals.

There was also, apparently, no reception after the service. Although, that was somewhat understandable, given the fact that Mimsy was the sole family. Receptions made more sense when there was a herd of out-of-town relations descending on the cemetery.

Estelle quickly and rather clumsily hugged Mimsy and her husband in an abrupt and uncomfortable-looking embrace. Then she hurried away toward her car, which led her past Florence and Luella. Myrtle sighed. Estelle was someone that she'd have asked for a ride from, but she couldn't very well do it in front of Florence. Florence did seem very defensive about her driving abilities.

Estelle pushed a strand of hair out of her face. "Nice service," she said, shifting from one foot to the other as if uncertain of really what to say.

"It was," said Myrtle.

Florence said, "I'm a little surprised to see you here, Estelle. I thought you were unhappy with Luella for being such a pill about your storm chasing van."

Estelle flushed. "I'm not here for Luella's sake—I'm here for Mimsy's. And I might say the same about you,

Florence. I know you weren't exactly pleased with Luella, yourself."

"That's right. But I'm here for the same reason you are—to support Mimsy," said Florence.

Actually, Florence was here because she thought it was Alma's funeral. But Myrtle decided not to press the point.

Myrtle summoned her fluffiest, most scatterbrained old lady persona and asked in a gossipy voice, "Isn't it just awful about poor Alma, Estelle? I suppose we'll be at her funeral next week. It's so tragic."

Estelle nodded. "I don't know what we're coming to here. I couldn't believe it when I heard. So terrible."

Myrtle said, "Red has been questioning everyone, of course. Trying to see if he can find someone who might have seen something. Maybe even something that they don't realize is important. I know you probably keep some unusual hours, don't you? As a storm chaser? Did you happen to see anything at Alma's house?"

Myrtle could tell that Estelle liked being recognized as a storm chaser. She puffed up a little bit and smiled. Maybe having someone acknowledge her profession made it seem a little more real.

"As a matter of fact, I *was* out night before last. I was actually coming back from a short jaunt to the coast to document some water spouts that were happening over the ocean," said Estelle.

"The ocean!" said Florence. "That's not exactly a day trip, is it?"

"It's a day trip if you don't have the money to stay overnight," said Estelle sadly.

Myrtle said, "When did you make it back into town?"

"Oh, it was probably around eleven. It's a good nearly four-hour drive. I did pass by Alma's house on the way in, although of course I wasn't paying a lot of attention. I didn't see anything," said Estelle, rather regretfully.

Myrtle got the impression that Estelle was enjoying being the center of attention, no matter how briefly or for what reason. Suddenly remembering the earring evidence, Myrtle leaned closer and peered at Estelle's ears underneath her short, sandy hair. She did have pierced ears and wore earrings, but they were gold studs. "That's too bad. But what do you make of all this, Estelle? Who might have been upset with Alma?"

Estelle looked thoughtfully at a nearby tombstone as the collected funeral goers moved slowly to their cars. "I can't really imagine anyone being upset with Alma. I guess family are usually the first to be considered suspects in these types of things. But I know Alma to be in the same financial situation that I'm in. In other words, she didn't have two pennies to rub together."

Then Estelle frowned. "You know, I did actually see something. Someone. You, Florence. I thought I spotted you wandering around outside when I was coming back into town."

"Me?" Florence colored. "Why on earth would I be outside that late?"

Estelle seemed to be kindly trying to help her out with ideas. "Maybe you were letting your dog out?"

"Haven't got one."

"Or feeding your cat?" asked Estelle helpfully.

"No cat either."

"Perhaps you were stretching your legs," said Myrtle briskly. "I often do that."

"At night?" asked Florence.

"Why not? If they need stretching, legs don't check with the clock," said Myrtle.

"Mine require very little stretching," said Florence indignantly. "Estelle, you must be mistaken."

Estelle bit her lip. She said nothing in response.

Myrtle swiftly changed tack. "I have a question for you both. Might anyone have something against *Mimsy*?"

Florence and Estelle both blinked at Myrtle as if she'd suddenly displayed signs of senility. Finally, Estelle said, "Don't you mean Alma? Or Luella?"

"No. No, I mean Mimsy."

There was a long pause. Florence said, "Well, her little dog is annoying. It barks outside all hours of the day and night. I honestly don't know why they don't bring it inside. It seems to be so distraught whenever it's outside."

Estelle said, "Mimsy is a really nice person. She's been one of the nicest people I've met here." Estelle, at least, seemed genuinely to like Mimsy. But when Florence wasn't looking, Estelle gave Myrtle a meaningful look. There was something Estelle didn't want to say in front of Florence.

Myrtle said quickly, "Estelle, I wonder if you might do me a favor. Florence was kind enough to drive me here, but she mentioned she might have an errand to run on the way back."

"Did I?" Florence's forehead wrinkled in confusion.

"Could you drop me back by my house?" asked Myrtle.

"I'd be happy to," said Estelle. "Especially if you're ready to leave."

Chapter Fifteen

The ride home wasn't nearly as harrowing as the ride to the funeral. Estelle, despite the fact that she chased storms for a living, appeared to drive at much more restrained pace than Florence. Once they'd left the cemetery, Myrtle got right to the point. "Estelle, it seemed as if you wanted to tell me something back there. Was it something about Florence?"

Estelle's hands briefly clenched the steering wheel. "Well, I hate to say anything. This is long-ago history. In fact, you may know it much better than I do. I've only heard it secondhand."

Myrtle frowned. "Well, you have whetted my interest. Although I can't say I remember anything about Florence from the past." There did seem to be some sort of faraway memory trying to poke its way to the surface, however.

"It's about Florence's favorite nephew. She doted on him, apparently. Seemed to care more for him than even her own daughter. And he ate it up. He was always dropping by and bringing her gifts and giving her a hand with her yard work or whatnot."

"And this nephew that she doted on had a connection to Mimsy?" asked Myrtle.

"Yes. He started dating Mimsy back in the day." She took her eyes off the road for a moment to glance over at Myrtle.

Myrtle said thoughtfully, "This is slowly coming back to me. So this young man—he had some sort of an accident, didn't he?"

"He apparently died tragically in a car accident," said Estelle.

"And Mimsy was driving? Surely, though, wouldn't she have faced some sort of charges of some kind?"

"That's just it, though. Mimsy *wasn't* driving. The nephew was. What's more, he'd been drinking. But at the time, Florence was inconsolable. From what I heard, she blamed Mimsy. The nephew had been a teetotaler until he'd started dating her. Mimsy's crowd was a little fast, Florence thought. She figured he'd still be around if it weren't for her," said Estelle.

"Hm. Well, she certainly doesn't run with a fast crowd *now*," said Myrtle.

Estelle read her mind and snorted. "Everyone changes, I guess. From what I gather, Poppy wasn't exactly in Mimsy's crowd back in school."

"Have you heard of anyone else who might have a grudge against Mimsy?" asked Myrtle.

"Everyone thinks she's wonderful," said Estelle with a shrug. "She's been nice to me since I've moved here. But why are you asking about Mimsy, Myrtle?"

Myrtle said, "Oh, just a hunch." She wasn't about to start blabbering on about psychics. Estelle seemed to be a woman of science, after all. If storm chasing were science. At any rate, she seemed to be on a first-name basis with science.

As Estelle pulled onto Magnolia Lane, Myrtle leaned forward and squinted through the windshield. "What on earth? Is that *Miles*?"

Estelle raised her eyebrows. "Seems to be. He's just doing a little yard work. Why? You seem surprised to see him."

"Surprised is an understatement. The man was practically on his deathbed yesterday and now he's pulling weeds? Just wait until I get my hands on him."

"Should I drop you off in your driveway? Or his?" asked Estelle.

"His. And thanks for driving me home, Estelle."

Myrtle got out of Estelle's car and walked slowly toward the oblivious Miles. He was sitting on the ground and busily pulling clover from a patch in his yard.

"Miles!" barked Myrtle.

Miles jumped, scattering clover wildly around him. "For heaven's sake, Myrtle!"

"What are you doing out here? If you think I'm nursing you back to health or dragging you off to the doctor again, you're sorely mistaken!" Myrtle brandished her cane at him.

Miles gave her a wary look and carefully put the remaining clover in the bucket next to him. "I was sick—"

"Indeed! I do remember!"

Miles continued coldly, "Sick of my *house*, Myrtle. And I don't feel ill anymore. The sun is shining and it's making me feel even stronger and better being outside. Or at least out of my living room. I think I may need to borrow your Puddin to get my house back to its normal state."

"I'm going to counteract your claim of being well. Because *no one* would think that Puddin would *improve* the state of their home unless they were feverishly hallucinating," said Myrtle. "However, if you're so sick of your living room, why not come over to my house? Our soap is about to start and I'm ready to put my feet up. It's been a long day and I haven't even made it to the car dealership yet."

Miles leaped to his feet. Myrtle decided it wasn't so much his eagerness to accept her invitation as it was for him to illustrate his excellent health. And potentially show off.

"Let's do that. And while we're getting settled, maybe you can fill me in on Alma's death and Luella's funeral. I have a feeling there's a lot of catching up to do."

They walked to Myrtle's. And before she could even fish her keys out of her pocketbook, she could hear screaming inside her house.

"What was *that*?" gasped Miles.

Myrtle sighed. "I assume it's an overtired grandson of mine who should be taking a nap." She unlocked the door.

"How is their plumbing project progressing?" asked Miles.

"You can ask Elaine, yourself," said Myrtle. "Although I image that the answer will be that it's not progressing too quickly since they still don't have running water."

Jack was apparently desperately unhappy. As soon as he spotted Myrtle, he darted away from a harassed-looking Elaine and hugged Myrtle around one leg, howling piteously. Myrtle gave Elaine a mock-stern frown. "Have you been upsetting my darling grandson?"

Elaine snorted. "I think it's the other way around." She pushed a strand of hair out of her eyes.

Myrtle asked, "May I give Jack a c-o-o-k-i-e?"

"That's fine. Hi, Miles."

Miles smiled at her. "Hi. You probably need a cookie, too."

Elaine said dryly, "I think it's going to take more than a cookie. I might be getting into Myrtle's sherry soon."

Myrtle moved into the kitchen and Jack trotted behind her, gathering that some sort of a treat was in order. He happily babbled to her, telling her about his day and the dog he'd seen at his friend's house. He gave a deep and rattling cough as he went.

Myrtle turned in time to see Miles's eyebrows shoot up in alarm. "Here's a cookie for you, Jack. And could you take this one to your mama?"

They rejoined Elaine and Miles in the living room.

Miles said hesitatingly, "So…is Jack feeling all right? That's quite a cough he's got there."

Elaine casually said, "Oh, you know how kids are. Jack has a cold. He's had it for a while now."

Miles eyed Jack cautiously and slowly moved away from him.

"Miles just got over that nasty bug," said Myrtle.

Elaine said, "I'm glad you're better, Miles. Myrtle was quite concerned yesterday when she was trying to borrow a car." Elaine sighed. "So much going on at the house right now. Plus the car issues. And also with Red's investigation. It's very disconcerting have one's husband investigating one's Bunco group."

"I'd imagine so," said Myrtle. She paused. "So, how's that going, by the way? Has Red mentioned which suspect might be at the top of his list?"

"He's been particularly guarded this time," said Elaine with a sigh.

"How annoying of him," said Myrtle.

Jack was dropping cookie crumbs in large bits as he spun around Myrtle's living room. He came precariously close to Miles and Miles came up with some excuse to visit Myrtle's kitchen as Jack gave another throaty cough.

"Cover your mouth, Jack," said Elaine automatically. Then she said to Myrtle, "Red does seem especially hard on Mimsy. Which is a bit embarrassing, since she's a friend. Well, they're *all* friends, of course."

"Hm. Interesting. Something else I wanted to ask you, Elaine. You see, I was talking to Estelle today at the funeral."

Elaine snapped her fingers. "Luella's funeral! I meant to ask you how that went. I'd have gone, of course, except that I didn't have anyone to watch Jack for me. And, well, a car to get there."

"And you know I'd have helped you out with both

things if I could have. I had a terrifying voyage to the cemetery with Florence Ainsworth. Anyway, Estelle was trying to recount some old gossip about Florence's nephew and Mimsy. She intimated that Florence had a grudge against Mimsy," said Myrtle.

Elaine took a thoughtful bite of her cookie. "I wouldn't have said that Florence *still* has a grudge against Mimsy. Heavens, that must have been ages ago. I do remember Mimsy mentioning to me before that she'd had a long-ago boyfriend who'd met a tragic end. I must have been pretty little at the time, so I don't remember anything about it."

"What did Mimsy tell you?" Myrtle heard Miles bumping around in her kitchen. He appeared to be finding snacks while he was waiting for the germy Jack to depart for home.

"Only that they'd been in a terrible car accident and that he'd been killed. Apparently they'd been at some sort of party and he'd been drinking. She said he was scaring her silly driving as fast and as recklessly as he did. But she survived the accident without a scratch on her." Elaine shook her head in wonder. "Probably because she had a seatbelt on."

Myrtle said, "I'm surprised that Mimsy would tell you such a story. Are you really that close?"

"We *are* friends. Not *especially* close. But she was telling me this story in context. Mimsy became a teetotaler immediately after the accident. Saw the entire thing as a sign, or something. At any rate, we always have a non-alcoholic option whenever we have Bunco, for that reason," said Elaine. "And Florence won't drink if she drives, either."

"I thought Mimsy *was* drinking at Bunco," said Myrtle, frowning. "It seemed as if everyone were drinking quite a lot, as a matter of fact."

"She puts her tonic water or water in a wine glass,"

said Elaine. "She says it makes her feel more festive. But she doesn't drink. Anyway, as I was saying, this was all ancient history. I can't imagine that Florence is still nursing hard feelings. She always seems very polite to Mimsy."

But polite wasn't the same as friendly.

"Ready, Jack?" asked Elaine. "Thanks for letting us use your facilities, Myrtle. And for the cookies. Bye Miles," she called.

"Bye!" came a fervent voice from the recesses of the kitchen.

Myrtle said, "Call me after Jack's nap and I'll run out to the dealership with you. Don't you think Red could drop us off there?"

"I'm sure he could. Picking us back *up* again might take a while, but I'm sure he can get us out there," said Elaine as she walked out.

The door closed behind her and Myrtle called, "It's safe to come out now."

Miles hovered in the kitchen door. "I'm waiting for the germy particles in the air to settle, first."

Myrtle sighed and walked past him into the kitchen. She rummaged under the sink until she found a jumbo sized can of Lysol. She then walked back to the living room and proceeded to spray its contents around the room, using large sweeping motions.

Then she put the Lysol away. "You've become quite the hypochondriac, Miles. But I think I've got you covered. Did you get snacks ready for us?"

"I just popped some popcorn."

"Then I'd say we're ready for our show."

Miles was apparently still smarting from the hypochondria remark. As he sat on Myrtle's sofa with his bowl of popcorn, he said, "I'm simply in no hurry to get sick again." His voice was cranky.

Myrtle nodded absently. "Thinking back—did you

really want Puddin to clean for you today? Don't you have anyone else to call?"

"If I called anyone else, they'd be booked," said Miles. "It's only the housekeepers who aren't any good who are available. Besides, even a bad cleaning job sounds better than the alternative … which is *me* cleaning it all up."

"I suppose I should go ahead and call her then. She needs a certain amount of lead-time, for sure. It's not as if she's going to just leap into action, you know."

Miles considered this. "How about if *I* call her? Have you got her number handy?"

Myrtle pushed across a small, spiral notebook full of jotted down phone numbers. Miles squinted at the page and then dialed.

"Puddin? It's Miles Bradford. That's right. Listen, I wondered if you might run by my house this afternoon and clean? I'm at Myrtle's house, so if you'd stop by and get the key? Thanks."

He hung up, looking pleased. "That wasn't nearly as painful as you made it out to be."

Myrtle scowled at him. "Wait until she's completely finished with the job before you evaluate her performance,." Myrtle glanced at the clock. "Wow, I think this is the first time I've watched the show live in forever! Usually I have to watch one I've taped."

"Oh boy," said Miles, swallowing down a bunch of popcorn. "So now we can't fast-forward through all the household cleaner commercials."

Myrtle sniffed. "It's called a *soap* opera for a reason. Besides, we need to watch the household cleaner commercials, Miles. Puddin is systematically annihilating mine and is about to do the same with yours."

Miles slumped on the sofa, a bit deflated. "She won't bring her own?"

"Of course not. That would be something a

professional would do. And this is Puddin."

The theme music for the soap opera started playing. Miles mumbled, "This is worst part of the whole show. The opening music. Sappy, sappy."

"It's historic, Miles. They *have* to play it. It's practically required. It's the same opening music they've had on the soap since the 1950s. If they started playing rap or hip-hop or something, no one would know what show this was."

Miles chuckled. "I think most rap artists would have a problem with their music being used to represent *Tomorrow's Promise*. So, after this, you're telling me how everything went at the funeral, right?"

Myrtle nodded and then put her finger to her lips. "Shh! It's starting."

Miles said idly, "Isn't it amazing how well dressed these people are? I mean, no one ever looks like we do. You even went to a funeral today and don't look as well dressed as these folks."

"Shh!"

The soap opera, in its attempt to produce an original storyline that had not made an appearance since the 1950s, veered into Extremely Unlikely territory. Still, it was pretty riveting stuff. And, as usual, the soap demonstrated to Myrtle some intriguing possibilities regarding the case.

A commercial break gave them the opportunity to discuss what they were seeing. Miles seemed, as usual, fixated on Briana. "The thing about this storyline that bothers me," he murmured, "is that Briana is by all accounts a woman with a very limited world view. Her entire universe is that salon. Her life revolves around doling out pixie cuts and perms."

"And melodrama," added Myrtle absently.

"Yes, and melodrama involving clients' love triangles and those of her own making. So how does someone with this very truncated world view end up as an international terrorist?" Miles's expression was bewildered.

"It's stunning that you have a problem with poor Briana when you've accepted the fact that little Johnny who was born a couple of months ago is now a four year old. What's interesting to me is that the show has developed her motive a little. Before, they were indicating that Briana was radicalized by her next door neighbor. And she's clearly impressionable. And disenfranchised. Isn't that how people who join cults or terrorists are described? Disenfranchised," said Myrtle. "But now we're seeing that Briana was actually sympathetic to the radicals for a long time, considering all the old literature that she's got in her house. But I have a bigger takeaway from the show so far today."

Miles raised his eyebrows. "Really? What's that? That all the women in the cast should put a bell around Alexandra's neck so they know when she's approaching their husbands?"

"No. That this case boils down to something very simple, very basic. What's the basis of all the storylines on *Tomorrow's Promise*?"

"Suspension of disbelief?" asked Miles.

"No. Passion. And it's one type of passion or another, but all very strong emotions. Very *real* emotions. Love, hate, fear, envy. And I have the feeling that's what we're dealing with with these murders," said Myrtle. "I'm just not sure which emotion it is."

She paused as there was a rustling outside, followed by a jangling of keys and someone unlocking her front door. Myrtle frowned at Puddin as the housekeeper walked right in. "Puddin! I didn't realize you still had a key to my house."

Puddin shrugged. "Didn't want to worry you to get up."

"I'll take that key back now, Puddin, *thank* you,"

Myrtle held out her hand and Puddin slouched over to return it.

Miles fished in his pocket for his own key. "Here you are, Puddin. Thanks so much for doing this for me at the last minute. You might want to wear gloves in there. I've been sick and I'd hate for you to catch something from me."

Puddin batted her eyelashes at him. "Ain't that sweet, sir? But I never do get sick none."

"Unless you count her thrown backs," muttered Myrtle.

"I'll get it real clean," she said to Miles. She quickly left, key in hand.

The entire encounter aggravated Myrtle. "She called you *sir*? And she didn't try to hang out with us and eat popcorn and watch the soap?"

Miles was pleased. "Puddin has always been very deferential to me. And I have a feeling that she'll do a good job with the cleaning. It's not such a big job, after all. The house was clean a few days ago."

"It's all very annoying."

Chapter Sixteen

They watched the rest of the soap opera, the plot of which was at least as unlikely as Briana's conversion to terrorist. After it was done, Miles stretched and idly said, "What did you think of your story in the paper today?"

"I didn't even have a chance to read it. Wait…why? Was there something different about the article?" asked Myrtle.

Miles wordlessly tossed the paper her way.

Myrtle scanned the front page. "Sloan has finally flipped his lid. I don't believe this. Is this the *Bradley Bugle* or the National Enquirer? 'Alien Spacecraft Reported by Local Resident?' That's Barney Shoemaker and he's reported aliens for the past fifty years…it's not news. It's all tied into his fond relationship with homemade moonshine."

"It's a very colorful newspaper," said Miles, looking sadly into his now-empty bowl.

"But what's this? 'Brainy Beauty Butchered?' *What*?" Myrtle gaped in horror at the story. "And *my name* is on the story?"

"Did you notice anyone looking oddly at you at the funeral today?" asked Miles. "Because that's the kind of story that might make people stare."

"No, I didn't see anyone looking oddly at me. Likely because they don't even subscribe to the paper anymore. What nonsense!" Myrtle crumpled up the paper and tossed it far away from her, fuming. "I'm going to have a talk with that Sloan Jones. I'll set him straight and not try to tiptoe around his feelings any longer."

"Before you do that, because I don't want to be around for the moment when that big man starts cowering under his desk, can you fill me in on the case? Who have you talked to, what have you learned, and how was the funeral?" asked Miles.

Myrtle was still thinking about the newspaper, but she gave him a very rote and factual representation of the events that had transpired since he'd become ill. Miles listened intently, nodding from time to time.

At the end of her recitation, he said, "Okay, so now I know all the facts. But what do *you* think, Myrtle? That's what I want to know. How are you processing all of the events and all of what you know? What kind of sense are you making out of it all?"

"Before I answer that," said Myrtle, "what do *you* make of it?"

"That's hard to say since I wasn't there and couldn't see the expressions of the suspects or hear their tone of voice. But I could take a stab at it." He thought for a moment. "I'm guessing that Alma simply got in the way somehow. She sure wasn't killed for her vast fortune. Maybe she'd seen the murderer or had some piece of information or evidence that tied the murderer to the crime. The murderer would have been desperate not to be arrested for Luella's death and would have eliminated Alma."

Myrtle said, "That's exactly what I'm thinking. Mostly. Actually, I'm taking it a step further. I think that not only did Alma know something, she attempted to improve her rather dire economic situation by blackmailing the person who was responsible for Luella's murder."

"Surely she must have known that was very dangerous though," demurred Miles. "After all, she would be dealing with someone who had killed once. And very brazenly, too—in a short period of time with a lot of people around."

"That's true, but you're forgetting one important fact. Alma was friends with whomever the murderer is. They played Bonkers together."

"Bunco," muttered Miles.

"Since they were friends, Alma may have underestimated the danger involved. This was likely a person that she'd known for years. She might have felt quite safe. And it must have seemed like a good way to get some extra spending money," said Myrtle.

Miles said, "But the killer wasn't a safe person to approach. And it was the kind of person who would not only murder a friend at a party, but would break into someone's house in the middle of the night to silence them."

"That's the thing, though…everyone would know that Alma kept her windows open at night to stay cool. She's the only person I know of who wasn't running her a/c. Clearly, she was trying to keep costs down. The only problem with that, is that it ultimately cost her her life." Myrtle stretched her legs out. She'd been sitting for a little while now. "What other conclusions did you reach, Miles? Or what else stood out to you? You're doing a good job."

Miles said slowly, "I suppose the mysterious earring. Do we know who wears earrings and who doesn't?

Myrtle counted on her fingers. "Poppy doesn't wear earrings or have pierced ears. Florence does wear earrings. Estelle wears earrings but they're just those stud kinds—not the big, dangly kinds. And Poppy reported that Mimsy wears earrings. Actually, Mimsy apparently lost an earring at my party."

"It sounds as if Mimsy is the most likely suspect then," said Miles.

"It does *sound* that way, doesn't it?" asked Myrtle.

"But you're thinking something else, it appears." Miles sounded a bit stiff at his lack of imagination.

"That's right. I'm thinking that *anyone* could have set Mimsy up. It would be very easy to have planted Mimsy's earring at the crime scene. Then you've nicely diverted attention from yourself if you're the killer," explained Myrtle.

"How would someone have ended up with Mimsy's earring?" asked Miles in exasperation. "Did they break into *her* house, too?"

"No, that wouldn't have been necessary. Remember? Mimsy lost an earring at my party. Someone could have seen it, taken it as an insurance policy of sorts, and then cleverly planted it as evidence against Mimsy at Alma's crime scene."

"But *why*? Why would someone do that? And really—do you think the killer spent that much time planning ahead?" asked Miles. He rubbed his temple as if he were getting a headache.

"I do think the murderer thought the crimes through, yes. Luella's murder was a crime of opportunity, but it wasn't something the killer hadn't thought about. This wasn't some sort of crime of passion where the murderer is suddenly boiling over with rage during an argument. As far as we can tell, there was *no* argument. Luella went outside to smoke. No one reports hearing loud voices, or an argument, or anything at all," said Myrtle.

"Maybe it was simply so loud *inside* that the guests couldn't hear the argument going on *outside*," suggested Miles.

"And that's a very good point, Miles. Except for one important fact—Erma Sherman was next door. And Erma is the nosiest, most obnoxious neighbor ever. If there had been a violent argument taking place mere yards from her house, she'd have known about it. She probably had all her windows open trying to listen in," said Myrtle.

Miles said, "This still doesn't explain the 'why.' Why

would someone try to set Mimsy up?"

"Plenty of reasons. It could have been a personal reason—maybe someone really dislikes Mimsy would like to see Mimsy hauled away in handcuffs. Or maybe it was just a very practical reason…the opportunity to divert suspicion away from the killer presented itself and the murderer leaped at the chance."

"So let's think who might have something against Mimsy," said Miles. He stared blankly at Myrtle's television. "You know, if I had to place a bet on someone, I'd pick Poppy."

"Maybe you're confused about who Poppy is. Remember, she's the one who's Mimsy's best friend. You might be thinking about Estelle," said Myrtle.

"I'm most definitely *not* thinking of Estelle. That's because I can't think of a reason on this earth why Estelle Rutledge would want to set up Mimsy Kessler."

"That's because you're not using your imagination, Miles. Estelle was angry with Luella for denying her a loan that would have saved or jumpstarted her storm chasing career. Alma may have spotted Estelle coming in from the backyard and decided to blackmail her," said Myrtle.

Miles interrupted. "But Alma would know that Estelle wasn't exactly rolling in cash. Wouldn't she be a poor mark in terms of blackmailing?"

"Well, yes, but beggars can't be choosers. And Estelle is certainly more solvent than Alma is. If Estelle were desperate enough, Alma could probably have gotten a couple of decent payments from her. I'm just saying that's what Alma might have *thought*. But perhaps Estelle really *is* as bad off as you're thinking. Then she might have had a very strong motive for murdering Alma…to keep her quiet because she couldn't afford to pay her and she didn't want to go to prison." Myrtle waved her hands around to demonstrate the importance of shutting down a blabbing

Alma.

Miles nodded slowly. "Okay. I'm following so far. And you're saying that she might have had an opportunity to take Mimsy's earring and snagged it, thinking that planted evidence could potentially be valuable in the future."

"Well, let's think about the order of events there. We don't really know when Mimsy's earring fell out. We know she reported it missing later in the party. What if Estelle or someone else saw the opportunity and grabbed the earring before Luella's murder, planning on planting it at the scene of the crime. ? And then, in the heat of the moment, maybe they forgot to plant it. Or perhaps they ran out of time—they thought that someone was about to come out the door, or something else spooked them and they weren't able to leave the earring, but they retained possession of it," said Myrtle. "It's the kind of thing that could come in useful later. And then there was a good use for it not long after."

Miles said, "This theory could work for just about everyone else, too. Poppy, for instance."

"I'm starting to think that you just don't like poor Poppy very much," said Myrtle.

"Let's consider it, though. This would be an example of someone wanting to set Mimsy up, since we couldn't find a motive for Poppy to kill Luella."

"And the motive for Poppy to kill her best friend?" asked Myrtle archly.

"Jealousy," said Miles decidedly.

"Okay, let's explore that. So you're saying that Poppy has had some sort of growing resentment against Mimsy. A resentment that got to the point where she couldn't stand it anymore and decided to plot her friend's downfall. Publicly humiliating Mimsy by having her dragged off to prison in handcuffs would surely accomplish that," mused Myrtle.

Miles was warming to his topic. "Think about it.

Poppy has a weak chin and a really beaky nose. She's incredibly awkward. She wears braces. She fights weight gain."

Myrtle murmured, "And Estelle intimated that Poppy and Mimsy were definitely not in the same crowd in school."

"Maybe Mimsy and her clique even bulled Poppy?" suggested Miles.

"Isn't that taking things a little far?" asked Myrtle. "Mimsy doesn't seem like the kind of person who'd participate in bullying."

"But adults frequently aren't the same people they were in high school," said Miles.

"What were you like in high school, Miles?" asked Myrtle. "What type of group did you hang out with?"

Miles flushed a bit.

"What kinds of clubs did you join, then?" pressed Myrtle.

"Well, I was in Future Business Leaders of America," said Miles. "And the Key Club."

"Any sports?"

"Not on school teams, no. I played a bit of table tennis sometimes," said Miles a little defensively.

"And your friends. What types of professions did they end up going into?"

"Medicine. Law. Engineering. Technology." Miles shrugged.

"Okay. So you hung out with the nerds," summed up Myrtle. "There's nothing wrong with that, Miles. Nerds rule the world. But my point is that you haven't changed all that much. It's hard to imagine Mimsy as a mean person when she's so pleasant now."

"Point taken. But even if Mimsy wasn't bullying Poppy in high school, it doesn't mean that Poppy isn't resentful of Mimsy. Mimsy is…cute," said Miles with that flush again.

Myrtle grinned at him. "Ah, so you think Mimsy is cute. I won't give you a hard time on that Miles. She *is* cute. She has a beautiful complexion and lovely black hair. She reminds me of Snow White, as a matter of fact."

"And she doesn't have to work two jobs, either," reminded Miles. "Poppy is slogging away to make ends meet by working as a preschool teacher and as a waitress. Mimsy stays at home."

"Well, she *does* volunteer quite a bit. But you're right, there's a big difference between having to work two jobs and volunteering. And she'd have to tamp down any of that resentment she showed when she was with Mimsy. I think it's definitely a possible motive," said Myrtle. "And then we have Florence."

Miles sighed. "Myrtle, I still just can't see it. So you're saying this slightly batty old lady is whacking people over the head with wrenches and climbing in through windows to murder her friend? Why is this difficult for me to picture?"

"Your bias against the elderly is showing, Miles. Florence Ainsworth isn't a stereotype. Florence has perhaps the strongest motive of the group. She is desperate to maintain her freedom and her treasured relationship. She would be forced to give both of them up if her daughter moved her hundreds of miles away or put her in assisted living. Florence may be a bit batty—or she may be playing it up y—. she's definitely not stupid. And she's a lot sprightlier than you're giving her credit for. I wouldn't sell her short at all," said Myrtle.

Miles sighed. "And then there's still Mimsy. I guess she's sort of the obvious choice, since she benefitted from Luella's death and since evidence that most likely points to her was found at the crime scene at Alma's house."

"We'd have to go with a financial motive if we're

considering Mimsy for Luella's murder. I think they got along just fine, so it wouldn't have been something personally *against* Luella, I don't think. And then Alma's death would have just been because she got in the way," said Myrtle. "Although Mimsy certainly seems financially solvent. And she's just so *stinkin' nice*."

Miles said thoughtfully, "What were you like in high school, Myrtle? Who did you hang out with?"

"*Amazing* people," said Myrtle with a sniff.

"Then some things really *don't* change," said Miles smugly.

After Miles had left to check on Puddin's progress, Elaine called to report that Jack had taken a short nap and that Red was available to drive them to Roger's Automotive.

As Myrtle suspected, Tim Rogers was glad to see them. He was very deferential to Myrtle and made sure to listen very carefully to Elaine when she was telling him what she was looking for in a new minivan. Apparently, business had been slow at the dealership lately, which explained why he pulled the expensive ad from the *Bradley Bugle*.

Myrtle said, "Red was going to drive us over to Creighton, Tim, but I told him I was *sure* we could work out a deal here and save us all the trouble. But my only requirements are that you give Elaine and Red an excellent deal and that you resume advertising at the *Bradley Bugle*. I'm prepared to send two other customers your way if you just agree to run those ads again."

"Miss Myrtle, you're an angel," said Tim, beaming.

Elaine strangled on something at these words and began violently coughing.

"No, I mean it. And I think that's a fine trade. Thanks, Miss Myrtle."

The afternoon went so well that by the end of it Elaine

was in the office signing paperwork for a new van while Myrtle attempted to entertain Jack in the showroom of the dealership. Once the dealer installed Jack's car seat in the van, Elaine drove them out of the lot. "This is wonderful!" she said in a happy voice. "And I think we got a very good deal for it."

"I think so, too," said Myrtle. She thought about having Elaine drop her off at the newspaper office but then decided that it might be nice to stretch her legs and walk over. And it would give her some time to think of a nice way to tell Sloan that everyone despised the paper now.

After getting home and having a short snack, Myrtle decided to head back out. Myrtle decided that the best approach with Sloan was to attempt to make him see reason. If that didn't work, she could always use intimidation. That would be a piece of cake since she intimidated Sloan anyway.

As soon as Myrtle walked out her front door, she had an Erma Sherman sighting. Fortunately, Erma appeared to be busily cleaning out her car with antiseptic wipes of some sort. Myrtle quietly slipped past her.

It only took a few minutes to walk to downtown Bradley. Myrtle was so busily mulling over the next things she wanted to do that she failed to notice that Pasha was trotting along behind her on the sidewalk.

Once Myrtle reached the splintery wooden door of the *Bradley Bugle* office, she turned to see Pasha standing right behind her. The black cat looked pleased with herself.

"Pasha! What are you doing, pretty girl? You shouldn't be here. You're supposed to be hunting the pesky squirrels at my feeders and causing havoc among small mammals. Subduing nature, and all that. This is no place for you."

Pasha seemed to disagree. For whatever reason, she was in the mood to be with Myrtle. Perhaps the animal sensed that Myrtle was on a mission and she'd decided to come along to help out … because, when Myrtle opened the door into the office, Pasha bounded in.

Chapter Seventeen

Sloan Jones wasn't in and he hadn't seemed to care enough about the contents of the newsroom to lock the door behind him. Pasha appeared to enjoy the dark space with its paper-laden desks and smell of old books. She darted around the large room, apparently looking for prey. Myrtle wondered, a bit uneasily, if there might be a few mice scampering around.

Myrtle looked for a place to sit and wait for Sloan. Sloan's own desk looked to be the most comfortable. He had a large rolling chair with a high back. The desk in front of the chair was as crammed with papers and old printed photos. Myrtle sat rather primly in the chair, clutching her purse and thinking over what she was going to say to Sloan.

Pasha stopped hunting and leaped up on Sloan's desk, scattering papers wildly. The black cat stared intently at Myrtle, batted some papers out of Sloan's inbox, and then leaped down to the floor to continue her search for a snack.

Myrtle discovered that the contents of Sloan's inbox were rather intriguing. "Precious Pasha," she murmured. Everything in the inbox appeared to be recent, according to the dates. Whenever Sloan got a lead for a story via email, he'd print it and stick it in his inbox. Consequently, it was jam-packed.

Leafing through the papers, Myrtle saw a story about Wilson Mayfield getting his Eagle Rank, high school student Priscilla Truman being chosen as a page in the state house, and Mrs. Flotman's weighty decision to plant peppers instead of continuing with her prize-winning tomatoes.

Frowning, Myrtle pulled the newspaper from her pocketbook. In the paper Myrtle was holding, she saw no mention of any peppers, Eagles, or pages. On the side of Sloan's desk, she saw the previous newspaper and flipped through it, too. No mention of the small-town topics she saw in his inbox. In fact, a running theme in both newspapers were bigger stories that were either taking place in the larger region or more sensationalistic stories—gossipy pieces about local residents.

"This is not good," muttered Myrtle. It wasn't that readers weren't submitting content to him. It was that Sloan wasn't printing it.

But what could she do? Oh, she could try to pressure Sloan. But hadn't she tried earlier? Wouldn't he just placate her, get her out of there, and then just do whatever he pleased? His vision for the newspaper was suddenly radically different from hers. And radically different, it seemed, from what his readers were actually looking for. Sloan needed to be *convinced*.

That's when Myrtle noticed Sloan's desktop on the next desk over. Its screen was dimmed as if it were sleeping. She paused a fraction of a second before scooting the rolling chair over and waking it with a jiggle of the mouse.

Judging from the sounds from the other side of the newsroom, Pasha appeared to have found a *real* mouse. Myrtle determinedly avoided watching the carnage taking place across the room.

Myrtle squinted at the screen. The homepage appeared to have some sort of scantily clad females on it. She sighed in distaste, hastily studied the shortcut icons on the desktop. She spotted the shortcuts for Facebook and Twitter. And smiled.

Myrtle held her breath as she clicked on the icons and

the pages came up. She released her breath in relief as she saw that Sloan, however unwisely, had chosen to have the computer automatically sign him in and remember his passwords.

So now she was looking at the *Bradley Bugle*'s social media. The newspaper's sites hadn't been updated for weeks. Myrtle decided it was time for a few helpful updates from the paper.

For the Facebook page, she wrote: *The* Bradley Bugle *congratulates Wilson Mayfield, Troop 39's 100th Eagle Scout*! She carefully tagged the Mayfields on the update to make sure it showed up on their profile page. Myrtle repeated this process with ten other neighborhood stories that had been cluttering Sloan's inbox.

The Twitter was a little harder. She stared at the page for a minute. Then she spotted the 'what's happening' status update bar at the top of the page. Myrtle thought a moment. Then she typed: Bradley Bugle *subscription giveaway! To enter, follow the paper online. Extra entries for sharing!* She noticed she still had forty-two characters remaining. Wasn't she supposed to do a hashtag thing with Twitter? She added #FreeBugle. She copied the post and shared it on the Facebook page, too.

Pasha ran up. She appeared to have a small creature in her mouth. Myrtle's response was to close the social media windows and carefully scoot Sloan's rolling chair away from the cat and its thankfully-dead prey.

Just in time, too. Myrtle heard Sloan whistling outside. She had no intention of telling him about the newspaper's updates or giveaway contest until it was a massive success. There was no reason to undermine the operation until it was over. It would be better if she knew the passwords, though. Otherwise, she'd have to keep sneaking into the newsroom and trying to figure out when Sloan would be out. That would require quite a bit more Sloan-tracking than she wanted.

It was then that she spotted a dingy, coffee tinged sticky note on the side of the monitor with the passwords on it. Myrtle snagged it and stuffed it into her pocketbook.

And not a moment too soon. Sloan's whistling stopped as soon as he opened the door. He clutched a McDonald's bag and wore a baseball cap, which he hastily removed. "Miss Myrtle! I didn't know you were going to be in here."

"You should have *guessed* I was going to be here."

Sloan looked blankly at her.

"Because of the way my article turned out," she added impatiently. "It was a lurid bit of yellow journalism."

Sloan backed up a little until his large frame hit the door. "Aww, don't say that, Miss Myrtle. It was just very *contemporary*, that's all. It had a strong hook."

"Let's face it, it read like pulp fiction. For heaven's sake, Sloan!"

Sloan slumped. "But Miss Myrtle, this is our best hope for saving the paper. We've got to move with the times. We've got to deliver what the people want."

"What people? Have you actually talked to real people?"

Sloan's face was hurt. "Of course I have."

"People who live in *Bradley*?"

Sloan looked away.

"See, that's where you're going wrong. You're communicating with journalists in other towns, right? Maybe think tank kinds of people who are trying to fix journalism. But you're not listening to the folks who actually *subscribe* to the paper," said Myrtle.

"Or unsubscribe," said Sloan glumly.

"Here's the thing. I've talked to a few readers and they've been adamantly against the direction in which the newspaper is heading. They love the folksy stuff. Give them Mabel's favorite recipe for tomato pie. Tell them about Jim's ham radio hobby. But for heaven's sake, keep out of the tabloid-style gossip," Myrtle said.

Sloan sighed. "I just don't know, Miss Myrtle."

"Trust me. Give it a try. Return to your old style of writing stories. Besides, I have some stuff I'm working on for you."

Now Sloan looked concerned. "What kind of stuff?"

"Nothing for you to worry about."

Sloan looked more worried than ever.

"Let's just say that it has something to do with your advertising. And there's something else I'm trying, too."

He was still backed against the door, still clutching the fast food bag. His expression was defensive. "All I want is what's good for the paper."

"Well then, you and I are on the same side," said Myrtle smoothly.

At that moment, Pasha decided to make herself known. She pranced up to Sloan and deposited the deceased rodent at his feet with a flourish.

Sloan squealed in response. "Where did that cat come from?"

Myrtle snorted. "Shouldn't you be more concerned about what the cat *caught*?"

Sloan paled. "I thought I heard rustlings along the edges of the back wall from time to time. But there's so much paper in the newsroom that I figured a draft was blowing it all around."

"I believe you've created the ultimate habitat for mice, Sloan. Lucky for you that my cat, Pasha, was bound and determined to get in here. I suppose she knew the kind of environment in here. And she is clearly an excellent mouser," said Myrtle proudly.

"What am I going to do about … that," asked Sloan, staring aghast at Pasha's deposit.

"You're going to thank Pasha profusely. It's what she

expects. And, if you're very lucky, she'll return for more hunting. Think of it—you might be able to rid yourself of an infestation for free! Perhaps a more appropriate thank-you would be a couple of cans of tuna or a container of cat treats. You could pick them up the next time you go out. If I know you're going to treat Pasha well, I could lease her to you to help you with your problem. But you need to let her back out before you lock up for the night. And you'll need to provide water and a litterbox," added Myrtle.

Sloan was staring at Pasha as if he wasn't sure if he'd rather have the cat or the mice.

Myrtle left the *Bradley Bugle* with a sense of accomplishment. She had the passwords for the social media accounts in her pocketbook. Sloan appeared to be *possibly* willing to back off from the lurid stories for the family newspaper. And she'd helped Pasha find entertainment.

Now she wanted to visit Mimsy. Since Mimsy had so kindly given her a casserole the last time, Myrtle figured she could return the favor. It would, after all, provide her with an excuse for visiting. And there *had* just been a family funeral that very morning. A casserole was practically required.

She supposed she should also see if Miles were up to visiting Mimsy, too. She'd missed her sidekick's input, along with his silent presence. And she thought that Miles had missed it, too.

Having a feeling that she really didn't have the ingredients to put any sort of casserole together, Myrtle stopped by the grocery store while she was in downtown. There weren't many people at the store, which suited Myrtle fine. She needed to remember what she had in her pantry and fridge and what type of recipe she could cook. This type of thinking required intense concentration on Myrtle's part and having Bradley residents ply her with chitchat wasn't going to help.

She had occasionally made a chicken casserole containing wild rice, green beans, and water chestnuts. One of the regular recipes on her rotation, it had the distinction of being the one that Red was most likely to eat while growing up. She thought again with vexation how annoying the day had been when he'd revealed that he'd fed many of his meals to their faithful dog, Sport. Even more vexing was the further revelation that his friends' parents had been feeding him meals to make up for the fact.

Myrtle decided that she did still have chicken in the freezer. She was positive she had French-style green beans, too. She found a can of water chestnuts, a box of wild rice mix, and—after a moment's hesitation—a jar of pimentos, which she believed was also part of the recipe.

Fortunately, she had completed her ingredient deliberations when a thin voice called out to her. "Miss Myrtle?"

Myrtle turned to see Poppy. She was wearing a stained top and was pushing a shopping buggy containing convenience items like boxed meal-makers, mac and cheese, toaster pastries, and frozen pizzas. Myrtle's stomach lurched just looking at them.

Poppy gave a trilling laugh. "And please excuse my appearance, Miss Myrtle. Someone spilled their lunch on me at the preschool."

"Hopefully a child?" asked Myrtle in concern.

Poppy laughed again. Her laughter was a nervous, high-pitched sound. "That's right. Although, maybe it would make a funnier story if it had been a coworker. There didn't seem to be any point in changing since I've got to get ready soon for waitressing."

Myrtle saw *plenty* of point in changing, but held her tongue. "Nice to see you, Poppy. I was just picking up some things to put together a casserole for Mimsy."

Poppy's face brightened. "Are you? That's very thoughtful. I know she'll enjoy it. She's been too busy to cook lately, what with planning and attending the funeral and going through Luella's effects and all."

"That's what friends are for, though, isn't it? To help out during a crisis." Myrtle paused for effect. "And you two have been friends for a long time, haven't you?"

Poppy gave a splotchy flush. "That's right. A very long time."

"And what a blessing that is," said Myrtle. "Many of my lifetime friends are sadly no longer with us."

Poppy seemed unsure how to react to this news. "Oh."

Myrtle said, "Were you friends in school? As long ago as that?"

Poppy rearranged a couple of boxes of instant food in her grocery cart. "Well, we were acquainted in school. , Mimsy and I."

"I'd imagine you were, as small as Bradley High School is. But you weren't in the same group?" asked Myrtle.

Poppy shook her head. "Not at the time. Mimsy was … well, she was a cheerleader for the football team and even the homecoming queen. And I … wasn't."

"No? What group did you belong to in high school?" asked Myrtle.

Poppy's flush grew a bit deeper. "I wasn't really in any groups at all. I think I must have been just trying to figure out who I was and how I fit into the whole scheme of things. I spent a lot of time by myself."

Myrtle could imagine that was the case. In fact, she could imagine that if it weren't for Mimsy's kindness, it would still *be* the case.

"Was Mimsy very different back then than she is now?" asked Myrtle. "Somehow I can't picture her as cheerleader and homecoming queen."

Poppy took a deep breath. "I don't think that maybe she was quite as understanding then as she is now. She cared a lot about her appearance and what other people thought and being in the right clique. She hung out with people who also cared what others thought." She shrugged. "I guess that's just the way high school is."

"It can be a rough time, can't it?" asked Myrtle softly.

Poppy's tensed muscles seemed to relax a little. "It can be. It was for me. Not so much for Mimsy, though." There was a tinge of bitterness to Poppy's words.

"Mimsy does seem to be one of the luckier ones, doesn't she?"

Poppy might have been holding back her true feelings about Mimsy at first. It certainly seemed that way to Myrtle as words started flowing quicker from Poppy's mouth.

"She is. She had an easy, fun time in school with lots of good friends and fun times. Then she married her high school sweetheart, and they've always gotten along great together. Mimsy hasn't really had to do any work—she just volunteers. She doesn't know what it's like to work two low-paying jobs that make your feet hurt by the end of the day. She's never been lonely. Her life has always been really comfortable." Poppy put a hand over her mouth as if trying to hold back any other words.

"What kind of work does her husband do again?" asked Myrtle.

Poppy was rather vague. "I think he does managerial work at the mill in Creighton. He does work from home a lot, I think. And then he does day-trading on the side. You know … like with stocks." She paused for a minute. "I guess I shouldn't be saying anything about either of them. Mimsy is my best friend now. People do change and get more mature when they get older, don't they?"

Sometimes. Myrtle had seen plenty who hadn't. They'd become more immature, as a matter of fact.

"And Mimsy isn't having things so easy now, is she? With Luella's death and all. Especially with the police checking into everything." Poppy waved a hand in the air.

"But you don't think Mimsy is responsible for Luella's death, do you? Or Alma's?"

"Of course not," said Poppy. But she looked away. "Mimsy would never do such a thing. Although the earring thing was pretty weird."

Myrtle looked curiously at Poppy. It almost seemed as if she *wanted* Mimsy to be a suspect. Could jealousy and resentfulness be behind it? Could Poppy have even taken things farther to make it appear that Mimsy was involved in the murders?

"Although there was something else that was weird. Besides Mimsy's earring, I mean. Florence. You know Florence, don't you?"

"I do indeed," said Myrtle. That harrowing car ride with Florence at the wheel was going to stick with her for a long while.

"The night that Alma died ... well, I saw something."

Myrtle frowned. "I thought you said that when you were coming back from waiting tables that you *didn't* see anyone."

Poppy looked away again. "Well, I was just so tired, you know? It's so exhausting waiting all those tables when I've already worked a full day with little kids."

Myrtle's eyes dropped again to the stained shirt.

"And then I have to be peppy and smiling at Geronimo's when I'm taking orders and so forth. I'm practically a zombie when I leave there. So I didn't immediately remember anything. But now that I've thought it over, I remember that I saw Florence outside. She was walking down the sidewalk."

Myrtle remembered that Estelle had also mentioned seeing Florence out late at night and that Florence had adamantly denied it. "You're sure it was Florence?"

Poppy gave a laugh that was more of a snort. "Well, of course I am. It was Florence, plain as day. The reason I remembered it is because I was concerned about her. I wondered if maybe she needed help or if maybe she'd gotten confused and was starting to wander—you know—that happens sometimes when people get dementia."

Myrtle said quickly, "But taking an evening stroll doesn't mean that someone has dementia. Seniors might want to stretch their legs. There's no law against it." Her tone was a mite more defensive than she'd intended.

Poppy's eyebrows rose in surprise. "Of course there's not. And if it had been *you*, Miss Myrtle, I wouldn't have thought twice about it."

"Why not?"

"Because you're so clearly *compos mentis* and because I've seen you walking late at night before. Or, I guess, very early in the morning. It's part of your routine. With Florence, it was outside her usual routine. Besides, she seems sort of scattered sometimes." Poppy stretched out her hands in front of her as if pleading her case.

Myrtle said, "True. All right. So you didn't stop and ask Florence what she was doing?"

"That's right. Oh, I thought about it. But as I was saying, I was super tired from Geronimo's, and on top of it all, Florence didn't look as if she were in any trouble."

"How *did* she look?"

"Furtive," said Poppy after a moment's hesitation.

Chapter Eighteen

Myrtle considered her conversation with Poppy as she walked back home with the small bag of groceries. She could feel the underlying resentment in her words. But Myrtle also got the impression that Poppy was proud of her friendship with Mimsy and grateful for it, too. Could Poppy possibly have both resentment and gratitude for Mimsy? Might her jealousy prompt her to do something that she regrets? Because Myrtle definitely also felt that sense of regret from her.

Myrtle walked up her front walk and set the bag down so that she could open her front door. As she did, Pasha bounded in front of her and into the house.

"Pasha! I didn't even know you were there," chided Myrtle. Then she frowned. "Can I check your mouth? You didn't bring any take-away bags home with you from the newsroom, did you?" She certainly hoped the end of her day would not involve trying to bribe Puddin to come by and dispose of a rodent for her.

Fortunately, Pasha didn't appear to have brought her own snacks. But whatever her hour in the newsroom had entailed, it seemed to have exhausted her. She curled up in a late-afternoon sunbeam and fell right asleep.

Myrtle went immediately to the kitchen. The whole point of the casserole was to keep Mimsy from having to cook supper tonight and it would be rather pointless if Myrtle didn't get it over to her in time. She quickly found her recipe card in the old metal box. It looked as if it had gone through battle, stained and bent from years of use.

Myrtle squinted at the card and then looked again at the rooster clock on her kitchen wall. She was going to have to hurry with this and take whatever shortcuts she could.

The recipe called for an oven temperature of 350 degrees so Myrtle preheated for 450 to make things go a bit faster. Then she started pulling the ingredients out. To her dismay and annoyance, she did *not* have either the chicken or the French-style green beans that she was so sure were at home. Rooting around in her pantry, however, she was able to put her hands on some canned tuna and a can of lima beans. She hesitated for a moment. No, tuna surely was bland enough to substitute. And limas were practically as bland as vegetables came.

The clock was ticking away, so Myrtle decided to go with her substitutions. She mixed the pimentos, the canned tuna, the wild rice, and the limas. The wild rice was uncooked, but Myrtle thought she remembered that it cooked fine with the juice from the canned veggie. If she added more water to the casserole it might be too soggy. And who wanted a soggy casserole?

Still a little worried about the potential blandness of the casserole, Myrtle added a generous portion of salt to the dish and popped it into the hot oven. She decided not to cover the dish, since time was of the essence and she really needed it cooked sooner rather than later. After her labors, she decided to sit in her living room for a while and read. Miles had gotten her to read *On the Beach* by Nevil Shute. He promised her that he would enjoy the dystopian tale but so far she had only been annoyed by one of the characters who appeared to be in denial that the apocalypse had taken place. She thought longingly of the *Little Men* book that she'd borrowed from Miles. Still, she was determined to force her way through *On the Beach*.

Thirty minutes later she was still annoyed with the book. But an interruption occurred with a light tap at the door. Miles stood on her front porch looking groggy. "Miles! Are you all right? You're not sick again, are you?"

Miles shook his head and walked in. "No, but I just woke up from a nap. I guess this virus must have taken more out of me than I thought."

"So why are you here? Why aren't you at home recovering from your nap?"

Miles said, "While I was napping, I had this very odd, very vivid dream that you were about to set out to do some more investigating. When I woke up, I felt as if I'd been left out of the process."

Myrtle felt herself flushing. She hadn't been planning on toting Miles to Mimsy's house with her, and that was a fact. If there was one thing that bothered her it was when someone else took credit for her own good deeds. Myrtle had taken the trouble to bake supper for poor Mimsy and Miles didn't need to horn in on her brownie points. Aloud she said, "You've been spending too much time with your cousin, Wanda. Clearly some of her prognosticating powers are rubbing off on you."

Miles winced. "I do wish you'd stop referring to her as my cousin. And I only want to come along, Myrtle. I'm your sidekick, after all."

"All right, you can come," said Myrtle ungraciously. "But just *absorb* everything, all right? I don't think you're in fit shape to really take part in an interrogation."

Miles's eyebrows shot up. "Is that what it's going to be? An interrogation of the bereaved?"

Myrtle said crossly, "Of course not. You've got me all out of sorts, Miles. But sure—feel free to come along."

"It sounds as if *you* could use a nap," said Miles.

Myrtle glared at him.

Miles said, "I also was wondering how things went with Sloan this afternoon. Did he decide to back off from the direction in which he's been taking the paper?"

"Well, he listened. But I'm not sure he was convinced. He thinks that the people I've been speaking with represent a very small portion of the town. The old portion. Fortunately, I was prepared for that attitude and I have some other tricks up my sleeve," said Myrtle.

"That's what I was wondering," said Miles. "Because a few minutes ago, when I was checking my phone after waking up, I noticed all kinds of alerts."

"Alerts? What—like severe weather alerts? Today?" Myrtle scowled at the sunlight still wafting in through the windows and covering the dozing Pasha. "Must mean a thunderstorm. Estelle should be excited. Wonder if she's chasing it."

"No, no. A notification kind of an alert. Doesn't your phone give you notifications?"

"Not if I don't want it to," said Myrtle with a sniff. "I don't want it to *presume*. I really just want the thing to let me make phone calls."

"Anyway, my phone tells me when people mention me on social media or when I have emails or whatnot," explained Miles.

"Sounds as if your phone thinks rather too highly of itself."

Miles was now studiously ignoring any interruptions. "I saw that I'd been mentioned on Facebook. So I pulled up the site and saw people had tagged me in a post. It seemed to have something to do with a contest and if you got other people to share the post, you got more entries or something? At any rate, the *Bradley Bugle* was all over the internet."

Myrtle beamed at him. "Really? Let me see that." She walked over to the desk across the small living room and sat down. Her pocketbook was on the top of the desk and she reached in and fumbled around until she found the tattered sticky note. Then she carefully logged into

Facebook.

Miles continued talking as she checked the *Bugle*'s profile page. "Did Sloan mention anything about his social media strategy? I have to say, this seems like a step in the right direction, but I was a little surprised that he'd try something like this campaign. Did he mention that he hired a publicist or a social media advisor to help him sort it all out?"

Then Miles gave a surprised yelp and Myrtle glanced over to see that Pasha had forsaken the sunbeam and had decided to scrutinize Miles in a very up close and personal way. From the vantage point of his lap. Miles eyed the black cat warily as she surveyed him. Finding Miles most disappointing, Pasha jumped back down again.

Myrtle turned back to the computer, distracted, still going from profile to profile and seeing all the mentions and the support that the newspaper was getting online.

Miles repeated his question about Sloan's strategy and Myrtle said, "Sloan has *no* strategy. He tends to be very mistrustful of social media because he believes so-called citizen journalists will end up putting him out of a job one day. They share news too, you know. I decided that the *Bugle* needs to actually use its Facebook and Twitter profiles. When I logged in, they hadn't been used for so long that they were starting to grow cobwebs in the corners."

Myrtle stopped talking for a moment to continue reading. Then she crowed, "Miles, everyone is saying just the right things! They all are supporting the *Bugle* and mentioning that they want the paper to be the way it *used* to be. And they're using the *hashtag*! Oh, this is very exciting."

Miles appeared to be still puzzling through Myrtle's previous statement. "So…you say that you *logged in*. Do you mean that Sloan has hired you on to help him sort out the social media for the newspaper?"

"No, I mean nothing of the sort," said Myrtle impatiently. "Sloan has one foot still stuck in the last century. As I said, he mistrusts the online world. Since he wasn't going to embrace it and he was going to continue making silly mistakes with our local newspaper—which is a treasure for the town—I needed to step in and work around him. Sloan unwisely had his social media passwords on a sticky note on his monitor and I took them."

"He won't make that mistake again," muttered Miles.

"That's how life lessons are learned," agreed Myrtle. "Although I'm sure the results of my clandestine operation will delight him."

Miles raised a skeptical eyebrow, but decided not to push the issue. Instead, he nodded his head to indicate the book on Myrtle's end table. "How is it going? *On the Beach*?"

"I declare, Miles, I can't imagine why this is one of your favorites. Are you sure I have the correct author and title? It's most unappealing at this point."

"Just stick with it," said Miles a little absently. Then he added, "Speaking of unappealing, what's that smell? I'm hoping I haven't been invited for dinner."

Myrtle gasped. "The casserole for poor Mimsy!" She hurried to the kitchen.

"Poor Mimsy indeed," muttered Miles as he followed her.

Myrtle hastily pulled out the casserole from the oven and studied it carefully. "Oh, it's fine."

Miles said, "What are those green, crunchy things?"

"Don't be deliberately obtuse, Miles. You know how it irritates me. Those are clearly lima beans."

"Those desiccated bits?" Miles sounded dubious.

"Of course they are. And I'll simply fish out the ones that are a bit overcooked," said Myrtle, pulling out a spoon.

"Will there be much casserole left once you do?" inquired Miles.

Myrtle narrowed her eyes.

Miles continued. "Is that *chicken* in the dish? Because it doesn't really *smell* like chicken. The aroma is quite distinctly different."

"It's tuna," said Myrtle, carefully removing a burned lima.

"But isn't this the chicken casserole that you usually cook?" asked Miles, peering over the side of the Pyrex.

"Yes. But we're allowed to be creative with our recipes, you know. Cooking is supposed to be an art form," said Myrtle.

Miles appeared to be trying very hard not to speak. Pasha gazed suspiciously at the casserole from the doorway.

"All right, well, that's done at least. But it's way too hot for me to carry over there. Let me just cover it with foil and we'll give it ten minutes to cool," said Myrtle.

"And turn the oven off," advised Miles. "Was *that* what the temperature was set to? No wonder it was scorched!"

Myrtle said, "It's so tedious when you're critical, Miles! Tell you what. While I'm covering this and we're waiting for it to cool, why don't you give me more tidbits for the social media updates."

Miles stared blankly at her. "Do I know any updates?"

"I'd imagine you do, if you can summon them to mind. I know how all the old biddies in town always corner you when you're shopping. You must know a lot about what's going on."

He sighed. "It's the truth. Let's see. Molly Tillis is thrilled to bits because she's going on her first cruise. I believe she's already told the whole town about it, but it still might be worthwhile to put online since she'd probably 'like' it and 'share' it some more."

"Exactly the kind of thing that Sloan *used* to put in the *Bugle*. And then someone like Molly, who has never left the town of Bradley, would buy up ten extra copies of the newspaper because it had her name in it and this trip. Okay, that's definitely going up." Myrtle walked back to her desk and Miles trailed behind, still thinking.

Miles snapped his fingers. "You know, I don't think Sloan has printed any hospital updates since this whole change-the-newspaper campaign started. And you know how people would always look forward to seeing the list of who was in the hospital."

"There are gobs of ghoulish people in this town," said Myrtle. "And Sloan isn't feeding the trolls. You're right. That list *has* to go in there. The only problem is that Sloan got the list by people calling the newsroom and reporting that they or their family member was in the hospital. And we don't have that list."

Miles said, "Sadly, I apparently *have* been spending too much time listening to the biddies. I believe I may have a fairly reliable current list. And then you can make an update saying to tag the *Bugle* or email if they're hospitalized. Do you have the newspaper's email password, too?"

"It was on the sticky. Silly Sloan." Myrtle spent a few minutes busily writing status updates on Facebook and Twitter. "This is genius, Miles. I think Sloan should pay us a huge bonus for saving the newspaper."

"Let's make sure your plan works, first," said Miles.

Myrtle glanced at her watch. "Okay, I think the casserole should be cool enough to take over there. Now remember, this is *my* casserole for Mimsy. You had nothing to do with it."

"I certainly didn't," agreed Miles calmly. "I'll be sure to reinforce that fact when we arrive. Since I'd hate to take any credit, of course. Although I likely will carry it for you…it's pretty heavy with all the rice in it. How did you think you were going to manage carrying it, holding a cane, and walking that distance?"

"It's not so far," said Myrtle.

"It is if you're carrying a casserole and a cane."

"I was going to use a tote bag and dangle it over my arm," said Myrtle breezily.

"This glass dish is extremely heavy, itself. Don't you want to transfer the casserole into something disposable so that Mimsy doesn't have to worry about returning it to you?" asked Miles.

"Of course not. The whole point is that I get to talk with Mimsy again and ask *more* questions. I'd only use a foil casserole container if I were genuinely trying to help," said Myrtle.

They walked out the front door and Pasha scampered out behind them.

Myrtle was about to lock the door when she heard Red call out from across the street. "Hold up, Mama! I'm going to need to be in your house."

Myrtle sighed and muttered to Miles, "This family togetherness is all getting rather tiresome."

Miles surveyed Red's front yard. "They still have backhoes over there. That's not a good sign."

"*None* of it is a good sign. I didn't realize how much I enjoyed being alone until I wasn't alone very often." As Red approached, Myrtle called out, "It's all yours, Red. How are things with the case coming along? Any new leads?"

Red gave her a wary glance as he walked up. "Hi, Miles. Mama, the case is coming along fine. No, I don't have any new leads. Do *you*? And I certainly hope the answer is no."

Myrtle said, "Why would I have leads when I'm not

even investigating?"

Red studied the bag that Miles carried. "Where are y'all off to, then?" There was a tinge of suspicion in his voice.

"Nowhere important. Just running by Mimsy's to drop off a casserole for her. Considering that the funeral was today and everything," said Myrtle.

Red nodded, still eyeing the bag. "Miles, did you have any input into this casserole?" He sounded hopeful.

Miles shook his head. "Not a bit."

"That's right," said Myrtle. "It was all my brainchild."

Red said under his breath, "That's what I was afraid of." Before Myrtle could lodge an indignant response, he said quickly, "Say, Mama, did you have anything to do with the newspaper campaign?"

Myrtle raised her eyebrows. "What campaign is that?"

"I noticed that the *Bradley Bugle*'s social media has really lit up. And then somebody put some poster board signs around town on the streetlights. They say '#SavetheBugle' and '#FreeBugle.' I was thinking that maybe you'd convinced Sloan to make some changes. I know you weren't happy with the direction the paper was going in," said Red.

"Its direction? You mean the fact that it was becoming an unproofed, unedited tabloid? Let's just say that I expressed my displeasure over it," said Myrtle. She wasn't ready to own up to her part in the social media thing. Maybe her hacking would actually be unlawful? She wasn't very good about keeping up with what was lawful and what wasn't. "But that's wonderful that people are being supportive about preserving the small-town feel of the paper."

Miles added, "I'm not very surprised that Sloan's changes have generated a movement. Folks can be very protective over their newspapers."

Red said, "I agree. I'm glad to have the paper back to normal or at least seemingly heading in that direction. But, 'movements' make me nervous, speaking solely as police chief. Oh, and Mama, thanks again for helping Elaine at the dealership today. Y'all picked a great van. I'll see y'all later. Tell Mimsy that Elaine and I said hi."

Which Myrtle did a few minutes later. Mimsy did seem pleased to see them. "Aren't y'all sweet? And wow … this is still warm. I can see we'll have this for supper. John was just saying a few minutes ago how hungry he was and I was just wondering if I'd have to pull some of the casseroles out of the freezer. So, so sweet."

Myrtle beamed.

Miles said quickly, "Actually, it's *Myrtle* being sweet. I can't take responsibility for the casserole."

Myrtle gave him a suspicious sidelong look. He grinned innocently at her.

"Well, thank you, Myrtle. That was really kind of you. And I so appreciated your being at the funeral this morning."

"Of *course* I attended. And it was such a nice turnout for Luella," said Myrtle.

Miles was now looking uncomfortable. "I'd have been there myself this morning, except I was still a bit peaked. It's amazing the difference a few hours can make. I'm so much better now than I was earlier."

Mimsy smiled at him. "That's kind of you, Miles, and I'm happy to hear you're better." She paused. "Could y'all excuse me for just one minute? I'm going to let John know there's supper out here for him and I've also got to pull some jeans out of the dryer before I'm not able to wear them anymore!" She gave an easy laugh and walked to the back.

Miles glanced nervously at the casserole.

"For heaven's sake, Miles. It's a chicken casserole, not

a bomb."

"It's a *tuna* casserole, remember?" Miles shifted uneasily. "You don't think they're going to invite us to eat with them, do you?"

"We'll tell them we have something else to do," said Myrtle. "That's very sensitive of you to try to spare them from having to entertain on such a trying day."

Miles's gaze returned to the casserole.

Chapter Nineteen

John Kessler walked into the kitchen. He'd always reminded Myrtle of a stork with his long neck and tall, thin frame. He wore glasses with black frames and had a kind smile. He reached out to shake their hands but Miles shook his head, "I'll refrain from the handshake since I've recently been ill."

Myrtle said, "Although he's been using hand sanitizer every five minutes. I don't believe you can find a more germ-free handshake anywhere."

"I appreciate the heads-up, though," said John. "That's probably the last thing we need over here—a virus."

Myrtle clucked. "You've both have had a hard time, haven't you?"

"It hasn't been easy. It would be better if the police would leave Mimsy alone." John stopped short and shook his head. "I'm sorry. I forgot for a second I was talking to the police chief's mother."

"Believe me, no offence taken. There are plenty of times when I'm mad at him, too," said Myrtle.

"The thing is that Mimsy had nothing to do with all of this. She was *very* fond of Luella and terribly upset about her demise. And this other lady? I'm sorry; I don't know her very well." John gave Myrtle and Miles a questioning look.

"Alma," supplied Miles.

"That's right. Anyway, Mimsy's been nothing but helpful to Alma in the past. Always brought her fresh vegetables from our garden because she thought she could use them. Things like that," said John.

"Besides," said Myrtle, "I suppose you're her alibi, aren't you? Since Alma's murder happened so late at night."

John said, "Unfortunately, I'm not. I'm just sort of a character witness. I think that's one reason why the police are still considering Mimsy a suspect—because I was out of town that night. I was interviewing for a job position. Mimsy thinks someone might be trying to set her up … between Mimsy's earring planted at the crime scene and the fact that I wasn't at home to provide her with an alibi. It's almost like someone planned it that way."

Miles eyes widened in alarm as John Kessler pulled a serving spoon out of a drawer, uncovered the casserole, and scooped out a large portion onto a plate.

"Oh, are you considering a position out of town?" asked Myrtle.

John got a fork out of the drawer. "I'm considering any position, anywhere. Management jobs aren't easy to find and I was downsized some time ago." He gestured to the casserole. "Won't the two of you join us? I can set the table and we can all enjoy this."

Miles made a strangled sound. Myrtle scowled at him and then said politely to John, "Thanks, but we brought it for you. Miles isn't completely a hundred-percent well yet."

Miles, as a matter of fact was starting to look as if his health were rapidly regressing. He was pale and rather haggard looking as he stared at John's plate in horrified fascination.

Myrtle gave him an irritated look. "For heaven's sake, sit down, Miles. You're starting to look like Frankenstein's monster."

Miles sank into a chair.

John put a substantial forkful of casserole in his mouth and then stopped short. He shifted the food around in his mouth, eyes growing bigger. Then he grabbed a nearby water bottle, unscrewed the top, and quickly washed down the food with a large amount of water.

It was then that Mimsy returned. "Sorry about that. Oh, John, did you start supper without me? Did you ask our guests if they wanted to join us?" She moved over to the cabinets to pull a plate out.

John said quickly, "I did ask, but they can't join us. And Mimsy, I'm not as hungry as I thought. I … ah, I think I'll enjoy this sometime later. Whenever you eat."

"I'm about to eat right now," said Mimsy, looking at John in surprise. "That's why I'm getting a plate out."

John said, "But you won't be able to eat this darling." He seemed to be trying to communicate something to Mimsy with his eyes, but she didn't appear to be picking up on it.

"Why ever not?"

"Don't you want to wait and eat until after our guests have gone?" John's voice had a note of pleading in it.

"I don't think they mind. I'm hungrier than I thought I was. It's been a busy day," said Mimsy.

Myrtle said, "Of course we don't mind."

John said urgently, "But Mimsy, you should really eat something else. Miss Myrtle was kind to bring food, but she didn't know about your food allergies."

Mimsy put her hands on her hips. "*What* food allergies?"

Miles made a sound that might have been a muffled, hysterical laugh.

John said slowly, "To…lima beans."

"Lima beans! No one's allergic to lima beans, silly." Mimsy gave her husband an affectionate smile.

Miles said, "Perhaps it *would* be better if you wait. My stomach is still sort of upset and who knows what the sight and sound of food might do to me."

Myrtle again studied him suspiciously. But indeed, Miles didn't appear at all well.

Mimsy seemed confused but obediently put down the plate. She abruptly changed the subject. "Myrtle, tell me what you've heard about the investigation. Does Red have any leads?"

"Unfortunately, my son is strangely opposed to sharing information about cases with me. It's a tendency I've been trying unsuccessfully to break him of."

Mimsy's face, which had been hopeful, fell. "Oh dear. I'm sorry to hear that. Not that I wish anything bad on someone else, but whoever is responsible for these terrible crimes does need to be brought to justice. And I've been so frightened by the attention on me. As a suspect."

Myrtle said, "It hasn't settled down, then? The attention on you?"

"Unfortunately not. It's because of that silly earring." Mimsy looked baffled. "I can't for the life of me figure out how one of my earrings ended up over at poor Alma's house."

Miles cleared his throat. "John was saying that you helped Alma out quite a bit. Alma always seemed a bit proud to me. You never had any problems getting her to accept your produce?"

"At first she resisted. But then I kept telling her that we had so *much* produce that we were going to have to throw it away and that John and I hated doing that. That made her accept it a lot easier. It was as if *she* were doing *us* a favor."

"Maybe your earring fell out while you were helping her? Don't you think during one of those visits to Alma's house that you might have had an earring fall out?" asked Myrtle.

"It *could* have happened. But it *didn't* happen. That's because I know when I lost that earring. It was the night of the Bunco party, Miss Myrtle," said Mimsy.

Myrtle and Miles stared at each other and at Mimsy. It sounded as if someone were trying to set Mimsy up. Perhaps the hapless Poppy?

"So this is the same earring that you'd mentioned earlier was missing? While you were at my house?" asked Myrtle.

Mimsy said, "That's right. I mentioned it in passing at Bunco, but naturally, it was overshadowed by the tragic events that night. I was so upset when we learned of Luella's death that I immediately forgot about my earring."

Miles looked confused. "So … the earring fell out? They do that?"

John said, "Exactly what I'd been wondering, Miles."

"They can fall out. This particular set of earrings is bad about falling out. And that earring didn't have a back on it," said Mimsy. "Anyway, I'd noticed it was missing fairly early on. But I didn't have a chance to look for it because it was then that you'd found Luella, Miss Myrtle."

Myrtle said, "So anyone seeing your earring at the party could have quickly put it in their pocket for later."

They were quiet for a moment. Then Mimsy said sadly, "Yes, I suppose that's true. They'd have to have been thinking ahead, of course. They'd have to plan to use the earring to make me look guilty. And how would they have known that they would need to murder Alma?"

John said, "Unless murdering Alma was part of the plan all along."

"I can't imagine that it was," said Myrtle thoughtfully. "No, I think someone saw an opportunity and grabbed it. The earring represented a sort of insurance policy, maybe. Against any future problems."

Mimsy slumped. She looked so devastated by the thought that Miles quickly came to the rescue with another change of subject. "Mimsy, it was very kind of you to help

Alma out. I'm sure she must have really appreciated it."

"I think she did. That's not why I did it, of course. But there's so much need, even in a small community like ours," said Mimsy.

John said, "Sort of like with Estelle, right? Aren't you trying to give her a hand? Although perhaps *we're* the ones who need a hand," he muttered.

Mimsy hesitated. "Well, I hate to bring up things like that because I don't want Estelle to be talked about. I know she'd hate that. But I know Miss Myrtle and Miles won't say anything." It was more of a question than a statement.

Myrtle made a zipping motion over her mouth. "My lips are sealed," she said.

Miles nodded in agreement.

"Well, I saw Estelle at the Piggly Wiggly grocery store customer service desk, filling out a long sheet of paper. And sort of dressed up," said Mimsy.

"Dressed up? Estelle?" asked Myrtle. Estelle hadn't even dressed up for the funeral that day.

"Sort of. In a skirt, at any rate. She must have seen me and been embarrassed or something because she turned away a little more. I went over to talk to her, though," said Mimsy.

"Was she filling out an application for employment?" asked Miles.

"She was. She said that she wasn't getting any traction with the storm chasing. Estelle said it was her one true love, but that a combination of things, starting with being turned down for the bank loan, meant that she could no longer do it full time. She was trying to get hours at the grocery store so that maybe she could still do some storm chasing on the side. But she said it would be tough because the whole point was that she had to *chase* the storms … going out of town long distances and gas was expensive." Mimsy shook her head.

Myrtle and Miles shared a look. Estelle certainly hadn't seemed to be swimming in money when they'd visited her.

John said, "So Mimsy is now putting Estelle on the free-produce list since Alma no longer needs to take advantage of it."

"Very, very sweet of you," said Myrtle. She paused. What she wanted now were Mimsy's thoughts on Poppy and whether Poppy could possibly be resentful enough of Mimsy's success that she'd actually set her friend up. But she had a feeling that Mimsy might be protective of her friend. "I did have one question for you, Mimsy. It was about Poppy, actually."

John snorted and Mimsy gave him a reproachful look. "What about Poppy, Miss Myrtle?" she asked.

John jumped in. "I'm sorry for my reaction. Poppy can be very … sweet."

"It was nice of her to bring us food from the diner," reminded Mimsy, loyally.

"That's very true. The only problem I have, and don't pretend you don't see it too, Mimsy, is that Poppy is clearly very envious of our lives. She doesn't see that we have struggles, too … she only sees what she wants to see."

Mimsy looked down at her shoes. "I suppose that's true. She never used to seem so … well, envious. I know she's having such a hard time, though. So *many* people are. I guess she really can't help it."

Myrtle carefully asked, "But do you think that Poppy *might* have acted out of jealousy? Could she possibly have taken your earring and left it at Alma's house?"

Mimsy looked shocked, mouth dropping open. "She couldn't. Not Poppy." But her eyes displayed doubt.

"And now, I really think Myrtle and I should leave so that you two can eat," said Miles, staring rather anxiously at the casserole dish still sitting ominously on the countertop.

"Thanks again, y'all," said Mimsy. Then she snapped her fingers. "I almost forgot. Tippy Chambers ran by right before you came. She was dropping by a frozen casserole, but she also mentioned that there was a new campaign afoot. She'd seen something on Facebook about the newspaper and got the brainchild to help try to get it back on track. Tippy is putting posters up with #SavetheBugle on them around town and she's started a Facebook page for people to say something supportive or scan in their favorite *Bradley Bugle* stories … you know … the ones they clipped and stuck in a scrapbook or something."

"Is that so?" asked Myrtle, beaming.

"I figured you should know, since you've been so involved with the newspaper," said Mimsy. She continued in a musing voice, "I'm planning on putting some posters out tomorrow. And I hope it helps. I can't handle any more stories about celebrities and aliens."

Miles and Myrtle were quiet on their walk back. The only sound was of Miles's intermittent yawns.

He apologized after the last one. "I think I've probably done too much today."

Myrtle nodded. "It's easy to overdo it when you're coming off an illness. You're wanting to get back into the swing of things, but you need to ease into it more." She paused. "How did Puddin do? With the housecleaning today?"

Miles gave Myrtle a sidelong glance. "My house is spotless."

Myrtle gritted her teeth. "That Puddin. Whenever she cleans anyone *else*'s house, she always does a better job."

"Maybe it's because no one was there," said Miles. "She wasn't distracted and she wasn't tempted to talk. She just got to it and finished her work."

"I'd like to think that's the case. But the last time I left her a key and allowed her to clean while I wasn't home, I returned to a messy house and Puddin on my sofa with a lemonade watching *Tomorrow's Promise*," said Myrtle.

"One day, I've often thought, I'm going to be investigating the case of a murdered Puddin," murmured Miles.

"If it weren't that she and Dusty were a package deal, I'd get rid of her for sure," said Myrtle fervently. "By now I know a little something about murder."

The next morning, Myrtle was up very early. She'd like to have said that she was up early to take on her day and formulate a plan of attack for the case, but the truth was that she had completely run out of laundry. It seemed that every time in the last few days that she had gotten a load together, Elaine had apologetically shown up with either Red's uniform or some of little Jack's soiled outfits. Naturally, Myrtle had insisted that Elaine should go first. Then, Myrtle had promptly forgotten about her own clothes by the time the washer and dryer were free.

So now, she was down to a rather disreputable looking nightgown with a torn seam and a tracksuit that a Red had inexplicably given her for the previous Christmas. The tracksuit was made from some sort of nylon material and was an unflattering shade of pink. Myrtle rarely wore pink anyway, finding that people were even more inclined to treat her like an infant when she wore it. If she did wear pink, it was the very lightest of shades … more white with a trace of pink.

Myrtle had been able to grimace a smile and pretend to be pleased when she'd opened the present. Elaine had just winced, but not said a word since she was simply happy not to have to do Red's Christmas shopping for him. Red, probably to be even more annoying, had continued to ask her when she was going to wear her tracksuit.

"I'm saving it for a special occasion," she'd told him.

"But Mama, it's supposed to be an *everyday* garment. It's easy-care and easy-wear. That's what the clerk at the store told me. And you won't believe what I bought it for. It was a real steal."

"Is that right?" asked Myrtle. She could only imagine. Perhaps the store had even paid Red to take it off their hands.

So today would mark the inaugural wearing of the tracksuit. And Myrtle had absolutely no intention of leaving her house while wearing the thing. It was hardly flattering and the color was vile on her.

After making this decision, Myrtle took a deep, cleansing breath. She wanted a peaceful, positive start to her day since it was very distressing to have no clean clothes. Occasionally, Myrtle *might have* allowed a getting-off-on-the-wrong-foot experience to wreck her entire day. She had no intention of letting that happen on this bright and sunny morning. No, today would go smoothly.

This happy thought and peaceful reverie was interrupted by some sort of screeching engine, a breaking noise, and someone vehemently cussing in her front yard. "What in heaven's name?" hissed Myrtle. A few seconds later, she'd already broken her promise not to step outside her house wearing the tracksuit as she hurried out, cane in hand.

Dusty was outside. He had a pair of cheap sunglasses pushed up on top of his head, a cigarette dangling out of the corner of his mouth and was saying rude things to one of her gnomes.

Chapter Twenty

"Dusty! Have you lost your mind? What's all the ruckus about?" Myrtle brandished her cane at him as his dire imprecations continued.

"Yer gnome! It bit my weed trimmer!" howled Dusty.

"What did you do to my gnome?" demanded Myrtle.

"What did *I* do?" Dusty scowled at her.

"Yes! Because you're the one with the power tool. The poor gnomes are completely defenseless." She peered closer. "That's my 'gone fishing' gnome! One of my favorites."

Dusty said, "Why's it got a rope hangin' off it? Killed off my trimmer!"

"It's supposed to be a fishing line, Dusty. It's hanging from the little guy's pole. Haven't you ever gone fishing?" asked Myrtle.

"Not with no rope, I ain't."

"Well the manufacturers couldn't very well use fishing line or it wouldn't be durable," said Myrtle.

"It done got wound up in my string trimmer line!" croaked Dusty, glowering at the offending gnome. "Now it won't start up none."

"I'm much more concerned about my damaged property," said Myrtle icily. "The gnome doesn't make sense anymore with the rope missing."

"An' my string trimmer don't make no sense without being able to run!" Dusty threw the equipment on the ground where it hit another gnome.

Myrtle glared at him through narrowed eyes. She was

about to debate who was the more injured party in this accident when Puddin loped by her carrying a notebook.

"Puddin? Did we plan for you to be here today?" asked Myrtle, frowning.

"Got bizness with you, Miz Myrtle," said Puddin, sauntering into her house.

Myrtle hurried to follow her. Besides, she was just realizing she was standing out in broad daylight with the hideous tracksuit on and would likely have her fashion transgression discovered soon if she remained.

"Wait," yelled Dusty as Myrtle walked away. "What about my string trimmer? Can't whack no weeds when it's broke!"

"When you figure out how to fix my gnome, I will figure out how to fix your trimmer," said Myrtle.

There was more cussing as Myrtle sailed through the front door and into her house.

Puddin guffawed. "Snazzy jumpsuit you got there, Miz Myrtle."

Myrtle glared at her. "It's a tracksuit, not a jumpsuit. Jumpsuits are for Elvis."

Puddin looked sadly at her. "Miss that Elvis. He sure was pretty. Need to get to Graceland one day."

"Let's leave your Graceland pilgrimage for another day. Tell me what you're prattling on about with this 'business' of yours."

"I'm looking for a payoff," said Puddin, attempting to look ominous.

Myrtle could only assume that Puddin had been watching too many Mafia movies. "Don't you mean a payout, Puddin? I think payoffs are for mortgages and car loans. And what have you done to deserve one? Did you find any useful information for me?"

Puddin glared at her. "I'd have had more if I hadn't gone to clean for Mr. Miles!"

"Yes, I know all about your cleaning stint for Mr. Miles … gleaming surfaces and all. I can't imagine for the life of me why you don't clean like that over here," said Myrtle.

Now Puddin appeared eager to get off of the subject of her clean-up at Miles's house. "Maybe I could persuade you somehow to give me the payoff. Payout. Thing."

Myrtle put her hands on her hips, which wasn't even all that easy to do with a cane in one's hand. "Are you clumsily attempting to blackmail me, Puddin? Because you, of all people, should know that's fundamentally impossible. I'm a paragon of virtue. What would you choose to release about me…that I enjoy a glass of sherry once a week? That I take a baby aspirin every day?"

Puddin gave her a sullen look and tried to backtrack. "That's not what I meant, Miz Myrtle. Touchy, aren't you?"

"Well, I was just wondering if my mild-mannered housekeeper had been hanging out with gangsters lately," said Myrtle.

"No, what I meant was that maybe I have more information for you. Maybe you'll find it useful enough to pay me for. You see, I heard that Miz Estelle had hit hard times. Not chasing storms no more. Going to have to work at the grocery. Maybe she got mad at Miz Luella for not giving her that bank loan," said Puddin. "And I hear Miz Mimsy is helping her out, since she's got a garden and all. And now Miz Mimsy is all rich and everything."

Myrtle picked through Puddin's words. "Well, you've basically just verified something I heard earlier. So you haven't presented me with any *new* information, although you've helped me fact-check what I already understood to be true. Although, perhaps you're even hearing it from the same source."

Puddin just squinted at her, trying to follow along. "So

I get the payoff?" she demanded.

"Puddin, what's going on with you and money lately? I've never known you to be quite so greedy."

Puddin blew out a sigh. "Dusty's birthday. Trying to get him something decent."

Myrtle nodded. "I see." She paused. "What kinds of things does Dusty like?"

Puddin shrugged. "Yard equipment. The TV. That's about it."

"It's not a lot to go on, is it? Although I guess a new string trimmer might be something he'd appreciate, since he's so ballistic over this one. How much do those things run?" asked Myrtle.

Puddin brightened. "That's true. He wanted a new one even before this one broke. Says he wants a 4 cycle and not a 2 cycle."

"I'm assuming that means more power. So how much would that run us?" asked Myrtle. She had a modest amount of money put aside for a rainy day.

"Reckon it might run around three hundred."

"Three hundred *dollars*?" gasped Myrtle. That wouldn't be a rainy day. That would be a tsunami. "I don't have that kind of money lying around to give to people for payouts. I thought you were going to say seventy-five dollars or something."

Puddin slumped. "Guess you're poor."

"I guess I am!"

"Maybe a gift card to the hardware store then," said Puddin helpfully.

"Is this a *significant* birthday, Puddin?"

Puddin narrowed her eyes. "What do you mean?"

"How old is Dusty turning?"

Puddin said, "This is his sixty-fifth. In a week."

He was certainly getting up there. Myrtle contemplated her options. She did always want to keep Dusty happy. The other options for alternate yardmen were not only too expensive for her and her retired teacher income, but they were also not as willing to trim the grass around her gnomes. One thing was for sure—Red had a vested interest in keeping Myrtle's yardman happy. Because if there were no Dusty, Red would be his most-likely replacement.

"Okay. I can't do anything today. But it's possible I might be able to piece something together very soon." If Red isn't completely tapped out with his plumbing emergency and car shopping. "I just need a little time."

Puddin shook her head. "He's really goin' to be fussin' over this broke trimmer."

"I'll come up with something to tell him. I'll tell him that Red is great at fixing yard equipment or something. That I'll get Red to take care of it if he'll just drop off the trimmer with me," said Myrtle.

"Mr. Red fixes yard equipment?" Puddin's voice was dubious.

"Well, not exactly. That is, he knows how to replace the string in them. But that's not important … it's just a way to buy time for me to figure something out," said Myrtle.

They were interrupted by Dusty sticking his head through the door. "I done fixed it."

"What?" asked Myrtle, a bit startled. "The trimmer, you mean?"

"No, the gnome," said Dusty. "I had something on my truck." He motioned her outside.

When Myrtle walked into her front yard, she saw that her "gone fishing" gnome now had a duct-taped bit of twine attached to his hand. She stared at it and then at Dusty. "Fixed? This is fixed?"

"Course it is," said Dusty scornfully. "Got a fishin' line and everything."

"But it's duct-taped!"

"You was missin' a duct-taped gnome," said Dusty simply. "This is the South."

"He's kinda cute like that," muttered Puddin.

Myrtle closed her eyes briefly and found when she opened them again that she was feeling much calmer. "You're probably right," she said. "I didn't have any duct tape representation here. Now we're good."

Dusty shook his head. "No we're not. What about my trimmer?"

"If you'll leave it with me, I can guarantee that Red will fix it for you," said Myrtle.

Dusty's eyes were suspicious. "Didn't know that Red was good with yard equipment."

"He's the best," said Myrtle simply. If buying replacement equipment counted.

Dusty was opening his mouth to continue questioning her when there was a dry cough behind them. It was Miles.

"Myrtle," he said, regarding her with amusement, "you look so fetching."

Myrtle scowled at him. "Desperate times call for desperate measures. I'm about to hole up back inside if we've resolved this particular crisis."

Puddin said thoughtfully, "You know, Miz Myrtle, I sorta think I might like to get one of them."

"One of them, I mean, one of *those* what?" asked Myrtle.

"One of them jumpsuits. Where'd you get it?"

Myrtle stared at her. "You were just laughing at me in it only a few minutes ago and now you want to buy one?"

"I was laughin' at *you* in it. But I kinda think I might look good in it. Might go with my hair." Puddin gestured to the lank, dirty-blonde hair that was falling in her face.

Miles's eyes were full of merriment.

Myrtle sighed. "I don't know … Red bought it for me for Christmas. He probably shopped at Brogan's. I can't imagine he'd have gone anywhere else. But I don't know if there are any left. It sounded as if Red picked it up on clearance."

Miles said softly, "Oh, I bet there are some left."

Puddin nodded, still looking at the tracksuit in an accessing way. "I'll have to run by there later."

It irritated Myrtle to think that she and Puddin might somehow end up looking like twins.

A truck pulled up across the street at what was becoming Red's Construction Site. Their front door opened and Myrtle heard Red's voice. "I have to get inside," hissed Myrtle. She grabbed onto Miles's arm and they scurried inside.

"I don't totally understand why we did that, but I don't think Red saw us," said Miles. He pushed his glasses up his nose and peered out one of Myrtle's windows. "He seems absorbed in the fact that someone apparently is indicating more digging to be done."

Myrtle rubbed her forehead as a thought occurred to her. "You know what? He's probably going to come right over here. He likely is going to put his clothes in a bag and come over for a shower. That's what he's done *every* day since this started." She raised her head for a moment and listened. "That huge load of laundry is nowhere near being finished, either."

Miles said, "Did I miss something? Why are you hiding from Red?"

"He gave me this tracksuit and I think he's *finally* forgotten about it. If he sees me in it, he's going to be so pleased that I'm going to have to wear the thing more often. The only reason I have it on is because *all* of my clothes need washing now," said Myrtle.

"You don't have *anything* else?"

"Not unless I want to wear a Halloween costume or a bathing suit," said Myrtle.

The phone rang and Myrtle hurried to answer it as Miles walked into the kitchen and poured himself a cup of coffee.

"Sloan?" Myrtle looked at Miles and made a face at him. She wasn't ready to be chastised for her part in the #SaveTheBugle campaign. But apparently, Sloan had other things on his mind.

"Do you think I could run by and bring your cat with me to the *Bugle*, Miss Myrtle?" he asked in an anxious voice. "She's quite the mouser. And now that I know the mice are in here, that's all I seem to hear. Rustling in the corners." He sounded quite disturbed.

"Oh, I don't think Pasha would like that, Sloan. She's not much of a fan of car rides. And I'm pretty sure she wouldn't willingly go with you to the newspaper, either. If she's not willing, there's no way you can make her … she *is* feral," reminded Myrtle.

Now Sloan sounded pitiful. "Can you think of a way to get her here, Miss Myrtle? I did call an exterminator, but the fee would be too high and the *Bugle* doesn't have the budget to handle it. Pasha did a really good job. And I've been having kind of a rough last twenty-four hours."

Myrtle didn't really want details about what made his last twenty-four hours so rough. She had a feeling it had something to do with his likely confusion over the social media campaign. But one thing she knew—leaving her house before Red came over would be a good tactic. Maybe she could throw a coat over herself for her walk downtown. "I think I could probably persuade Pasha to follow me to the office. This is the time of day she's usually hunting in my backyard. I'll pull treats out."

Sloan said, "Don't pull out too many or she won't be hungry enough to hunt!"

"I don't think that will be a problem. Okay, I'll see you in a few minutes," said Myrtle and hung up.

Miles looked nervous. "Mice in the newsroom? I never did care for the thought of the little varmints running around."

"That's because you're so fastidious. Any self-respecting mouse wouldn't dream of invading your house … there wouldn't be any crumbs to eat. Yes, Pasha was unfortunately impressive yesterday and eliminated part of Sloan's mouse problem. Now he wants her back. Want to go with me to the *Bugle*?"

Miles didn't appear reassured by Myrtle's words. "I think I'll pass. What else do you have on tap for today and I'll try to catch up with you then?"

"Laundry. And laundry. And I probably want to follow up with Florence to find out why she was wandering around the night Alma died. Although she'll probably deny it, as she did earlier," said Myrtle.

"I'll go along with you when you talk to her," said Miles. "I'm feeling a little shortchanged as a sidekick this time. That virus really knocked me for a loop."

"I'll let you know," said Myrtle. She sighed. "And the laundry is still running so I can't even put anything in the dryer before I leave. I need to rush out of here before Red shows up."

She walked to her coat closet and found the longest coat she could find. It was, unfortunately, wool, which might not be the most comfortable choice for such a warm day.

Miles crinkled his forehead. "I know you're wanting to cover up the tracksuit, but are you sure that a wool coat is wise? You might have a heat stroke out on the street."

Myrtle waved him away. "I'll be fine. I may not look fashionable or weather appropriate, but at least I won't be funny looking."

"So you say," murmured Miles.

When Miles left for home, Myrtle rooted around under

her kitchen sink for the cat treats. Finding them, she gave them a quick shake. "Kitty, kitty?" she called.

Pasha immediately jumped up from the backyard into her kitchen window, eyes gleaming. "Want to go for a walk, Pasha?" asked Myrtle in as polite a voice as she could muster. It always paid to be deferential to cats, Myrtle thought.

Pasha, thankfully, agreed that she would stroll along beside Myrtle as she walked to downtown Bradley. Myrtle gave her a treat from time to time. Halfway there, she turned around briefly to see Red's figure hurrying across to her house. It had been a close call.

She glanced down at the cat, which was moving steadily beside her, tail held high. She hoped Pasha would enjoy her hunting expedition. Who knows? Pasha may not be in the mood, though, despite the fact Myrtle had assured Sloan that she would be. Everyone knows that you can't force a cat to do anything it doesn't want to do.

A car pulled up alongside them. Florence rolled down the window and said, "Myrtle, do you need a ride?" She squinted at Myrtle's outfit. "And—are you feeling all right? Isn't it very hot for a wool coat?"

Myrtle suppressed a shudder. No, she thought she'd pass on another ride with Florence. In fact, she didn't feel all that safe standing on the sidewalk with Florence around. "It's only a wool blend," said Myrtle. "And I've got my cat with me so, no thanks." She paused. "I know you're worried about your driving, Florence. Or, at least, you're worried that your daughter might take your keys away."

Florence beamed at her. "But the most amazing thing has happened, Myrtle. An answer to a prayer."

Myrtle frowned. "What was the answer to a prayer?"

"Puddin. She cleans for you, too, doesn't she? What a sweet woman!"

"Puddin? Sweet?" Myrtle stared at Florence. Perhaps

she was more far gone than Myrtle had suspected.

"Yes. She was cleaning for me recently and was such a comfort the day Luella threatened to call my daughter and report my driving. I was so distraught. Then, this morning, Puddin offered to drive me to see my friend every day. She'll drop me off and pick me up at an assigned time…and that time might be dependent on her cleaning schedule. You can't imagine my relief!" Florence beamed. "I think I drive fine around town…well, most of the time. But I'm a little sketchy when driving longer distances."

Myrtle knew Puddin was no saint. And she remembered Puddin's recent interest in "payoffs". "So I suppose there is some sort of remuneration involved? For Puddin driving you?"

"Oh, certainly. Gas and wear and tear on Puddin's car, naturally. And then I insisted on paying her a daily stipend. It's worth every penny," said Florence, gratitude laced through her voice.

Myrtle wondered how Puddin's new driving arrangement would impact Myrtle's ability to schedule her to clean. She sighed. But it seemed as though it was something that would work out well for both Puddin *and* Florence. And perhaps the sidewalks would be a bit safer without Florence driving as often.

"That's wonderful, Florence. I'm so happy that worked out for you," said Myrtle.

Pasha swished her tail as she spotted a squirrel across the street. She gazed at it through slitted eyes.

"Before you head out, there is one thing you can do for me, Florence." Myrtle knew that Miles had wanted to be in on her interview of Florence, but this was too good of an opportunity to pass up. "I was visiting with a few folks and I heard a few things. For one, I heard that many years ago Mimsy had been dating a favorite nephew of yours and you felt that she might have been involved in his accidental death."

Florence blinked at her. "Goodness! That *is* old news. What are people saying?"

Pasha had redirected her attention to a large black ant on the sidewalk. She deftly killed it with a powerful paw, causing it to fall apart in more than one section. She swiftly ate it and looked at Myrtle as if to say that she could provide her own treats.

Myrtle pulled her gaze away from the cat. Hopefully the feline wouldn't concentrate on Florence next. She seemed to be in a feisty mood. "I believe that the idea is that someone may be setting Mimsy up for Luella's death. That perhaps it would have been a way for you to avenge your nephew's death."

Florence gave a dry laugh. "His death was decades ago. I'd have to be a very petty person to exact revenge at this point. After all these years of volunteering with Mimsy and going to church barbeques with her?" She shook her head. But then her expression was reminiscent. "Did I ever tell you about Denny? He was such a sweet boy. He'd always walk by my house on his way to school and toss my paper on my porch from the driveway. He'd take me out to lunch and we'd have such laughs together!" Her blue eyes were wistful.

"Something else folks are saying," interrupted Myrtle, "is that you *were* out the night that Alma died. Although I know you say you weren't."

Florence looked directly at Myrtle now. "I was out. I couldn't sleep. This horrible restlessness had come over me and I felt like I needed to walk. Do you ever lie in bed and your mind races so fast that you can't possibly sleep?"

"No," answered Myrtle truthfully. "And that's because I don't ever lie in bed when that happens. I get right up and start doing housework or go visit Miles. Miles is usually awake at night, too."

"Well, that's what happened. I was thinking about my friend … the one who I met playing bridge. I'm on my way to visit him now, actually. I started thinking about how awful it would be if my daughter moved me away from here or if she insisted I stop driving. So, I got up after a while of tossing and turning. I put some clothes on. I took a walk. I did see headlights a couple of times, which made me feel worried—like someone would think I was demented or something for walking so late."

Maybe that was the basis of the "furtive" behavior that Poppy reported, reflected Myrtle.

"When I heard what happened with Alma, I was worried that someone might think that's why I was walking near Alma's house. Because the police were talking to me about Luella's death, you know. I thought I'd look even more suspicious. So I went for a walk." Florence shrugged a thin shoulder.

What struck Myrtle was how completely lucid Florence seemed. She didn't seem confused and she didn't look foggy. She was still a perfectly dreadful driver, but she didn't appear confused at all. Not now, anyway.

"Besides," said Florence, "I just don't understand the whole setting-up-Mimsy thing. Why do people think she's being set up? Just because she was a beneficiary of Luella's will?"

"Not only that, no. She also lost an earring the night we played Bunco and someone apparently put the earring near Alma when Alma was murdered. To make it look as if Mimsy had been there," said Myrtle.

Florence said slowly, "Does Mimsy lose a lot of earrings? I mean, all the time?"

Myrtle wondered if she'd been too quick to think that Florence was clear-headed. "What do you mean? As far as I'm aware, she's only lost the one earring."

Florence shook her head. "I saw her put her earring in

her purse that night at Bunco. I thought it was odd then. Especially when I overheard her telling Elaine that she'd lost it. I thought, 'and people think *I'm* confused.'"

Myrtle caught her breath and felt an icy chill go up her spine despite the wool coat. Even Pasha stood still.

"Did you say anything about it? Did you remind Mimsy where the earring was?"

"No. Because it wasn't long after that when you found poor Luella. I didn't really think about the earring anymore," said Florence.

Myrtle nodded slowly. "That's very interesting, Florence. I won't keep you … I have to get my cat to the newsroom at the *Bugle*."

Florence gave her an odd look. It made Myrtle think that Florence was going to go around talking about Myrtle and saying, "And people say that *I'm* confused…."

Chapter Twenty-One

Myrtle held out a treat to Pasha, who quickly bounded after her. Mimsy. Mimsy was responsible for Luella's death? And Alma's? It hardly seemed possible. Could Florence have been mistaken? But other things seemed to fall into place.

Mimsy had seemed very financially stable. Poppy, for one, even seemed envious of her apparent stability … according to Mimsy. But when Myrtle and Miles had been dropping off the casserole, John had said that he was interviewing for a job out of town. Maybe they hadn't been as financially stable as they'd appeared, if John had been unemployed. And, since John had also done day trading on the side, perhaps he'd lost a lot of money on the stock market.

What if Mimsy had wanted to maintain her lifestyle and killed to do so? Could she be so calculating? Had she hidden away her own earring as a possible insurance policy for potential future crimes? Acted as if someone were trying to set her up? Pointed suspicion at her own friend, Poppy, by subtly acting as if Poppy had been envious of her all along?

Had she taken advantage of her husband's trip to kill Alma?

Myrtle, for once, felt a strong urge to talk to her son. She took out her phone from her pocketbook. As far as smartphones went, it wasn't a *genius*, but it was fairly clever. Sometimes she wondered if it were sharper than she was.

She pulled up her contacts and found Red's number. It rang until his voice mail answered. Myrtle hung up, sighing in irritation. He was probably taking that shower at her house. Plus, it always took him a while to check his voice mails on his personal phone. Then she realized Red seemed a lot more responsive to his text messages. The text message screen was so small that she had to fumble around in her purse for her reading glasses in order to type on it. Finally, she typed *need to talk to you about Mimsy, Red.* Maybe that would pique Red's interest enough to give her a call back.

"Myrtle?" asked Mimsy's voice, very close.

Myrtle just about jumped through her skin. "Mimsy!" she gasped.

Mimsy said solicitously, "Oh, Miss Myrtle, I'm so sorry. I didn't mean to scare you. You must have been deep in your thoughts."

"I must have been, yes. I was thinking about Pasha, my cat," she said in a rush. Pasha sprawled out on the sidewalk, enjoying the sun on her stomach. "Are you out running errands?" she asked. She glanced around for Mimsy's car, but didn't see it.

Mimsy held up some poster board she was carrying. "Just walking around and putting up signs supporting the *Bradley Bugle*. I'm amazed how that social media campaign has caught on. It's like the whole town is coming together in support of the newspaper."

"A newspaper is important to small towns," said Myrtle in a rather perfunctory voice.

"Are you feeling all right, Miss Myrtle?" asked Mimsy, staring closely at her. "You don't quite seem like yourself."

"I'm a little tired, maybe," said Myrtle. As if to emphasize that point, she wove a bit unsteadily, still trying to clutch her cane, the bag of cat treats, her reading glasses, and her phone. She was able to regain her balance, but she dropped the cane and the phone in the process.

Mimsy swiftly stooped down to retrieve them. She hesitated while picking up the phone, then rose and gave Myrtle a quick smile. "Here you are, Miss Myrtle. I don't think the phone is broken and the cane is in good shape."

"Thanks," said Myrtle quickly. She noticed that the phone's screen was still on her text messages. Had Mimsy seen her message to Red?

But Mimsy's gaze was impassive as she gave Myrtle a friendly smile. "Maybe if you put everything in your purse it would help."

"Yes, I suppose it would. Thank you, Mimsy. Hope you have a good day."

Myrtle walked off toward the *Bugle*, clicking her tongue to Pasha who bounded after her to catch up. After walking for a moment, she felt as though eyes were trained on her back. She paused and swiftly turned around, but felt foolish when she saw that Mimsy was placidly taping a poster board to a stop sign.

There was a sticky note on the old wooden door of the *Bugle* that said *back soon*. Myrtle sighed. Sloan could be so flaky sometimes. At least he'd left the door unlocked. She opened the door to the dimness of the newsroom and Pasha, now looking alert, leaped in. Pasha must recognize her hunting ground from the day before. Myrtle was sure the furry creatures were cowering in the shadows somewhere as this master predator entered.

Myrtle strolled over to Sloan's desk, took off the heavy, wool coat, and sat down at his desk to wait. She figured she'd fess up to her social media dabblings so that he wouldn't keep thinking they'd somehow been hacked. If she pulled up the *Bugle*'s accounts, she could explain why the publicity was such a good thing, and maybe tell him about the car dealership and her plans for getting the advertisers back.

She jiggled the computer mouse on the desk and saw that Sloan was still logged in to the Twitter and Facebook accounts. Myrtle would have thought that he'd have learned his lesson about not signing out, but it certainly made it easier for her. Looking at the updates, she saw that everyone was uploading their own news and pictures and tagging the *Bradley Bugle* in them. Robert Finley had apparently caught a huge fish in the lake yesterday and he'd just uploaded a picture of him, the fish, and a yardstick. Myrtle made a face. She hated to think she sometimes swam in the lake with creatures that big in it.

Pasha bounded past her and she drew her feet up a little. Thinking of creatures, she'd just as soon not have one brush against her in its attempt to escape.

Myrtle was so absorbed in the Twitter and Facebook windows that she didn't immediately notice when the door to the *Bugle* opened. But when she glanced up and saw that it was Mimsy, and that Mimsy had a hammer and was still trying to adjust her eyes from going from bright sunshine outside to the dark interior of the newsroom, she quickly and silently typed on the Twitter and Facebook accounts *Help! It's Myrtle Clover. Trapped in the* Bugle *downtown office with killer!* There was no time to dig out her phone or grab the desk phone because Mimsy had already spotted her. But she did close the windows to the sites.

Mimsy said in a too-calm voice, "Stop right there, Miss Myrtle. There will be no phone calls or texting now. And if Red calls or texts you, you're not picking it up. I saw your last text message to him."

Myrtle said, equally calmly, "If Red calls or texts me and I *don't* pick up, then he's going to start looking for me. And there are only a few places I'd be. This is one of them." This wasn't completely true, but Myrtle figured that Mimsy wouldn't know otherwise.

"Then when he comes looking, he'll find your body. Which probably would work out better than Sloan finding it. Sloan is in such poor condition that he might have a heart attack. And I'd hate it if anything happened to our local paper. Changes in leadership aren't always good," said Mimsy thoughtfully.

Myrtle's chill up her spine was back. Mimsy was completely cold. Completely calculating. Completely dangerous. She could only hope that either Sloan would come back and be somewhat helpful and brave or that somebody … anybody … was on Facebook or Twitter and could see her message in time.

Mimsy continued talking in her calm monotone. "I really do hate to do this. You're sort of the matriarch of the town, aren't you, Miss Myrtle? I've always rather admired you. You never had to play sweet to fit in, did you? You never pretended to be anyone but yourself."

Myrtle frowned at her. "Who else would I be? What kind of a life is it if you're putting on an act all the time? Is that what you've done, Mimsy? Put on an act? You weren't the Lady Bountiful, actually, were you? Did you have contempt for all those people you were helping through your volunteering?" She needed to keep her talking. That hammer was way too close and Mimsy was much younger and much stronger.

Mimsy stared at her. "Contempt for them? Why on earth would I volunteer so much if I felt that way?"

To Myrtle, though, it seemed as if Mimsy were genuinely asking a question. As if she wanted to hear the answer herself.

"Do you watch *Tomorrow's Promise*, Mimsy? The soap opera?"

Now she really appeared to have gotten Mimsy's attention. "Sometimes. Not always, though."

"Have you watched the storyline with Briana in it?"

asked Myrtle. Her hand was shaking so much that she put it in her lap so that she could match Mimsy's calmness.

Mimsy tilted her head slightly to the side. "The one with Briana turning into a terrorist?"

"That's right," said Myrtle in a very measured voice. "Briana, who has always been sort of a clueless hair stylist, suddenly took a very visible role in the soap opera when she joined a radical terrorist cell."

Mimsy said, "Which wasn't very believable."

"I'm not so sure. You may not have watched the more recent episodes, but it takes us inside Briana's *house*, not just the salon where we usually see her. There we see that maybe she's been having something of a double life. She has some material around her home that shows us that she's been interested in various fringe groups. She's bookmarked websites that show that she is sympathetic to these very radical Middle Eastern religious groups. So we see that it *wasn't* such an abrupt transformation, but something that's been happening all along," said Myrtle.

Mimsy's face was curious. "And you're saying that Briana was a terrorist all along … that it was everyone else who just saw a mild-mannered beautician."

"Exactly." Myrtle thought she heard voices outside. But then she realized it was only squirrels fussing at each other on a limb outside the window.

"But what makes you think that *I'm* like Briana?" asked Mimsy. She absently hit the hammer on the palm of her other hand.

Myrtle took a deep, calming breath. "I've heard that you ran with a fast crowd in high school. Florence even blamed you for her nephew's death. If there's one thing I know after decades of teaching, it's that people usually are fundamentally the same as when they're in high school. They're in different situations as adults, yes. Yes, as adults they have more experience to pull from when they make their decisions. But their character, their personality, their ethics … most of these things stayed the same for the students that I had."

Mimsy shrugged. "Maybe Denny's death was a wake-up call for me."

Myrtle gave Mimsy the direct, piercing stare that she used to train on students most in need of correcting. "There were no wake-up calls for you, Mimsy. That's why you have to be stopped. This all started because you needed money, didn't it? To maintain this storybook lifestyle you had? John is out of work and who knows how long that's been going on, since he commutes out of town. So you killed Luella, knowing that you were the only heir to an inheritance. There was nothing personal against Luella. I kept looking for someone who resented Luella. But you were only looking for what you could *get* from her." Wanda's croaking words came back to Myrtle: *Ain't nothin' personal with that Luella.*

"Her death was merely a means to an end. I'd no hard feelings for Luella. And your yardman left such a handy weapon nearby," said Mimsy with a smirk.

"What would you have done if there *hadn't* been a handy weapon?" asked Myrtle.

"I'd just have had a casual conversation with Luella while she smoked," said Mimsy.

Myrtle said, "You created a diversion by saying you'd lost your earring. That brought in several people from the kitchen to the living room. You were taking a tremendous risk. Anyone from the party might have seen you go out. Anyone might have seen you come back in."

Mimsy laughed. "If someone had seen me come back in, I'd have been shuddering with fear and grief because I'd just discovered poor Luella dead in your backyard."

Myrtle gazed at her thoughtfully for a moment. "You needed the thrill, didn't you? Killing Luella on such a tight deadline. Breaking into Alma's home and murdering her while your husband was out of town. Making it appear as if someone was setting you up for the crimes when, actually, you *were* committing the crimes. And why was it necessary for poor Alma to die?"

"Because Alma was desperate for money and she spotted me coming out of the backyard after killing Luella. She unwisely decided to blackmail me, realizing that I would soon come into an inheritance. But Alma was demanding a lot of money that I didn't yet have. John has lost a mint with his day trading. So money *was* the key motive for murdering both Luella and Alma. But, sure, boredom played into it, too. Let's face it, Miss Myrtle. I've been a little bored here in Bradley. Maybe you're right about leopards not changing their spots. I've been playing nice for a long, long time. I've participated in all the available activities in Bradley."

Myrtle actually felt a tiny twinge of sympathy toward Mimsy. "Of which there aren't many. Activities, I mean."

"That's right. You and I have been in something of the same boat, haven't we, Miss Myrtle?" Mimsy seemed startled by the realization.

"Except that my boat isn't sinking. If *I* get bored, I investigate crimes. I don't commit crimes," said Myrtle. She furtively raised her hand to search for *some* kind of weapon to use against Mimsy since she wasn't sure she could raise her cane up in time, especially with Mimsy being so close to her. Her fingers only came in contact with paper, however. Did Sloan have *nothing* but piles of paper on his desk? Myrtle was starting to feel helpless and it wasn't a feeling she was accustomed to or enjoyed.

"And now you've driven me to have to commit another," said Mimsy.

She actually managed to sound regretful. Myrtle trained her stern gaze on Mimsy again. "You don't have to do this. Turn yourself in peacefully to Red. It's better to be tried for only two deaths."

Mimsy said laconically, "I have a feeling it doesn't matter much once you get past two murders."

"Don't be silly. Besides, Sloan will be here any minute," said Myrtle.

"I doubt that. Because once I saw where you were headed, I slashed the tire on Sloan's truck. Besides, he was also juggling what appeared to be an angry mob upset about the changes at the newspaper. I do believe he'll be delayed for a while." Mimsy's eyes glinted with satisfaction. "Face it, Miss Myrtle—no one's coming."

With that, the door burst open and a crowd of people rushed in. Myrtle spotted an odd assortment of Miles, Dusty, Erma, the fisherman from the Facebook post, and Georgia Simpson. What's more, they appeared to all be armed with various weapons. Dusty wielded a rake, Georgia a tire iron, Erma waved a hideous plaster vase, the fisherman gripped a 2x4 plank of wood, and Miles inexplicably held a shovel. It looked like a revolt of the peasants.

Mimsy gaped at them for a moment before howling and lifting the hammer at Myrtle. Myrtle ducked down, at the same time whacking at Mimsy's legs with her cane. Mimsy cursed but still stood and was ready to strike with the hammer … until Pasha chose that moment to run across Sloan's desk chasing her scampering furry prey.

Once Mimsy spotted the mouse, which was now pausing and trying to decide if Pasha or Mimsy were scarier, she shrieked and directed the hammer at the mouse, instead. But Mimsy appeared to have bad aim. The mouse escaped and made a run for the door as more screaming ensued … this time from the collective rescue party, which dashed toward Mimsy and Myrtle.

Mimsy abandoned killing Myrtle and ran away from

the door toward the back of the newsroom. But Erma Sherman was running straight at her, in terrified escape from Pasha.

Pasha was clearly disturbed from all the screaming and running around by the humans in the room, and leapt at Mimsy, who caught her neatly and screamed behind her, "Everyone stay back! You're all going to let me out of here or I kill the cat."

Pasha the Feral Cat didn't make a good hostage, however. She savagely bit and clawed until Mimsy gave a sharp exclamation and let her go. Mimsy then bolted for the front door and right into Red's arms as he pushed open the door.

Red took one look at the band of Bradley residents, metaphorical pitchforks in hand and all yelling at him, took out his handcuffs, and restrained Mimsy.

Fifteen minutes later, Red had called the state police to pick up and process Mimsy who was spitefully keeping silent. In the meantime, he'd contacted his deputy, Darrell Smith to sit with her in the nearby police station while Red spoke with everyone in the *Bradley Bugle* newsroom.

Sloan had returned by this time, dismayed at having missed all the action. "You'll come up with a write-up of Mimsy's arrest, won't you?" he asked Myrtle in a low voice.

Myrtle was about to answer him when she was distracted by the realization that she no longer had the long, wool coat on. But it was too late to cover up. Red finally took a good look at her and lit up. "Mama! You're wearing your present!"

Myrtle bared her teeth in a smile. "Why, of course I am. You know how much I loved it."

Miles gave her a sympathetic look.

Myrtle said to Sloan, "Yes, of course I'll write up the story. Just keep my words *as-is*."

Myrtle waited at Sloan's desk as Red carefully talked to everyone who'd come to her rescue, everyone who was now a witness to a very different Mimsy. From time to time Red glanced Myrtle's way as if hearing something alarming and wanting to see with his own eyes that she was completely intact. She gave him a small wave whenever he did so.

Sloan stood near Myrtle and was surreptitiously snapping pictures of everyone. Including Myrtle. "Stop that!" she hissed at Sloan.

Miles and Georgia Simpson were beside them, waiting their turn to give a statement to Red.

Sloan said, "So what was behind everyone showing up at the *Bugle* office?" He gave a nervous laugh. "I guess y'all didn't show up, armed, because of the editorial direction of the newspaper?"

Georgia had pulled out a cigarette and Sloan appeared unable to offer even a weak protest. Georgia's eyebrows were plucked nearly away so that she could draw her own expressions in. Today's expression was fairly hostile. Miles could only stare at her in horrified fascination. Between the cigarette, the big helmet of hair, the tattoos, and the glowering eyebrows, and the tire iron she wielded, no one was going to get in her way today. After taking a big puff from the cigarette, Georgia responded, "We got the frantic tweet and Facebook update. Figured, if somebody put Myrtle in danger, I was going after them. Nobody messes with Myrtle."

Sloan still looked puzzled, so Miles explained, "Myrtle sent out social media updates that she was here and needed help."

Georgia nodded and took another large drag on the cigarette. "That's right. And everybody who was online and saw it stopped what they were doing, grabbed a weapon, and ran to the *Bugle*."

Sloan gave Myrtle a reproachful look. "So *you're* the hacker?"

Myrtle snorted in irritation. "There was no hacking required, Sloan. I merely updated the social media sites while you left your computer unlocked. And the passwords were on a sticky note, for heaven's sake. That hardly passes for computer security."

Sloan shook his head. "So … Mimsy. I can hardly believe it."

"You'd have believed it if she'd been heaving a hammer at you," said Myrtle succinctly. "Sometimes people aren't totally what they seem."

Miles said under his breath, "Briana the terrorist?"

Myrtle nodded and together they waited for Red.

It didn't take long until Red plopped down in a wheeled chair next to Myrtle and took out his notebook. Pasha had calmed back down once all the people were behaving once again in a normal, people-like manner and she was now curled up on Sloan's desk by Myrtle. Myrtle scratched her under her chin. "Good kitty," she murmured.

Red said, "Mama, I've got to hand it to you. You were able to figure out who was behind the murders when I was still thinking that Mimsy Kessler was being set up by someone jealous of her."

Myrtle nodded. "Someone like Poppy, you mean?"

Red said, "Exactly. I guess you must have come to that conclusion along the way, too."

"Because that's the conclusion Mimsy *wanted* us to reach. She was the one talking about how envious Poppy was of her success and her lifestyle and the fact that she didn't have a job. She fed all those ideas to us so that we'd think poor Poppy was setting Mimsy up to look like the killer."

"Was her financial situation really that bad?" asked Red, shaking his head. "It's hard to believe that Mimsy would do something like this just because she'd fallen on bad times."

Myrtle said, "I don't think she *was* doing it merely because she'd fallen on bad times. For one thing, I think she's always been a little dangerous. Even when she was a teenager, she liked pushing things to the limit. She ran with a fast crowd back then."

"She sure doesn't now, though," mumbled Red.

"Right. But she got that same thrill from murdering Luella at my Bonkers party. Can you imagine? Killing a family member at a party after pretending to lose her earring. Everyone came into the living room to try to help her find it. She was just as cool as clams. And anyone could have spotted her breaking into Alma's house," said Myrtle, waving her arms around excitedly.

"Anyone who was up very late at night and outside," reminded Miles.

"Which, as it happens, are a lot more people than we thought," said Myrtle. "I'd have only said it was you and me until very recently."

Red said, "What I don't get is how you knew it was Mimsy. *Suspecting* it was Mimsy is one thing. *Knowing* it is something entirely different.

"Florence gave me the final piece of the puzzle," said Myrtle. "She told me that she'd seen Mimsy put her earring in her purse and thought she might be absentminded."

Red's eyebrows shot up. "I must have spoken to Florence Ainsworth five times since Luella's death and she never told me any such thing."

"But did you ask her about the earring?" asked Myrtle.

"No, but that's because it was evidence. I was trying not to divulge the evidence we had in the case," said Red.

Myrtle shrugged. "I had no such concerns. So I brought up the earring thing with Florence."

Miles cleared his throat. "People also find it easy to

talk to your mother, Red. Maybe they're a little intimidated that you're the police. They open up with Myrtle more."

"I think you ended this whole investigation very quickly, Mama. Good job. Not that I ever want you to do this again," he added ominously.

"Duly noted," said Myrtle, promptly and deliberately forgetting his addendum. "If you wanted to thank me, I know just how you can go about it."

"I just *did* thank you, I thought," said Red warily.

"Yes, but my solving the case qualifies for a special thank you. Like replacing Dusty's string trimmer," said Myrtle.

"What? But that will be expensive," said Red. "And I'm paying for a plumbing emergency and a new car."

"I don't think it will be all that bad. He wouldn't want anything top of the line, I don't think." Actually, he *would*. But since Dusty wasn't aware of any of it, he'd be none the wiser. "It's his birthday. Plus, he just broke his string trimmer. And I have a feeling that you're not in any hurry to step in and substitute your services for Dusty's."

Red said hastily, "No, that's for sure. I suppose I do have my police discount at the hardware store."

"Just remember, it's a secret. And if Dusty should ask you about repairing his trimmer, you just nod and smile and say that you're getting right on it," said Myrtle.

Red tilted his head quizzically at her. "Repairing it?"

"He thinks you are. Repairing it, I mean. So just go along with it."

Red said to Miles, "Sometimes I feel like I don't know what's going on."

"Join the club," said Miles. "Sometimes I feel like *Myrtle* is the only one who knows what's going on."

Sloan, who'd been outside talking on his cell phone, came into the building again. The expression on his face was stunned. "I just heard some amazing news," he said slowly. "Rogers Automotive says they want to resume advertising with the *Bugle*."

Myrtle beamed at him. "Well, isn't that nice!"

"And Tim Rogers said to give Miss Myrtle his regards," said Sloan. He and Red stared at Myrtle.

"There are many ways of being persuasive," said Myrtle with a shrug. "I just hope this means that you can hire Tilly Morris back as copyeditor again. My red pen has run dry with all the correcting of the paper."

"I will," said Sloan with a sigh. "Although I still need a new part-time salesman to get more advertisers."

Myrtle snapped her fingers. "I have a great idea. I just happen to know someone who would do a fantastic job and would be happy to work part-time. Robert Wiggins."

Red said, "Alma's son?"

Sloan's eyes opened wide. "But I thought I heard something about him. Something that might make me worried about hiring him at the *Bugle*."

Myrtle put her hands on her hips. "Red, have you arrested Robert Wiggins for fraud?"

"I sure haven't," he said.

"Then I think you'll be fine with him, Sloan. He's very well-spoken. Besides, the *Bugle* doesn't have any money to steal anyway," said Myrtle.

"Isn't that the truth," said Sloan glumly.

"And I certainly hope it means you don't try any radical means of getting readers for the paper. Clearly, they like the *Bugle* the way it was."

Red snorted. "You think? I passed about ten #SaveTheBugle signs on the way over here."

Sloan colored a bit. "I got the message, too. I think you'll find that everything with the newspaper will be returning to normal soon."

Myrtle said, "And you'll bring back the horoscopes, recipes, and the Good Neighbors column? Because the paper isn't the same without them, Sloan."

Sloan nodded. "I will. I give up. People want what they want and there's nothing I can do to convince them otherwise."

The next morning, Myrtle figured Sloan was *trying* to thank her by featuring her on the front page of the newspaper in living color alongside her story on Mimsy's arrest. Even though she was now immortalized for all time in a pink nylon tracksuit.

Next Myrtle Clover: Murder on Opening Night

Sign up for Elizabeth's free newsletter to stay updated on its release:

http://eepurl.com/kCy5j

When Myrtle Clover and her friend Miles attend a play in their small town, there's a full house on opening night.

It's clear to Myrtle that one of the actresses is a stage hog who loves stealing the spotlight. Nandina Marshall certainly does upstage everyone—when her murder forces an unexpected intermission.

Can Myrtle and Miles discover who was behind her final curtain call….before murder makes an encore?

About the Author

Elizabeth writes the Southern Quilting mysteries and Memphis Barbeque mysteries for Penguin Random House and the Myrtle Clover series for Midnight Ink and independently. She blogs at ElizabethSpannCraig.com/blog , named by Writer's Digest as one of the 101 Best Websites for Writers. Elizabeth makes her home in Matthews, North Carolina, with her husband and two teenage children.

Other Works by the Author:

Myrtle Clover Series in Order:
Pretty is as Pretty Dies
Progressive Dinner Deadly
A Dyeing Shame
A Body in the Backyard
Death at a Drop-In
A Body at Book Club
Death Pays a Visit
A Body at Bunco

Southern Quilting Mysteries in Order:
Quilt or Innocence
Knot What it Seams
Quilt Trip
Shear Trouble
Tying the Knot (June 2015)

Memphis Barbeque Mysteries in Order (Written as Riley Adams):
Delicious and Suspicious
Finger Lickin' Dead
Hickory Smoked Homicide
Rubbed Out

Where to Connect With Elizabeth

Please sign up for Elizabeth's free newsletter to learn about new releases, and receive special deals for subscribers: http://eepurl.com/kCy5j
Facebook: Elizabeth Spann Craig Author
Riley Adams, Author
Twitter: @elizabethscraig
Website: www.elizabethspanncraig.com

Thanks so much for reading my book…I appreciate it. If you enjoyed the story, would you please leave a short review on the site where you purchased it? Just a few words would be great. Not only do I feel encouraged reading them, but they also help other readers discover my books. Thank you!

Printed in Great Britain
by Amazon